HAZY LOVE

HANNAH SMITH

First edition March 2022

ISBN: 978-0-6452802-0-3 (ebook)
ISBN: 978-0-6452802-1-0 (paperback)

Edited by Rachel Collins
Cover Design by ©Emily Wittig Designs

*For every single person who encouraged me
to keep writing.*

AUTHOR'S NOTE

This book contains references to sensitive topics such as anxiety, depression, infidelity, sexual assault, drug use and death. It also contains profanity and sex scenes and is intended for audiences 18 years or older.

Happy reading!

I WONDER if people would ever suspect Reuben of murder.

Six-foot tall, man-bun of sun-streaked brown hair, eyes the colour of the Maldivian ocean. He's got a kind face, with a welcoming smile to boot. I bet lots of people would never consider it.

Of course, *I'd* suspect him. I know better than to think serial killers look a certain way, despite how some people think they're predominantly sketchy and unkempt, with creepy eyes and bad vibes. *Anyone* can be a murderer, or a rapist, or capable of other horrific things. Look at Richard Ramirez (sans the teeth) or Paul John Knowles (the Casanova Killer) or the infamous Ted Bundy. Harold Shipman was a doctor, for God's sake, and he murdered multiple elderly patients in his care. No one is immune from suspicion in my book.

"Did you run a marathon today, Hazy?"

A snort escapes my nose at Reuben's words, interrupting my train of thought. Whilst I can't see my reflection, I'm willing to bet my face is still tomato-red from my run, covered in a sheen of sweat that won't quit. What was once a neat ponytail, is now a wad of matted hair sticking to the back of my neck. That's going to be hell to brush out later.

"It was only ten kilometres, but it felt never ending," I sigh, leaning against the counter. "My head wasn't in it today."

You'd think running the coastal paths of South East Queensland's beautiful beaches would be enough to snap anyone out of a funk. Unfortunately for me, I still feel like I woke up on the wrong side of the bed.

Reuben offers me a sympathetic head tilt as he taps away at the coffee machine. "But you did it. The hardest task of the day, done. Whatever you face from here on out will be a walk in the park."

I scowl. "You haven't met my boss."

Reuben chuckles. "God knows why you still work for that woman."

"Don't start."

Reuben lifts a hand in surrender, using the other to pour milk into a steel jug. "What's on for the weekend? Something to turn your week around? Netflix hire you as an ambassador yet?"

"Not yet, but I'm pretty sure I single-handedly keep them in business," I reply, before perking up. "There's a new documentary about Issei Sagawa dropping on Sunday."

"Should I know who that is?"

My mouth drops open in mock protest. "The Kobe Cannibal? He's a Japanese murderer and necrophile who ate—"

"Alright, alright! Jesus," Reuben interjects, shooting me a warning glare. I can't say I blame him. Exploring the darkest corners of the human psyche isn't everyone's cup of tea. There's no way Reuben could be capable of murder.

"If it makes you feel any better, I've got old faithful *The Vampire Diaries* when I need to switch to something light-hearted and heartbreaking at the same time."

Reuben shakes his head. "You're such a nerd."

"Don't knock *The Vampire Diaries* until you've tried it."

"Believe me, I've tried it. It was terrible."

"How dare you, sir?"

"You've watched so much Netflix you're looping back to repeats." Reuben watches carefully as he froths milk in a steel jug, scratching the stubble on his face absentmindedly. "Maybe you could consider finding other ways to use your time?"

"Doing what?"

Reuben glances up at me and grins. "I've got some fit mates I could set you up with."

I drop my gaze, pretending to busy myself with pulling my bank card out of my wallet. "I'd prefer to stick with Netflix. It keeps me out of trouble."

"Hazel Jones, I can't imagine you ever getting into any sort of trouble." Reuben delicately pours warm milk into two cups before placing them both in front of me. "Unless, of course, Kali has something to do with it. The two of you together are a force to be reckoned with. Lest we forget."

"I don't know what you're talking about."

The corners of Reuben's mouth turn up as he snaps a lid on each of the cups. "No pressure, Hazy, but you've known me how long now? Two years? You know the company I keep. My friends are decent human beings. Decent human beings who you might hit it off with."

My cheeks heat and my jaw clenches. At twenty-seven years old, I've experienced enough flirting, partying, and heartache to last a lifetime. Heartache being the major sticking point and Reuben knows it. He saw me when I was at my worst and gave me so much free coffee, I'm pretty sure I owe him quadruple figures.

"I'm not saying you *need* to date anyone," Reuben assures me. "But you never know. A fun night out with Engineer Eddy or Pistol Pete might be good for you."

I allow myself to smile, imagining that I interrupt my weekend of self-loathing to meet one of Reuben's friends on a romantic date on the beach, or in a cosy corner of a swanky restaurant. What are the odds of me changing out of my weekend sloth attire and voluntarily leaving the house to meet a total stranger and remembering how to flirt, as if I haven't been a zombie floating through life the past few months?

Those odds don't exist.

"Thanks for the offer, but I think I'll stick to the likes of John Wayne Gacy and Ed Kemper for now."

Reuben offers a half-smile, and I'm grateful he doesn't push the topic further. "Don't say that out loud too often. People will think you enjoy the company of TV serial killers more than actual people."

I tap my card to pay. "It's kind of true."

Reuben laughs at my joke, waving to a customer behind me. "You weirdo. Enjoy your quality time with the TV this weekend and remember to bring your keep-cups next time. You and Kali should know better."

Reuben whistles to Rosie, his Golden Retriever, who's begging one of his customers for a piece of banana bread. She bounds across, her claws clacking against the wooden floors.

"I promise I'll bring the keep-cups next time." I reach to scratch Rosie behind the ears as she arrives at my feet, tail wagging, and try to feed off her happy vibes. "Rosie, tell your daddy to stop being a bully."

"Rosie, tell Hazy she needs to stop killing turtles with her poor lifestyle choices," Reuben fires back.

Despite the way a chuckle rings out from my mouth and the joy I find in our regular banter, I can't help but hone in on the familiar sensation in the centre of my chest. A feeling that most people would say isn't a feeling, it's sort of nothing. A nothing feeling. It's been sitting there, bleeding into my organs and bloodstream for the past few months.

No. No matter how much I might appreciate him looking out for me, the mere mention of me going on a date has me rattled.

It's also reminded me that the only thing I'm interested in doing in my spare time involves snacks and a screen.

Kali is in the kitchen when I get home, shuffling her feet and groaning as she fixes her breakfast. The instant she spots the coffee in my hand, her eyes widen.

"Woman, I fucking love you." She takes the coffee and smells it with her eyes closed, before taking a sip. "I mean it Hazel. I love you more than life itself."

"More than coffee?"

"Mmmm." Kali takes another sip of liquid gold before snapping her eyes open. "How was Reuben this morning?"

"Meddlesome. Offered to set me up with one of his friends," I say, shaking my head at the idea.

As if she can read my mind, Kali chimes, "I'm going to take a stab in the dark and say you passed on the offer."

Instead of acknowledging anything about my lack of sex drive or something more serious, I squeeze past Kali to get the ingredients for my morning smoothie. "He also scolded both of us for not using our keep-cups."

"An attractive man who loves the planet."

"He's still very much gay, Kali."

"I dunno. I reckon we could sway him." Kali grins, bringing her sleepy face to life. "Are we still on for pizza and wine tonight?"

"Of course, after the gym." I toss a bag of spinach onto the bench and grab a banana from the fruit bowl, knowing that Kali's eyes are on me. Fortunately, she decides not to lecture me on my exercise regime today. She used to get on my case about over-training and burning myself out, but she's mostly given up.

"Good," she says, as she helps herself to a handful of spinach. "But don't let me drink too much. I don't want to have a haggard face for Alex's party tomorrow." I feign interest in breaking up my banana, switching the blender on at the wall, hoping that Kali will be oblivious to my silence, and jump to her next thought without noticing. She doesn't.

"Hazel," she says, swallowing the fistful of spinach leaves she'd shoved into her mouth and placing both her hands on the bench in front of her. She leans back as if gearing up for a race. "You are coming to Alex's birthday. I'm sick of seeing you walk around like a shell of a human being because of that dickhead."

I bite the inside of my cheek to steady myself. Kali's never been one to hold back. "I am not a shell of a human being." I refuse to look at her as I thrust the ingredients into the blender. "I don't want to go."

"You never want to go. You haven't gone anywhere for months. We're going and we're going to have fun."

"I *am* having fun," I say. "Eating take away and watching Netflix in my pyjamas by six pm is fun for me. It's fun for lots of people, actually."

"You need human interaction," Kali argues. "You need conversation. Dare I say it, you could use a bit of dick–for all our sakes."

I fill a cup with ice from the fridge, hoping the loud noise will put her off talking. Of course, Kali doesn't let up. "When was the last time you saw a penis? In real life?" A dramatic eye roll gets me nothing but raised brows in response. "See? You've probably re-virginised, for God's sake."

I groan, tipping ice into the blender. "I don't need penis to be happy."

Kali scoffs. "Do you even hear yourself? '*I don't need penis to be happy.*' That's proof you're long overdue for some."

My head shakes in disagreement. Despite me briefly toying with the idea of going on a date with one of Reuben's friends this morning, the thought of talking, flirting, or touching a guy stirs nothing but disinterest in me. I don't feel sexy or horny. I don't want to listen to some guy spill a heap of bullshit as he tries to get into my pants and I certainly don't want to pretend to be someone I'm not, so I can have meaningless sex and wake up filled with regret.

Oats. I need oats. I keep my hands moving and my mind busy. I need Kali to drop the subject of sex. I don't want Kali to bring *him* up. I don't want to talk about *him*, or how I've been coping since *him*.

Clearly Kali's not interested in what I need, because she keeps pushing. "I'm not saying go out and meet another asshole to waste three years of your life with. I'm saying find yourself a piece of Gold Coast man meat and treat yourself. You've got to live again."

"And in order for me to live again, I need to fuck someone?" I ask.

"Mate, I don't care if you just *talk* to a guy for five minutes," she cries. "Do something productive for yourself, something other than running or going to the gym...start drawing again. Sketch a design! Anything! Anything's better than this robot version of my best friend."

Kali notices me wince at her comment about drawing, and knows she's touched a nerve. My plans of starting my own business and illustrating book covers for authors went on hold when he ended things. It was as if my desire to create disappeared overnight.

I avoid her comments about me existing as a robot and divert instead to the least painful of the topics brought up this morning. "I talk to guys plenty." I pour way too many oats into the blender and slam the lid into place, allowing the blender to come to life and drown out any further conversation. My eyes snap to Kali's and I can tell she's not done. She folds her arms and leans against the bench, waiting for the noise to stop so she can continue. When I finally let up and flick the switch, she's already rattling out words.

"Arguments on Tinder about destroying the patriarchy do not count as talking to guys," Kali berates.

Probably true.

"I talk to Reuben nearly every day," I point out.

"That doesn't count. He's a *gay* friend you're not attracted to and you spend more time paying attention to Rosie than him anyway."

"That's *not* true! It's an even split."

"Even if he was straight and you were into him, you'd do everything in your power to guarantee you stayed two metres from him at all times."

I frown at the thickness of my smoothie. "I don't like being that close to people."

"No, because you've been avoiding male attention for weeks. God, even longer. The last guy I remember you seeing was that rugby player—"

"He was going through a high-profile divorce!" I cut in, waving my hand for emphasis. "His wife was on the *Real Housewives of Melbourne,* for fuck's sake. I ended that for my protection *and* yours. We would've been dragged into a fucking D-grade celebrity shit fight."

"At least that might have livened you up a bit." Kali's eyes are ablaze. "Instead, you went down the road of becoming a gym-obsessed, work-obsessed Sober Sally, and not that I don't agree with your decision to stop partying, because *Jesus.*"

I agree that the partying from both of us had gotten ridiculously out of hand.

"But come on, Hazy." Kali lowers her voice, the ferocity fading and her gentleness taking over. "This isn't you. This isn't living to your full potential. It's not even close. You seem so... sad."

There it is. This is what Kali's been avoiding saying to me *again* because she thought maybe this time was different. It's not different, but I don't have the energy to get into it with her. Not today, not ever.

"All right," I say, and Kali fist-pumps the air, her mood switching from concerned to victorious. "I will come to Alex's and I will *try* to have fun."

"And I can dress you?" Kali's eyes brighten.

I sigh, the tightness in my chest constricting further. "Yes, you can dress me."

If she suspects I've agreed to her pleas to get her off my back, she doesn't show it as she launches into how excited she is to finally hang out with her latest man crush at his thirtieth birthday party. I make a point of blasting the blender during crucial sections of her storytelling and cut her off when she asks me what she should do if Alex's penis and sexual skills don't live up to the ones she's created in her head.

"Let's save the penis talk for this evening," I suggest, grabbing my smoothie and walking towards my bedroom, secretly praying we don't talk about sex, or penises or my lack of either, for the rest of the day.

After showering, I spend far too long staring at my reflection. Despite Kali's best efforts, the bags under my eyes seem to have become permanent. No amount of gel pads or creams have rid my face of them completely, but I'm pretty sure they're getting smaller.

Is she right? Do I seem sad? Despite my tired appearance, I believe I've been doing a pretty good job of at least appearing to be happy. My skincare routine is helping my pale skin seem dewy. I mix things up with different lipsticks at least twice a week and eyelash extensions mean less work in giving my eyes life. I thought I certainly *looked* the part of someone who had her life together.

Sometimes I'm not even pretending. I've noticed myself genuinely smiling. I'm sleeping better. I no longer obsess about *him* every waking minute of the day and how *he* crushed my heart—

Stop.

I can't afford those memories. I've done a bloody good job of blocking them out, of blocking out that entire three-year period, and I can't afford a weak day. A weak day is a step backwards and I've worked too hard to go anywhere but forward. If anything, I'd say my focus on forward-planning is teetering somewhere on the verge of unhealthy since the break-up.

My diary is laid out with plans, appointments, gym session times and to-do lists. My online work calendar is colour-coded and checked every night before leaving my desk, so I know what's in store the following day. The calendar in my bedroom is for personal items, such as birthdays and upcoming events. Even though I have no desire to attend Alex's thirtieth birthday tomorrow night, the event is written neatly for this coming Saturday. It's the only event on the calendar for the entire month.

I don't need to view the other pages of the calendar to see it's the only event I've added since Luke left.

2

LIKE CLOCKWORK, I pull into the car park of the Gold Coast hub of Green and Acre. I'm nothing if not consistent and getting to work half an hour before my boss gives me thirty minutes to brace myself for the day and prepare as much as I can, so the day runs smoothly. Nobody wants to be around the haughty and condescending Executive Director, Lisa Fox, on a bad day, and I'm the person who has the best shot of ensuring she's in a good mood.

I check my reflection in the rear-view mirror, noticing the constant frown is still very much there. Kali's words about my lack of creative work and enthusiasm about life have been playing on repeat ever since. I'll keep topping her wine up tonight, so she's got a haggard face for Alex's birthday tomorrow. *Ha!*

The pleasant warmth of the building hits my skin as I walk inside, and I reach up to loosen the light scarf from around my neck. It's September and although we're in the early days of spring, the morning chill won't be disappearing for a few more weeks. I'm a sook when it comes to the cold.

"Good morning, Hazel!" The loud and bubbly voice startles

me slightly and I slow down to see Rachel, an administration assistant from the retail team, striding towards me. Despite my dry sense of humour and lack of enthusiasm about pretty much anything to do with absolutely *anything,* she continues to strike up conversations with me. After what Kali said this morning, I believe the reason Rachel chats to me is that she, too, can see my sadness. If that's true, I might be even more pathetic than I thought. Though there is the remote possibility she's a sociopath, persisting in her efforts to ingratiate herself into my world for her own entertainment.

Maybe I do need to lay off the true crime.

"Hey, Rachel, how are you? Ready for the weekend?"

"Ugh, not really." Rachel flips her vibrant red hair over her shoulder. Despite her lack of enthusiasm, she still looks like she's beaming. "I'm moving into a new house on Hedges Avenue this weekend."

"Oh wow." I hear the surprise in my voice as I press the button for the elevator. Hedges Avenue is a prestigious street which runs parallel to the beach north of my suburb, and it ain't cheap.

"It's one of the smaller houses," she assures me with a chuckle. "I haven't met three of the women yet. There will be five of us living there."

"What a nightmare," I blurt out, and Rachel smiles with surprise. "No offence. I mean, five women who don't know each other under one roof could be problematic."

Rachel giggles again. "Oh, I know, but somehow, I got a room with an ocean view, so I'm not complaining."

"Is the umbrella girl moving with you?" I ask as we step inside the elevator.

Rachel once told me about the time one of her housemates had a screaming match in the driveway with her boyfriend after she caught him out in a lie. She'd smashed a neighbour's windscreen with an umbrella in a fit of rage, sending shards of glass onto her boyfriend's arm.

"Yep, she and I are moving in with three newbies. I'll be sure to give you any umbrella updates. What are you getting up to?"

She asks out of politeness, because I usually give the same answer of "nothing much" followed by a random comment about Netflix. I've never shared anything else with Rachel, but today a strange part of me wants to tell her the truth as a thanks for taking the time to chat with me.

"I've got a friend's thirtieth birthday tomorrow night," I tell her. Rachel's eyes widen with welcome surprise. Me having plans for the first time in several months has knocked her over.

"That's *great*, Hazel," she says earnestly, beaming at me as a proud parent would. Not once have I ever found Rachel condescending, patronising or annoying. Her genuine happiness at me leaving the house to be social is evident, and my cold, boring heart warms for a second at her kindness. "Where's the party?"

"Kygo in Burleigh."

"It's meant to be awesome," she coos, smiling brightly at two men joining us in the lift. "I haven't been, but everyone's raving about it."

Yeah, that's exactly what I'm dreading. A tiny, over-priced bar, filled with Instagram influencer-wannabes, and people who take too many selfies.

When we reach Rachel's floor, she farewells me with a smile, stalking across the shiny floor in her giant heels, the gazes of the two ogling men following her. A pang of jealousy spasms through me, and it's not because of Rachel's beauty. While she's stunning, it's her confidence I envy. Mine was like that once.

When I reach my floor, I shake my head to clear the barrage of insecure thoughts running through my brain. I need to focus. Lisa Fox doesn't appreciate sloppiness and neither do I.

With straightened shoulders, I march across the wide-open

spaced foyer to my office nook and dump my bag on the table. I let myself into Lisa's glass-walled office to switch on her computer and pull the blinds halfway, leaving them slightly open. She loves the view, but the heat from the morning sun reflects off her screen, and she complains if the blinds aren't tilted at the perfect angle. Heaven forbid she get up and fix the issue herself.

Once I've ensured her office is in order, with the temperature set to 22.5 degrees Celsius and plenty of bottles of sparkling water in her bar fridge, I head back to my nook of heaven. It might not be much to others, but to me it's my little oasis, complete with exposed brick and a pot plant named Audrey. She's a great listener and hears plenty of my complaints and worries day in, day out.

As my computer powers up, I receive a photo and text message from Kali.

KALI

> May this be your second reminder for the day to get your ass moving on your career aspirations. Also, please have a think about what sort of dick I should line up for you for tomorrow night. Alex has some BIG friends ;)

A tut escapes me at her comments, but I allow myself to smile at the photo. It's a mock book cover I designed for Kali's birthday several years ago. Using my drawing tablet, I created a cartoon illustration of Kali, walking down Fifth Avenue in New York, ladened with shopping bags and stalking towards the cover, exaggerating her long, dark brown legs. I called it 'An Australian in New York', slapped some fake quotes from authors and celebrities on the cover and had it framed. She keeps it in her locker at the gym she works at across town and tells anyone who will listen that the cartoon version of herself is on book covers all around the world.

The ache in my stomach tells me Kali's right. I haven't been creative in months. I don't spend hours admiring book covers anymore or stalking graphic artists on Instagram. I've stopped designing worlds and illustrating. I've stopped everything that used to bring me joy.

For as long as I can remember, I've drawn for fun. I'd spend hours cooped up in my room getting lost in other worlds created from my brain, and so I studied graphic design at university. Many people around me struggled to figure out what they wanted to do with their lives, but I knew the general direction I was headed: illustration or graphic design. I wanted to create art and do something I would love.

I dabbled in a few jobs post-graduation, but when the opportunity came to work for one of the largest retail corporations in Australia, I couldn't refuse. I planned to work full time and then spend my evenings and weekends working on my own ideas. Once I got my foot in the door, there'd be chances for me to branch off into design or marketing. I'd be able to make connections of my own and doors would open for me. I was only twenty-two; I had time.

Cut to me, five years later, still in the lucrative, yet gruelling job of executive personal assistant. The assistant to someone living *her* dream. With Lisa Fox taking up a lot of my mental and physical energy, dedicated time working on my projects and designs fell to the wayside, and even more so when I met Luke. His goals of opening his own surf store, and a bar with a friend, and launching a venture via *Amazon* ended up taking priority.

Not quite how I'd imagined things going in my twenties. Nothing's really turned out how I thought. Especially with Luke breaking my heart.

Everything stalled after Luke.

I hate that I miss him.

After four months, the ache for him has died a bit, and the pain in my chest has faded a little. I'm no longer crying, sobbing, and living in a black hole of despair. I partied hard, really hard, for a while, until I found working out was a much healthier option than copious amounts of booze and the occasional illicit substance. Kali and I had a hell of a few weeks post-Luke, but like Kali said this morning, I haven't really wanted to do anything else since I found physical exercise. I work hard. I run or show up to the gym, sometimes twice a day, and I commit to wine and pizza night every Friday. I go about my business during the week and lock myself indoors on weekends. Repeat, repeat, repeat. Robot Hazel is very much here, and if I'm being honest, I hadn't noticed, until today.

"Hazel! Great, you're here. Could you join me in my office?" Lisa Fox snaps me out of my daydream as she stalks down the hallway, wearing one of her trademark power suits, with her blow-dried blonde hair bouncing on her shoulders.

With my palms flat on the desk in front of me, I crack my neck out of habit as I push myself out of my seat. Not only is she in much earlier than usual, but I can tell by her clipped tone that she's also in a mood. *Fantastic.*

As I follow Lisa into her office, the scent of her over-sprayed Chanel perfume lingers in my nostrils. The gold jewellery on her wrists jingles with every step as she stomps around, throws her designer bag onto her desk, and shimmies out of her blazer with fervour.

"Good morning, Lisa."

"I just got off the phone with that weasel in Sydney!" She puts her blazer on the back of her chair, a deliberate exhale shooting from her nostrils. "He's always trying to tell me how to do my job. That snivelling rat has got his head so far up George's ass it makes me sick."

Ah, she's in a *delightful* mood.

Lisa Fox is the Executive of Property for the company. She's in charge of international leasing, store design and development, and has overseen the expansion of Green and Acre stores in New York, Los Angeles, London, and Tokyo. She's an expert in development and construction, is a no-bullshit dealmaker when it comes to the international market and last year, was listed in the top fifty most powerful and influential women in Australia.

She's never short on enemies, confrontation, and colleagues trying to tear her down, being such a prominent, dominating figure in the industry. Although in her defence, I'd say as the leading woman in the organisation, she has to fight harder than most males.

"What did Julian say?" I ask. I've learnt from experience that the calmer I stay, the quicker Lisa joins me back on Earth once she's screamed out her profanities. It makes for an easier day for everybody in the building, and I like to think of myself as a team player.

"He had the nerve to *review* my proposal for the storefront in Sao Paulo and said it wasn't viable," she snaps. "Who does he think he is?"

I refrain from saying "I told you so" or anything else obnoxious. I knew she made a mistake the minute she asked me to proof it for typos. The beauty of working under someone so experienced is that I've learned a lot, even if property has never interested me. When Lisa asked me to go over some specifics, I spent my entire weekend poring over it, noting that the cost of the space was very high compared to others in the area. The projections were a bit of a stretch and the risks seemed to outweigh the potential rewards. When I tried to bring it up, Lisa told me to stick to what I know best, such as diarising her life and photocopying.

So, I shut my mouth. Lisa's known for taking risks. That's how she's had so much success and why, despite her regular outbursts, she's well respected.

"He's trying to butter up George for the chief retail role," Lisa continues, dropping into her high-backed chair with a huff. "He thinks because they're both in Sydney, go to lunch and golf together, that he's a goddamned shoo-in. I bet he's sitting on George's lap at the gala."

I head to Lisa's fridge and pour a glass of sparkling water, which she accepts without question. "Speaking of the gala, George Wilson's assistant called and left a message after hours last night. She wanted to double check your RSVP."

"How stupid is that woman?" Lisa snarls, sipping her water with narrowed eyes. "I've got a room confirmed, hair and makeup booked, and a dress that costs more than her monthly salary. Didn't you tell her I'd be attending?"

"Yes, I put in your acceptance months ago. Everyone at Mr Wilson's table is being contacted to confirm their attendance. They don't want any empty seats near the stage."

Lisa holds her empty glass out to me and I take it so she can start tapping away at her computer. "Tell them I'll definitely be there. I'm not missing the biggest event of the year. Even if I have to sit next to Julian the entire night."

I reach for the pile of paperwork I left on her desk this morning when I sense she is cooling down already. "The brief for your two o'clock meeting with Gary is in here and I've emailed you a copy. Susan called to confirm your lunch with her today."

Lisa squints at her screen through her black frames, her red lips pursed with scrutiny. "Honestly, I have an assistant. Why do people contact me directly? Michael Miller's sent a link for a live video webinar tomorrow night. You can watch it on my behalf. I'm happy to pay you overtime."

I open my mouth to agree, but remember my weekend plans. I can't remember the last time I had plans, and this would be the perfect way to get out of them. But Kali's right, despite her constant meddling and lecturing, about me needing to do things again.

At my hesitation, Lisa's dark gaze leaves her screen and lands on me, burning a hole through my skull.

Deep breath, Hazel. "I sort of have plans tomorrow night."

Lisa peers over her horn-rimmed glasses, mild surprise plastered on her face. "Well, what do you know? She has a life."

Her gaze drops back to her computer screen. I can't say I blame her reaction to my revelation. Even I'm surprised.

"Watch the webinar once the recording is available. It'll be up on Sunday, so I expect notes on Monday morning," she orders, clicking away at the keyboard.

Great. "No problem."

As I leave a re-filled glass of water on a coaster by her computer, she orders me to close the door, muttering to herself about how she can't wait to be rid of this place, something she says daily. Lisa says a lot of things.

She's said multiple times I'd get to accompany her on some of her exotic trips around the world. Once, I got to go with her on a trip to Perth and I visited New Zealand with her for two days, where I stayed in my hotel room sorting out her life. For whatever reason, she can look after herself and sort out her own appointments when she's travelling first class on a weeklong trip to London.

She's also said for the entire time I've been working for her, she'd help get me into the marketing or creative design department. Still waiting on that, otherwise I'd be days away from throwing in the towel.

I mentally pat myself on the back for having the courage to tell her I have plans and have almost made it back to my desk, when I hear, "Wait, Jonesy!"

My legs stall and I pivot to see Lisa hanging out of her office. If she's using her nickname for me, she's either in a better mood, or about to ask me to do something I won't want to do. "Tanya is going to drop Lulu here in about an hour. She needs to be at her appointment at ten."

Ah, Lulu. Lisa's precious chihuahua.

Another reminder of why I so often contemplate throwing in the towel.

3

I SLIP INSIDE THE HOUSE, *holding my breath.*

A quick scan of the hallway and living room confirms I still haven't been detected, and I place my overnight bag gently on the floor. I had to pull one too many favours to leave the conference early, and I'm not about to sabotage my surprise by being heavy-handed.

When I hear running water coming from our ensuite, I push down my shorts and kick them off in the hallway. I tiptoe towards our bedroom, biting my lip with anticipation. I don't want to scare him, or it could end in one or both of us getting injured.

As I approach the ajar bedroom door, a moan halts me in my tracks.

My stomach drops.

I swallow down the sudden dryness in my throat, as I see him through the open bathroom door.

Luke, his sculpted torso flexing and contorting, as he thrusts in and out of someone who isn't me. Wet, blonde hair, and perfect breasts push against the glass as he slides in and out of her, over and over and over again. Her moans imitate a pornstar's.

It's an eternity before Luke looks up and locks his gaze with mine through the steam.

"*Fuck!*" *barks from his mouth, as he pulls out of the woman. He's scrambling to get to me. "Hazel, wait!"*

I run out of the room before my heart can catch up with my brain. Seconds later, Luke comes screaming into the foyer with a towel wrapped around his waist, his chest heaving, his eyes panicked.

"Please, wait, let me explain!"

My throat and chest constrict as my world crumbles in front of me. I'm on fire. It's so hot in here, even with the air conditioner blasting through the house. Is it working? Why is it so hot?

"I'm sorry, I'm so sorry," he says.

"What...when..." I can't piece together a sentence. Days earlier, I wondered what sort of ring I'd choose should he propose. Salty tears are in my mouth and I can't breathe.

"Hazel, I'm sorry," he pants.

"You were...you were with another woman in the shower we chose together," I utter, my hand clutching my chest.

"I..." Luke winces as he meets my expression, which is undoubtedly mascara stained. I don't even care that I have no pants on. "I fucked up. I fucked up really bad."

"You think?"

Luke reaches for me and I slap his hand away, only to regret it seconds later. I've never lashed out at him and despite what's happening, part of me wants him to hold me. I can't see straight. I can't think straight.

"How long?" I whisper, dreading the answer.

Luke runs a hand through his hair, his gaze darting towards the bedroom. Is he worried she'll overhear his answer? Does he care about her? Who is she?

I bend over and place my hands on my knees to control my breathing. My chest hurts and my breaths are sharp and shallow. Painful.

"Since my work Christmas party," he answers.

That was six months ago. Six. Months.

An off-kilter sounding sob escapes my lips before I can stop it. Luke closes the distance between us, ignoring my protests.

"Shit, Hazel. I'm such an asshole." Luke hovers in front of me, unsure of how to comfort me or what to do next.

When I look into Luke's wide eyes, with one hand on my chest and the other steadying myself from falling, the pain on his face barrels into me. "Do you love her?"

Luke hesitates and a fresh wave of tears burst from my eyes. The noises coming from my mouth mimic a baby whale crying in the ocean, but I don't care.

I'm going to pass out.

Right here, with no pants on and my heart breaking under my hand.

I take a too-large gulp of red wine to wipe out the memory.

"You all good?" Kali casts me a sideways glance with manicured eyebrows perked in concern.

"I'm thinking about stupid stuff."

"By stupid, I assume you mean fuckface."

I smile but say nothing.

"I hate what he did to you," Kali snarls. "I bet that's what happened with this dude and his wife. She found out he was cheating, confronted him, and he pushed her down the stairs." Kali nods her head towards the television in front of us.

"I thought an owl flew in and caused her to fall?" I ask dryly.

Kali shrugs, helping herself to a slice of pizza. "We'll never know the truth."

"It wasn't a goddamned owl."

This is where we sit most Friday evenings, on the floor, heads resting against our couch as we devour pizza and red wine, dissecting crime docos, the latest television shows or watching classic movies with nostalgia. Tonight's choice is one we've watched several times before and it has us throwing theories back and forth, with more confidence, the more wine we drink.

I only allow myself to drink around Kali in the safety of our home these days. Drinking pulls down the walls I've worked hard to put up. Not to mention, my partying ways had me contemplate full-on sobriety for the rest of my life. When you wake on someone's front lawn, on a street you don't recognise with your wallet missing, you question who you are.

"I checked his Instagram today." It takes me a second to realise I said it aloud, the red wine allowing me to confess my shame. Kali shifts in my peripheral, grabbing her phone from the coffee table.

"And?"

Grateful she's not chastising me for my stupidity, I say, "He's in Western Australia."

Luke's latest photo is of him standing against a stunning desert backdrop, his muscular torso on display and arms outstretched. My stalker skills revealed he's on the other side of the country working for a mining company and there are no signs of another woman. I'm positive we'll never get back together, but I'm not ready to see him with someone else. Especially *her*.

"Ugh, what a show pony," Kali grumbles, scrolling through Luke's feed. "He could put a shirt on once in a while."

I nod in agreement, wondering how Luke coped in the immediate days and weeks after we fell apart. Perhaps he's using physical exercise as a coping mechanism as much as me.

"You're going to be so amazing tomorrow night you'll have your choice of the hottest guys the Gold Coast has to offer." Kali drops her phone, a gleam in her eye. "Hell, you can choose more than one for all I care, and dickhead won't be on your mind ever again."

"Why are any of these men going to want to go home with me?"

Kali holds a finger up. "Knock it off with the insecure, self-condescending bullshit. I don't want to hear it and neither do guys."

"Kali—"

"You don't have to do anything you don't want to," Kali interrupts. "But *promise* me, you'll try to have a good time. Promise me. Right now."

With a loud exhale, I loll my head to the side. "I promise." Kali nods with satisfaction and I allow a glimmer of hope to ripple through me. Maybe she's right and a fun night out is what I need to get out of this rut.

"I'm doing this for you," I remind her.

Kali grins.

"I'm not going." The words slip from my mouth as I curl into the foetal position on my bed, watching an underwear-clad Kali raid my wardrobe.

She doesn't pause in her task. "Hazel Jones, you're going if I have to drag you out of here by your damned hair." She dumps a stack of dresses onto the back of the grey armchair in the corner of my room. Most of them still have the tags on. Our wardrobes are bursting with clothing samples from Green and Acre. Kali, the sometimes ethical and sustainable hippy, loves the perks of my job as much as I do.

A low growl escapes my lips as I roll onto my stomach and shove my face into a satin pillow.

"Can't you take someone else?" I plead, tilting my head to the side. Kali's holding a baby-pink jumpsuit to her tall body, assessing its suitability in the mirror. "Don't wear that."

She casts it aside. "There's no one else in my circle whose life is as pathetic as yours right now."

"I hate you."

"You love me," Kali selects a black feathery dress from the

pile of potential outfits for the evening, studying her reflection, lip curling upwards. She tosses that one aside too. "And as I've been saying to you endlessly, you need to get out of the house and talk to some other humans." Kali locks her wide chocolate gaze with mine via the mirror. "Sitting around here all-day moping doesn't look good on you."

"Says who?"

"Says me, and my opinion is the most important one in your life."

"I don't want to talk to strangers," I moan, curling up again. The idea of going out wasn't one I was keen on to begin with and, now we're getting ready for the night, my stomach rolls with anxiety. The notion of leaving the comfort of our cosy townhouse, to mingle with beautiful people I'll have nothing in common with, elicits sweat from my palms. Even with Kali's promise to do my hair and makeup so I appear flawless doesn't help. Whilst I can appreciate the glitz and glam, I want nothing to do with the extra attention, and with Kali at the helm she'll force me to wear something ridiculously tight and short to 'show off what I've got' and 'get me heaps of dick.'

"Alex isn't a stranger," Kali argues.

"I've met him twice and say hi to him at the gym some-times," I reply. "I'm your sympathy plus one."

"There will be other guys from the gym who you'll recog-nise." Kali smiles as she decides on her outfit for the evening; a skin-tight, burnt-orange dress designed for the Kali's of the world, people addicted to Pilates, with dark skin, perky tits, and legs for days.

"Hazel, it's entirely your choice." Kali has her matter-of-fact face on. "You can either get ready now or you can lie on that bed until it's time to leave and accompany me in your pyjamas. Either way, you are coming."

I flip restlessly onto my back, snapping at her, "You can at least get me a beer. If I'm going out to hang with a bunch of strangers, I deserve to be pleasantly buzzed before I arrive."

She grins and saunters out of the room, her chocolate waves bouncing on her shoulders. I smile to myself. She might be a pest for not leaving me alone, but I'll be damned if she isn't the best friend a girl could ask for.

Kali returns holding two open bottles of cold beer and slaps one into my hand, her smile wide and cheeky as she chinks her bottle to mine. "Tonight's going to be fun, I promise," she says, turning my music speaker on. "Alex's friends are hot and don't seem repulsive. Plus, it's an *open* bar. You know what that means."

"We can abuse the bar tab to our hearts' content and not spend a cent?" I muse.

"Exactly." Music radiates from the speaker as she places it on my bookcase.

Despite my grumbling, a tiny part of me is hopeful tonight won't be terrible. Which surprises me. It's comforting to feel hope again. The old Hazel, the pre-Luke Hazel, would be the first to admit I enjoyed a few drinks on the weekend. With a few drinks comes a more confident and flirtatious Hazel. I know from previous experiences; I need to remember to draw the line between sexy and fun Hazel and completely-obliterated-swear-at-strangers-and-fall-over-because-I'm-terrible-at-walking-in-heels-Hazel.

A smile creeps across my face as I think of the potentially good outcomes tonight could bring. I take an ambitious sip of beer, sighing as the cool liquid slides down my throat.

Kali clicks her fingers to get my attention, dragging my desk chair to sit in front of the full-length mirror, and pats the seat with vigour. She holds up a makeup brush and waves it at me, as if she's a predator taunting her prey.

4

KYGO IS EXACTLY what I've been dreading.

Situated in Burleigh Heads, right across from the ocean, it's the Coast's latest 'it' spot. An open-roofed, two-storey bar pumping with loud music and, apparently, the entire population of the Gold Coast.

Three beers prior to showing up are not enough to put up with the sheer number of people. Nausea festers in the pit of my stomach as we try to weave our way through the throng of everybody who wants to be seen. Local wannabe (and some fairly legitimate) Instagram 'influencers' mingle in loud groups scattered in every room, as I'd suspected they would. It's a sea of high hair and manbuns, stiletto heels and chino pants, perfect makeup, flowy skirts, fake tan, tight dresses, and sunglasses to mask dinner-plate pupils. Almost every person we pass has their phone in hand, taking selfies in front of the pink neon sign that reads 'Don't Tequila My Vibe'.

Naturally, every place to be seen is also a place to see, and heads turn as Kali leads the way through the crowd. She is in her element, her slender shoulders rolled up and back as she

marches through the gawping crowd, leading me by my hand as
I apologise for brushing against people.

I do not belong here.

At the very least, Kali can be proud of her work. After a lot of
bickering and excuses, she got me into a pair of black cropped
pants and a midriff top, teamed with a cape in case there were
no heating lamps in the outdoor area to ward off the chill still in
the air.

I couldn't argue. If I had to be dressed against my will, at
least it's in my favourite colours: black on black on black. She
also tamed my thick mass of hair into soft ribbons down my
back and painted little wings to accentuate my almond-shaped
eyes. I at least *look* part of the crowd here, but I can say without
a doubt I'm the ultimate wolf in sheep's clothing. Except I'm the
sheep and the beautiful people here are the wolves, ready to tear
me to shreds.

When we reach the second floor, the outdoor rooftop is
roped off for Alex's function, to which we gain instant access
and wristbands for the private bar. Lord knows how busy this
place would be if there wasn't someone on crowd control.

Beautiful people are *everywhere*, covering the backdrop of the
blackened ocean with their desperate need to get photos before
everybody looks too trashed. Hastily, I scan the crowd in a
desperate hope for at least one other familiar face, but it's
useless. I only spot Alex, who's treated himself to an over-the-
top teeth-whitening job and is almost bursting out of a too-tight
navy dress shirt. The minute he spots Kali, he raises a giant
hand and waves.

Kali's face breaks into an enormous smile and she returns
the gesture, indicating that she and I are going to get a drink.
She leads me to the bar and orders us two beers before letting
out a quiet squeal under her breath.

"I'm excited," she admits. Even though she's confident and
fierce most of the time, it's always endearing to see her act like a

schoolgirl, jittering with nerves. She runs her fingers through her hair and tousles it. "How do I look?"

"Flawless." I glance towards the crowd and see Alex's enormous frame edging closer to us. "Incoming."

"Fuck," she hisses, graciously accepting her beer from the bartender and taking three large gulps. I thank the bartender and sip on my drink, making no effort to hide the fact that seeing Kali nervous or intimidated raises my levels of smugness.

Alex's welcoming face appears over Kali's shoulder in a matter of seconds, and I smile up at his goofy expression while Kali does her best to act nonchalant. "Happy birthday," I say, raising my bottle to him.

Kali, ever the award-winning actress, throws Alex her best set of sex eyes. "Happy birthday."

Alex looks like Kali's type of guy, a young Arnold Schwarzenegger on twenty-first century steroids. "Pretty cool, huh?" He looks around at the jampacked rooftop with a proud grin. "It's great so many people could make it. Thanks for coming. You too, Hazel."

He might be way too into his appearance, but underneath that muscle is a sweet and sexy teddy bear dentist (Kali's words, not mine). He also remembered my name, which was more than Kali's previous love interest managed.

Kali and I follow Alex to a group of his friends, some of whom I unfairly judge as self-absorbed and stupid because their enormous muscles don't fit properly in their overly tight pants. Kali's right: pulling back from most human contact for two months has had some negative side effects.

Kali effortlessly jumps right into their conversation. She's exceptional at getting people to adore her without even trying. She's bold, loud, and charming. I have zero resentment towards her about it, but sometimes wish I could adopt some of her skills. Instead of socialising, I stand with my back against the closest wall, assessing everyone within view for red flags and distinguishable features, in case one of them ends up 'wanted' on the morning news. I *know* that's ridiculous, but when you coop yourself up for months on end listening to true crime podcasts and watching every serial killer documentary ever made, unconventional habits start to form.

"How do you know this lot?" A slender woman with milky skin stands beside me, slurping on a vodka soda-like drink.

"I'm here with Kali," I reply, nodding towards Kali's back. "Alex and I see each other at the gym sometimes."

"How do you people find the energy to even go to the gym?" she tuts.

"Have your boyfriend destroy your life. That always helps." Words tumble out of my mouth before I know what I'm saying, and I mentally slap myself. Maybe the earlier beers are taking effect.

"Guys are dickheads," the woman says, and then she holds out her hand. "I'm Meg. Alex's only cousin."

I shake her hand. "Hazel, Kali's only friend."

Meg laughs and indicates for me to follow her to the cushioned bench in the corner close to us. "Excuse me!" Meg waves a manicured hand to a passing server as we take a seat.

"What can I get for you ladies?"

"Hazel, what are you having?" Meg grabs my half-empty bottle to read the label. "Another one of these and I'll have an espresso martini, please, and two tequila shots, with salt and lime."

My stomach knots. "Uh, no. No—"

"Come on Hazel, it's a party with free booze!" Meg cries with a giant smile. "And the best way to forget about the dicks in your life is by letting loose and having a bit of fun. Don't you agree?" She turns her question to the server, whose cheeky grin has widened.

"Absolutely. Your order is coming right up." He winks at Meg's victorious face before disappearing.

"Just the one shot," I warn her.

"Of course." Her face is one of mock-innocence. "Do you think that waiter is cute?"

"Very, and very into you."

"Do you think so?" Meg asks, wide-eyed. It takes everything in my power not to scoff. I'm pretty sure men *and* women are ogling her as they walk past. "I know most of the guys here, but so many of them are basically brothers to me, and Alex never lets any of them look at me."

"My guess is Alex is going to be preoccupied tonight, so I'd say everyone is fair game." I glance across to where Alex stands, Kali by his side, his hand on the small of her back. I sense by the end of the evening, he won't be so gentlemanly and her, not so ladylike. She'd explicitly said so on the taxi ride here.

"So, what do you do with yourself Hazel?" Meg asks.

Eat. Train. Work. Sleep. All the above to stop myself from thinking about my ex.

"I'm an executive assistant for a director at Green and Acre," I reply.

"Shut up!" Meg cries. "My friend works there too! I *love* Green and Acre. Maybe you'd know my friend. Which department do you work in?"

"I work for the person in charge of property–"

"Meg!"

The two of us whip our heads around to see a woman with bright red hair in a *very* short black dress walking towards us. To my surprise, it's Rachel from my building. Meg squeals with excitement. "I'm so glad you could come on such short notice!" Meg says, pulling Rachel into our lounge area. "Come here, you might know—"

"Hazel! I was hoping I'd see you here!" Rachel cries.

"So, you guys *do* know each other?" Meg claps with excitement before halting abruptly. "Please tell me you guys aren't rivals or something stupid."

I grimace at Meg. "Rachel's kind of a bitch." For a split second, I wonder if my lame attempt at humour isn't going over so well, but then Rachel cackles and sits down at my other side. It's got to be the first time I've offered blatant sarcasm in front of her since we met.

"We work in the same building," Rachel explains. "I would've told you I'd be here tonight when I saw you yesterday, but *someone* only invited me a few hours ago as a last-minute replacement friend." Rachel shoots a scowl at Meg, who sits up to protest.

"You were my initial invite months ago, but couldn't make it remember? So, I invited Chanelle, but she's got gastro and Alex said I was only allowed *one* friend because he didn't want his friends hitting on everyone—"

Rachel giggles. "I'm joking! I know, I know, I'm messing with you."

Meg huffs, but plasters her award-winning smile onto her face when our server returns with a tray of drinks. "Here we are ladies," he sings, placing our drinks and three tequila shots on the low table.

"How did you know we needed three?" Meg asks.

"I saw your friend arrive," he replies, a grin spreading across his handsome face.

Even in the darkness, I see Meg blush as her gaze flicks to his name badge. "Thank you…Frankie."

"Let me know if you need anything else. He holds Meg's gaze for a few seconds before he walks away.

Rachel leans across me to give Meg a raised eyebrow. "Waiter boy is *sooo* cute."

"He is, isn't he?" Meg reaches greedily for the saltshaker in front of us. "Alright ladies, lick your place of choice."

I groan. "I can't believe I'm doing this."

"You don't like tequila, Hazel?" Rachel asks, licking the top of her hand and holding it out for salt.

"No, I don't," I grumble, snatching the salt from Meg and passing it to Rachel. Meg grins at me, bouncing in her seat as she waits for us to set ourselves up.

"At least you've got a chaser," Rachel points out, nodding to my beer. "It won't be that bad."

"You won't be saying that when I vomit it straight back up." I lick my wrist and sprinkle salt on it, bracing myself for what's coming.

"You've got this." Rachel hands me my shot and I shudder at the whiff of liquor.

Meg holds her phone above the table, ready to capture the moment. "Ready girls? Cheers!"

Three hours later, I am drunk. Super drunkkkk.

I've had two tequilas, one wet pussy shot, countless beers and a slice of birthday cake. On two separate trips to the bathroom, cocaine was offered like pieces of gum. Flashbacks of my party phase shot through my brain and I said no to both offers, escaping before my brain had time to catch up. I'm not willing to re-open that door anytime soon, even if I am totally inebriated.

Rachel, Meg, and I have barely moved from our corner of the rooftop, squealing, and giggling as we exchange stories about our exes, our bosses and who here we think is hot. I did move to dance to a couple of songs. It's mindless and effortless and, for the first time in months, I'm having fun.

An eclectic mix of beautiful and interesting people finds their way into our corner to rest their sore feet, or to hit on one of us, the free-flowing alcohol lowering everybody's inhibitions. Kali comes by multiple times to mingle with the three of us, as well as update us on how much she adores Alex. She's gone from 'he's the sweetest guy I've ever met' to 'I'm going to fuck his brains out tonight', much to Meg's dismay. Kali also lets me know how many guys have hit on me, which I brush off, not wanting her to see my giddiness at the prospect. Although, I *had* noticed the number of guys squeezing in to chat us up.

The rooftop is a sight to take in as the night goes on. What started as polite conversation and courteous laughter has escalated to provocative dancing, boisterous cheering, and a lot of grinding. The sexual energy sizzles amongst the guests, none of whom seem keen on leaving.

Frankie, our new favourite staff member, is becoming more and more ballsy with his advances to Meg. She's fairly liquored up and matching him in the brazen department. When Frankie arrives with a tray filled with shots for whoever wants them, I watch Meg lock eyes with him. She leans forward so her breasts conveniently press together and reaches for the saltshaker. Without a hint of shyness, she lifts her hand and slowly licks the inside of her wrist, maintaining eye contact with a rock-hard-in-the-pants Frankie. Rachel's mouth hangs open in shock, and I do my best to stifle my drunken giggles. He shifts to adjust his pants as he walks away with a breathless smile. Yep, that would've turned anyone on.

"And here I was thinking you were sweet and innocent," I say, poking her in the ribs. Meg bats her eyes a couple of times before reaching for her shot.

My fuzzy gaze wanders around the balcony. I know I'm somewhere along the line between a good time and the point of no return. The tequila's helped in my newfound friendships with Meg and Rachel, but it also tugs at the emotional part of me I've worked so hard to stomp down and lock up since Luke and I ended.

I decide to dip my toe into a few of the memories I'd pushed to the deepest corners of my mind, such as, how in the beginning, Luke and I couldn't keep our hands off each other, especially when we went out with friends. We spent hours at bars, getting drunk, touching each other every chance we could. I proudly showed him off as mine. Women would throw him sex eyes or try to chat him up and then I'd sweep in, their annoyed expressions priceless.

Kygo is somewhere he would've loved; a place to be seen, a new spot to scope out.

My choice in men is somewhat stereotypical of the Gold Coast, but Luke was unique to me. He loved to look after himself and liked to be liked. He was charming and funny, and cared too much about his reputation as a loveable rascal, but he was sweet and kind and caring. He made me laugh and knew how to cheer me up when I was down.

I imagine Luke's face, on the guy standing behind the bar and again on a man crossing the dancefloor. My gaze lands on the broad back of another man nearby, wearing a light blue shirt. Luke loved that colour because it made his eyes pop. One of the man's toned arms curls around the waist of a tiny, willowy blonde. Their backs are to me and I watch as she traces her left hand up and down his lower back, before giving his butt a squeeze.

My heart aches a little.

He turns his head to the side with a wicked grin on his face and pulls the woman closer to nuzzle her neck.

My stomach drops.

Oh, Christ.

I'm going to be sick.

Even though the party's outdoors, a cold tingling sensation dances from my hands to my chest, and I'm transported to the foyer of my old home with Luke, his torso covered with droplets of water.

Her slender hand hypnotises me as it wanders the body which used to be mine.

Up and down.

Up and down.

And then I see it.

The sparkling rock on her finger.

I've died and gone to hell only to continue re-living the moment I realise my boyfriend of three years might be engaged to the woman he cheated on me with.

Tears form in my eyes. I place my beer on the table in front of me and rise unsteadily to my feet. I cross the luminous dance-floor, my head ducked in shame.

I don't want him to see me. He can't see me. This is why I never come out. I need to get out of here.

"Hazel! Hazel Jones, where do you think you're going?"

Shit.

I spin deliberately to see Kali shimmying towards me with a bright yellow cocktail in her hand. Her level of intoxication is clear as she doesn't notice anything wrong with me and pulls me in for a tight hug. "Do you want to do a shot?" Luke's large frame looms in the corner of my eye. *Please don't see me.*

"I need to pee. I'll be back in a second," I lie, kissing her on the cheek and spinning her around. With perfect timing, Alex dances across the floor, and she hurries towards him. She's so drunk she'll be leaving here to bang him any minute.

I dare a glance in Luke's direction and freeze. I shouldn't have looked.

His piercing blue gaze locks on mine, and my stomach falls out of my body.

It's the first time I've seen him in person since that day, and the way he stares at me sends a volt of electricity to my core. Too broken to return and get my things, Kali took care of that. I never got to say goodbye or yell, or ask a million questions. Now he's in front of me, it's as though I'm imagining someone from beyond the grave.

I need to leave. Before I cry. Before I vomit. Before Drunk Hazel causes a scene. I snap my gaze away and move as fast as my feet will carry me.

My vision blurs as I trudge down the narrow staircase towards the exit, the lump in my throat swelling with each passing second. As I reach the ground floor, I pick up my pace into a run, pushing past the line of people waiting to come inside. Not knowing where to turn, I stumble into the empty side street next to Kygo and walk halfway along before letting the tears fall in dramatic sobs.

My heart is shattering inside my chest. Again. Seeing *him*, with *her*, is all it took to tip me over the edge. I've spent months compartmentalising my darkest thoughts, burying them where they would stay until they fizzled out, but tonight, leaving my safety net, has let them break free to suffocate me.

I stabilise myself against the graffitied brick wall and do my best to stop wailing, but it gets worse. Not only is it more unbearable, but I also know how drunk I am now that I've sprinted from the bar. My head is fuzzy. I'm warm, but it's too cold out here to feel this way.

I squeeze my eyes shut, willing myself to calm.

"Are you okay?"

The deep voice next to me hardly registers as I squeeze my eyes shut, trying desperately to get a handle on my breathing. "Anxiety...attack," I get out, without opening my eyes. I'm not sure if the nausea burning in my gut is from the alcohol or seeing Luke, but I know opening my eyes will make it worse.

Inhale one ... two ... three ... four ... exhale one ... two ... three ... four. Breathe Hazel, breathe.

I'm not sure how much time passes before I get control of my body again. The familiar noises from the nearby street and the bar upstairs remind me where I am and I relax a little as I keep my hands on my knees, my body hunched over.

Somebody or something touches my arm and I jump. THWACK. My head smacks on something behind me and before I can curse loudly, my vision blackens.

5

"HEY! HEY! WAKE UP!"

Owww. My head hurts.

A groan escapes my lips as I open my eyes to see dark brown dashed with golden flakes.

"Are you okay?" The man asks.

"What happened?"

"I startled you." A flicker of relief flashes across his face at my newfound consciousness. "You jumped and hit your head on a wall bracket. You were out for a few seconds."

The man reaches down and gingerly lifts me to my feet, keeping his warm hands on either side of my waist as I steady myself. His angular face creases with concern, his dark brows knit together in a frown.

In a fitted dark grey suit, he looks as if he's stepped straight out of a Mediterranean-inspired fashion magazine, complete with dark tousled hair and an olive complexion. I'm jealous of the prominence of his high cheekbones, noting a tidy, straight white scar on his left cheek. A light smattering of immaculately trimmed stubble covers his chin and the space between his nose and top lip. My eyes stare at his mouth.

"Hey." He squeezes my hips at my lack of response, his fingers skimming the exposed flesh of my midriff. An unexpected shiver ripples through me.

He's not a figment of my imagination. He's real. Very real.

"I'm fine," I say. I wipe my face, which is likely red, blotchy, and stained with mascara. *Great.*

"Can you tell me what day it is? Do you know where you are?" he asks.

Thoughts of how I look vanish. He moves his hands away as I cross my arms like a petulant child, scrambling to remember what's going on. "*Yes*. It's ... Saturday and ... I was getting some fresh air. Women *are* allowed to walk around unchaperoned, you know."

A small smile threatens to crack his beautiful face. "I didn't mean it like that."

"Sure, you didn't."

"In my defence, you didn't exactly look like you had things under control."

"If you'd left me alone, I would've handled it and not smacked my skull against a rusty piece of metal."

He cocks his head to one side. "You know, I think you were more pleasant when you were unconscious." The light sarcasm in his tone causes me to scoff.

"Thanks for your help." My head hurts too much to deal with any more men tonight, no matter how handsome. Plus, the way he's peering at me–a mix of arrogance and pity–isn't something I need right now.

I turn to head towards the road, but I'm woozy. As my vision sways, the man comes back into focus, steadying me again, pulling me so close his chest is in front of my face. My taste buds tingle as I inhale his pine-scented cologne.

"I think you may have a concussion," he says. His voice is deep, but not threatening.

"I'm fine." I try to push him off, but it's no use. I can't stand upright without leaning into him. How did I allow myself to get into such a vulnerable position? I don't just hate tonight, I hate myself.

"Why don't you wait here a couple of minutes?"

I don't argue as he tenderly steers me to lean against the brick wall, where I let my head fall back. After ensuring I won't topple over, he steps back to give me some space and a calm silence settles between us; the sounds of music and hum of conversation drift from the noisy bar above.

"What were you doing out here?" he asks, scanning both ends of the alley. I frown as I try to remember why I left the bar to begin with.

Oh, yeah.

A humourless laugh escapes my lips. "If you must know, I saw the man I spent three years of my life with and who shattered my heart into a million pieces, flaunting his new fiancée."

The alcohol coursing through my veins takes away any embarrassment I would normally feel at blurting out my problems to a stranger. The man says nothing, and I need to fill the silence. "It turns out when faced with danger, my instinct is to run. I guess my anxiety got the better of me when I got here." My words trail off as I re-live the helplessness from minutes ago. How my breath caught in my throat and my chest constricted.

The man's eyes crinkle in the corners. "You're out here because you ran away from your ex?"

"Would you suggest I cause a big scene in the middle of a friend's birthday?" I ask. "Scream at him like a lunatic?"

"I'm relieved you're not out here crying because of something more sinister, to be honest." The man offers me another small smile. "It's a shame you weren't able to take the opportunity to get your pent-up rage out. I bet screaming in his face would've felt far more satisfying than crying in a random alley with a suspected concussion, right?"

Sober Hazel would have laughed at those words. But not Drunk Hazel.

Drunk Hazel hates tonight.

Drunk Hazel hates herself.

And Drunk Hazel hates this douchebag.

"You know what? I don't need this!" I shout, and his eyes widen in surprise. For a second, I even surprise myself, but it doesn't stop me from ranting. "You know nothing about me. Yes, I'm drunk and might *appear* slightly pathetic crying over a man who broke my heart, but for the record I went through the wringer with that guy, and I don't need some random dude waltzing into my life while I'm having an anxiety attack, giving me his two cents on what I should've done!"

I'm gasping for breath by the end and the man puts his hands up in a defensive pose.

"My apologies. That's not what I meant, but you're right, I clearly don't know the situation or you."

"You think?"

Does everyone get this worked up when they run into exes with their new fiancées? It turns out I'm someone who *does* and now I've told this random dude about it. I'm not one for blabbing my emotions and I silently curse myself and the alcohol I've consumed for my incessant babbling. Even Drunk Hazel knows she's acting like a spoilt child. *Please God, let me wake up from this nightmare.*

A gasp escapes my lips when I run my fingers over the warm bump at the back of my head. It's slightly swollen and tender to the touch.

"I meant what I said about the concussion," he says, eyeing me as I assess my head. "We should get you an ambulance or—"

"I'm not getting in an ambulance, for God's sake," I groan, dropping my hand. "I'm *fine*."

I ignore his deliberate gaze and survey his towering frame. He's blessed with broad shoulders, but he's not bulky. Fit, undoubtedly, the expensive suit clinging to the right curves in his chest and legs, but not big enough to have taken steroids. I've found men who are sans-substance abuse to be a rarity on the Gold Coast. Well, if you have a habit of searching in the wrong spots, like I do.

He's older than I first thought. Older than me. The fine lines marking the edges of his mocha eyes show someone with life experience. Even so, he's still got the genetic blessings of a European model. The bridge of his nose is slightly crooked, and I bet he's broken it at some time. Probably from getting into fights in darkened alleyways. I'm not one for violence, but the image of this man shirtless and covered in a sheen of glistening sweat, channelling adrenaline, dances before my eyes—

Not helping, Hazel.

He's attractive, but I'll bet he's a troublemaker. With a face like that, it'd be easy for him to scope out women in trouble, so they'll thank him with their vaginas. He must be disappointed to have come across one who can't stand up straight, string an intelligent sentence together and whose vagina has healed over.

"You hit your head pretty hard," he adds, and I blush at how long I spaced out, thinking about him as a shirtless and fighting womaniser.

"Enough about that. What are *you* doing in this alleyway?" I probe, adjusting my stance against the brick wall. My head throbs, but I refuse to let him know. He pauses, likely to weigh up whether I'm going to fall over.

"Drug deal?" I probe. "Preying on potential victims?"

He could pass for an unsuspecting psychopath, dazzling would-be victims with his handsome face.

"How about saving damsels in distress?" he asks, mimicking my actions and taking a couple of steps back to lean against the opposite wall, his arms behind his back.

"You *caused* my concussion, remember?"

"So, you *do* think you have a concussion," he counters. He

looks up and down the alleyway, something he's done several times since arriving. He looks mildly annoyed, although that could be his normal expression.

"If you need to get going, don't let me stop you. I need to get home, anyway." *I need bed.*

"Where are your friends?" he asks.

I think of Kali, Meg and Rachel. They're about an hour away from leaving to pass out or an hour away from getting kicked out.

"They're inside having a good time," I brush off. "I don't need a babysitter; I need an Uber." I stumble again as I leave the wall and hear him sigh.

"You can't go off on your own. You can't even walk properly," he mutters.

"It's these stupid shoes," I insist, continuing my graceful walk towards the road.

"Wait ... hang on a second ... miss!"

When I turn to face him, he is close enough for me to smell his minty breath. "My *name* is Hazel Jones." I reach my hand out for him to shake, concentrating with everything I have left to keep my balance. He hesitates, his eyes flickering to my hand, before meeting my eyes.

"Hazel Jones?" he questions, genuine curiosity on his face.

"I know it sounds made up because it's so boring," I snap, retrieving my hand before he can shake it. "But it's my actual name, I swear. Here—" I fumble around in my bag and fish out my driver's licence. "See? *See?* That's my name. Hazel No-Middle-Name Jones."

The man squints at my licence. "I didn't say I didn't believe you, Hazel."

As if I'm a child throwing a tantrum, I stick my tongue out as I shove the card back into my clutch bag.

"My name is Patrick," he says, as I roll my ankle and fall

forwards. Patrick reaches out and catches me before I tumble ass-over-tit. I hear him curse under his breath.

"Help me get an Uber and I'll get out of your hair," I grumble into his shirt.

"Do you even know where you are right now?"

I narrow my eyes as I straighten, doing my best to ignore the rock-hard chest underneath my fingertips. "Do I look useless to you?"

He raises both eyebrows. "Do you want me to answer that question honestly?"

"Are you always this much of a smartass?"

"Are you always this stubborn?" he snaps.

"Yes, actually."

"What a surprise."

My eyes travel down to where his hands still rest on my hips, holding me upright. He must notice because he steadies me and pulls his hands away.

"Like I said," Patrick says. "You hit your head pretty hard. Whereabouts do you live?"

I pause, deciding whether I want to answer. "Mermaid Beach."

"Let me drive you home."

My vision is fuzzy from the alcohol and emotions, but somehow my brain has some function. "I think I'll take my chances with a service that has tracking devices and verifies their drivers."

He pauses before sighing, as if I've somehow beaten him down.

"You could be a serial killer," I add. Heaven forbid I act sensual and flirtatious, like Kali would. Instead, I blurt out the first logical yet extreme response that pops into my brain. Seriously though, what if he is a serial killer? Albeit a devilishly handsome serial killer, but still …

"Fine, get an Uber," Patrick growls, shaking his head.

As I open my mouth to say something clever, a high-pitched squeal interrupts me.

"Hazel! There you are!" Meg and Rachel are all giggles and long legs as they stumble along the alleyway toward us. I sense Patrick assessing them and a part of my drunken brain feels a stab of jealousy. I'm sure he's checking them out.

"Kali said you were peeing, but we couldn't find you," Meg slurs on approach, her eyes moving between myself and Patrick.

"Jesus, *hello!*" Rachel whoops, her gaze locking on Patrick without shame. She turns to me and waggles her eyebrows, a giggle escaping her lips.

"Wow, you have a beautiful face," Meg says, her eyes glassy.

Patrick chuckles. "Tequila will do that to a person's vision."

Trust me, it's not the tequila.

Meg giggles and Rachel lets out a noise of agreement, and I realise I didn't think it. I said it out loud. There's enough booze in my system to take the edge off me experiencing pure mortification, but I'm too nervous to look at Patrick's face.

"Are you coming with us to Archie's? Alex organised a private bus to take everyone there," Meg explains. "There's no way we'll get Ubers tonight because of the footy game."

I groan. Local footy games mean taxis, Ubers and every other ride-sharing company are backlogged with pre-booked trips.

"Drunk with a concussion and a *long* wait to get home." Patrick's voice sounds smug.

I glare at him. "No Archie's for me. I'm going home."

Rachel and Meg exchange knowing glances. "Right, *okay.*"

Rachel links her arm with Meg's as she turns her attention to Patrick. "Pleasure to meet you, man with the beautiful face. You should definitely take our friend Hazel home."

"Definitely," Meg agrees. "Maybe even take her pants off."

"Christ," I mutter to myself, but they're too drunk to care whether they're crossing a line.

"We'll let Kali know you're heading home," Meg says, with

wide-eyed innocence as Rachel giggles. My two new friends envelop me in their warmth as they throw their arms around me in a messy farewell hug.

"Get her home safely!" Rachel barks, holding her phone up and snapping a photo of Patrick before he can object. "I've got your picture now, so no murdering and all that."

"No murdering and all that," Patrick says with a nod. "I'll get her home safely."

The two of them stumble back towards the entrance of Kygo, and I wonder if they'll have any luck getting into another establishment in their state.

"What's it going to be, Hazel?" he asks, glancing at his watch. "I don't have all night."

I can't tell what he's thinking. Does he want me to accept the offer of a ride home, or is he doing it out of politeness? And what do I want to do? It's always a bad idea to get into a car with a stranger. Every single true crime podcast I've listened to says to never do it. *But* I have two witnesses and the chances of me getting home otherwise are bloody slim.

And my feet hurt.

"Okay, but no locking the doors."

6

I SEND Kali a text saying I had a great time but need my bed. If she hears about me seeing Luke, having a panic attack and being rescued by a moody man in a suit, she'll insist on coming home with me, but I want her to enjoy the night out. She replies saying she's sad I've left but relieved I'm safe. Guilt trickles into my chest about lying to her, but my throbbing head wants to get home. Hopefully Meg and Rachel don't mention Patrick and his offer of a ride until I'm safely in bed.

Patrick leads me to the street running parallel to Kygo, where a small car park sits behind a row of shops. I let out an exaggerated whistle as the lights of a sleek, sporty black Mercedes flash in front of us.

"You know, for a potential serial killer, you sure know how to travel in style," I say. Patrick rolls his eyes for the thousandth time as he steps forward and opens the passenger door for me. "And he's a gentleman too."

Patrick's chest rises as he inhales deeply. "Please get in the car before I change my mind." The huskiness and finality in his voice send a mix of pleasure and danger through me.

I hesitate before reminding myself there were plenty of

witnesses who saw us leave the bar, including two reliable, albeit drunk, women. I'm not a totally clueless idiot for getting into a stranger's car that has windows blacker than sin.

Definitely not.

I slide into the passenger seat, the scent of fresh leather hitting my nostrils. The interior is immaculate, every surface free from dust and clutter. It's black and pristine. Serial killers are anal about cleanliness. I guess I should be grateful the car doesn't smell of bleach.

Patrick closes the door behind me and makes his way to the other side, gracefully sliding into the driver's seat. I can't help but look across at him, admiring the way his hair is styled; a little messy, but perfectly so, with a few dark locks falling into his eyes. My gaze drifts to the side of his jaw again, the close shave and five o'clock shadow like a piece of art up close.

His dark eyes sense mine on him because he sends me a curious look. "What?"

My drunken, concussed brain smiles at him, and he looks away. "I guess Dirty Bird is *not* allowed in this car?" I click my seat belt on and curl my hands around the leather seat under my thighs.

Patrick stares at me with a puzzled expression. "Dirty Bird?"

I gape at him. "Dirty Bird. KFC. Kentucky Fried Chicken. Come on, old man."

Patrick looks perplexed. "Old man?"

"Everyone born after 1950 knows what Dirty Bird is," I say matter-of-factly. "Wait a second. *Were* you born after 1950?"

The corner of his mouth curls up slightly. "Just," he replies.

"How old are you?"

"Why is it important?"

"Why do people get weird about sharing how many years they've been on the planet? I'm twenty-seven. Now, stop being such a baby."

Patrick smirks, and I wonder if he's thought of the irony of the situation. Me, a waffling, drunken adult, calling *him* a baby.

"I'm thirty-seven."

A ten-year age gap. Which is completely appropriate when you're two mature adults.

"And you're right, *Dirty Bird* isn't allowed in my car."

The car comes to life without Patrick appearing to touch anything, the sound of the engine powerful, but quiet and soothing. I swallow a bit of fear as the central locking kicks in. I immediately hit the button on my side to unlock the door.

"Don't even think about it," I say to him. He shakes his head but doesn't re-lock the doors.

It should only be about a seven-minute drive at this time of night. I will not be murdered.

"So, Patrick," I say, to break through the tension. "If you're not a serial killer, why are you going out of your way to help me?"

Patrick focuses on the road while I look at the way his long fingers curve around the steering wheel. He's not wearing a wedding band. Not that I care.

"One could argue you're the serial killer here," he replies. "Pretending to have an injury so you can lure me alone and beat me to death with a hidden weapon. You could be a classic Ted Bundy, although maybe not *as* charming."

My mouth drops open as Patrick offers a close-lipped smile at his attempt at humour. He notices the horror on my face because he raises a hand off the steering wheel in surrender. "It was a joke."

"You think bringing up specifics of Ted Bundy's MO to the woman you convinced to get in your car is *funny?*" I snap.

"I was making conversation!" Patrick cries. "You're the one who keeps bringing up serial killers!"

"Because I want to avoid crossing paths with one at all costs!" I shriek.

"I'm sorry! I'm sorry!" Patrick shouts, slowing the car at a stop sign. Patrick spins his body towards mine, eyes wide with panicked earnest. "Honestly, it was a poorly perceived joke."

A few seconds pass and I take deep, deliberate breaths to slow my heart rate. Despite my outburst, my instincts aren't warning me I'm in danger. Before he raised his voice to shout his apologies, Patrick's cool headedness brought on a sense of calm.

"How do you even know Ted Bundy's MO?" I huff, leaning back against the headrest.

Patrick's face flickers with relief as he continues driving in the direction of my house. "Doesn't everybody?"

"I suppose he's one of the well-known ones, yes," I mumble. "Will you at least tell me what you're doing lurking in an alleyway tonight? I'm still not sold on you being a random passer-by good Samaritan."

Patrick lets out a raspy chuckle. "Fair enough. I had dinner with a client."

"A client? *In* the alleyway? What sort of client? What do you do for work?"

"You ask a lot of questions."

"You should've picked a less nosy victim." A small smile curls at the corner of his mouth, but he doesn't answer, so I continue, "In a suit like that, I assume you attended some sort of cliched, pretentious event involving tiny canapes and cigars."

"Pot calling the kettle black, don't you think?" Patrick asks.

"How exactly?"

Patrick's jaw pulses, but he keeps his eyes on the road. "You're dressed for a sponsored Instagram ad and you came stumbling out of the newest bar on the Gold Coast. If anyone's being accused of attending something pretentious and clichéd, it's you."

His sharp response surprises me, but the tequila brushes it off. "Touché Patrick. If it makes any difference, my best friend dressed me in these clothes with a gun to my head." I peer down at my black outfit. "She said it made me look like one of my illustrations." A giggle escapes my mouth as I remember Kali insisting my get-up for the evening was identical to that of an American teenage villain I created. The character got her power from other people's grief and having her wear black and a modern-day cape seemed fitting.

Patrick turns to assess me. "You're an artist?"

I yawn and loll my head to the side to observe his profile, his scar shining under the rolling streetlights. "I wish. I used to draw. A *lot*. I used to create some of the most beautiful things you had ever laid your eyes on Patrick. I used to use *all* the bright colours. All of them."

"You don't anymore?"

I sigh. "No, I don't anymore."

"Why not?"

"Because Luke ..." But I don't know how to finish.

Wrapping my arms around myself, I take a deep breath as an emotional wave hits me, reminding me of the things I denied and pushed deep down about Luke; that maybe we weren't on the same trajectory, that he never really supported me in my ambitions, that maybe he stayed with me because it was easier than breaking up with me, that he was in love with someone else towards the end.

That he's engaged.

In my shattered stupor none of it makes sense.

Patrick is quiet as he changes lanes, but I sense his stare to the side of my face as we slow at an intersection. "Luke is your ex? The one you ran away from tonight?"

I shrug but can't help word-vomiting my disdain. "We broke up in May. I think the woman he brought tonight is the one who ... I'm an idiot to think I would wear a ring. Do you know how many surfing documentaries I sat through with that guy feigning interest? Five hundred million! Do you know how many hours of *his* life he spent taking an interest in my art? Or offering to listen to my business idea? Sweet fuck all.

"He'd never leave a night out with *his* friends to come home with me. Once he paid some guy at a bar to drop me home because I was tired and when I asked him to come with me, he pretended he couldn't hear me and said *cheerio* as he closed the door."

Patrick is silent. Am I boring him to death with my whiney stories?

"Sounds like you dodged a bullet," he says as we accelerate from the junction.

Tension locks my entire body as the usual defensiveness washes over me. It's my own fault for even raising the topic with a complete outsider and exposing a part of my life I'm not proud of.

"That came out wrong," I reply. "Luke and I went through a lot. He was good to me." *For the most part.*

"He strung you along for several years, didn't support you in your career aspirations, and showed up at the busiest place on the Coast, flaunting some woman he messed around with. In my experience, that's dick behaviour."

"You know nothing about him," I growl.

"Except everything you told me, which sounds awful."

"Alright Judge Judy, can you just drop it?"

"And who the hell says *'cheerio'*?"

"Okay, I get it!" I snap, turning to face the front.

As I wonder why the hell this sporty car can't get me to my place any quicker, a hot flush wipes everything from my mind, and my fingers curl to grip the seat beneath me. Whether it's that I'm in a moving vehicle, have a potential concussion, am drunk, or a combination of everything, I'm hit with a wave of nausea that sends bubbling heat through my body.

"Tell me you're not about to be sick." There's an edge to Patrick's voice.

Before I have time to process what's happening, I lean forward in my seat, legs apart, as a wave of vomit surges from my mouth. I shut my eyes from the dizziness and the complete humiliation.

"Oh my God, I'm so sorry!" I cry, keeping my eyes closed.

The car stops and I'm certain Patrick is in shock, or has abandoned his vehicle, because he says nothing, but scoops me out of the passenger seat and carries me to sit on the curb. I vomit onto a patch of grass, and squeeze my eyes shut again, cursing Kali and Meg and Rachel and anyone else who played a part in this evening. I hear myself say sorry between breaths.

"Stop apologising, Hazel," he says, although if I could see his face right now, I would imagine it's full of disgust. I bet he's contemplating leaving me here and walking away after he's torched the car my stomach acid destroyed.

By the time the world stops spinning, I'm exhausted and couldn't sink lower if I tried.

"I should never have left the house," I mutter. I scoot along the curb away from my vomit and hunch over, head hanging between my legs. "Bet you're wishing you'd left me in the alley."

To my surprise, Patrick sits next to me, his intoxicating cologne travelling into my nostrils and wiping out the bitter taste of regurgitated beer. "And miss the wondrous experience this is turning out to be? Please." I hear the humour in his voice, but I can't smile.

"Have you ever felt so shit about everything in your life, you wonder what the hell the point is?" As the words leave my lips, I know I don't mean them to sound as heavy as they come out. This sort of bold statement is one of the many reasons I stopped drinking excessively; my emotions get the better of me.

To my surprise, Patrick exhales next to me. "Yeah, I have an idea."

I turn to see his face screwed up, lost in thought. A part of me wonders if he's thinking about his vomit-filled car, but something tells me whatever he's thinking goes deeper.

A faint ringing breaks the silence, and Patrick reaches into his pocket to retrieve his phone.

"Hi … yes, I did … no, there's been a change of plans." If it were possible to hang my head lower, I would. I've messed up whatever he had on tonight and the guilt is real.

"Your concern isn't needed. I've got it covered." He pauses, the muffled voice on the other end sounding impatient. I sense Patrick lean away from me. "In case you've forgotten, I'm the one in charge here. Stop breathing down my neck while I do my job. If you want to find work elsewhere, be my guest." Patrick clicks the side button to end his call, an obvious tension hanging over us.

"You sound like a pretty tough boss," I mutter.

His concerned face shines under the streetlights, his hair ruffling every time a car drives past. "I am. Especially when it comes to my know-it-all younger brother."

"I owe you and your know-it-all brother an apology for whatever I cocked up tonight," I say, ducking my head again.

"We'll survive." Patrick shifts so his arm skims mine and my heart skips a beat. It's not skin-to-skin contact, but I can't concentrate. The last time I felt something, an actual spark of electricity, was when I first met Luke.

From what I've gathered so far, Patrick is the opposite of Luke; work-focused, serious, and determined. He's also sarcastic and witty. The way he's taken charge of the evening and looked after me, reaming out his brother, being sure within himself … I can't deny he turns me on.

"So, how'd you get that scar on your cheek? Saving damsels like me?" I joke, tilting my head to look at him again. Patrick's expression darkens and I regret asking him anything.

Patrick's gaze flitters across my face, almost as if he's assessing whether he wants to engage in a conversation. He doesn't answer my questions and turns to look at the passing traffic, chewing the inside of his cheek.

Eventually, Patrick snaps out of his daze and stands with a fresh wave of determination in his demeanour. "Let's get you home, Hazel."

I don't argue and let Patrick help me to my feet, as I shamefully wipe my mouth with my hand. Patrick opens the back door of his car and I climb in; grateful he doesn't force me to sit near my pile of spew. I'm also grateful the car doesn't reek of it.

My tired eyes encourage me to lie down.

After Patrick switches the engine on, he turns to me. "Don't fall asleep yet. You might have a concussion, remember?"

"Yeah, yeah." I deserve to slip into a coma for acting like such a fool. Not only tonight, but for the years I wasted with Luke, a man now engaged to the woman he cheated on me with.

"Hazel, I mean it." Patrick's voice is piercing, as if he's turned the volume up a few decibels. *Did I fall asleep?* "Talk to me while I drive."

I groan and close my eyes. "You mean about how I wasted three years of my life with a guy who didn't love me as much as I loved him?"

"Sure, whatever helps."

"God, I'm so pathetic."

"This definitely isn't your finest moment." I ignore his comment. "Hazel! Do *not* fall asleep."

"I'm not," I slur, my eyelids closing of their own accord. My thoughts travel back to Luke, with his arm curved around *that* woman. He used to touch *me* like that. I don't bother to fight with my whirling thoughts as they pick up at the memory of when I walked in on *him* with *her* in *our* shower. The walls I worked hard to erect are crumbling.

A hand shakes my arm and I jump, as if coming out of a falling dream. "Wake up Hazel. We're here."

The car still moves as I sluggishly sit up, rubbing my eyes

and blinking several times to remember where I am. Weren't we minutes from home?

Oh fuck. Patrick, the psychopath, has brought me to his sex-dungeon and this is where it ends. I knew I shouldn't have got in the car.

I blink a few more times and realise he hasn't driven me to his torture chamber. No. He's driven me to a large grey building, lit up in the darkness.

I'm definitely sober now.

7

"How are you feeling?"

"Like I drank too much and whacked my head on something hard."

Liam, a sweet, broad-shouldered nurse, chuckles as he checks me over. He's come by a few times since I got given a bed. I've drifted in and out of uncomfortable sleep ever since, drinking all the water I can get my hands on and feeling progressively worse about how my night has turned out. Particularly the part about my ex moving forward with the girl he cheated on me with. Vomiting in Patrick's car is a close second.

And, yes, Patrick is still here.

I've been in this hospital bed for three hours and apart from when I changed into my hospital gown and discussed some confidential information with the assessing nurse, Patrick has been by my side.

If I'm honest, a part of me *likes* that Patrick stayed. I like that he brought me here and didn't ditch me at the side of the road when my guts left my body via my mouth. *Ugh.* I like that he insisted on driving me home.

In a perfect world, the handsome knight in shining armour

would be charming, funny, and gentle. Maybe if we'd met under different circumstances, Patrick would be all those things, and until we were sitting side by side on the curb, I thought I saw snippets of his softer side. I must have imagined it.

He's been cold, impatient and taking sarcasm to a whole new level since we got here. It's as if a switch flipped from *be kind to drunk damsel* to *make this drunk damsel feel the size of an ant for her stupidity*. Although, to be fair, I haven't given him anything other than my worst tonight.

He's sitting in the low chair next to my bed, stony-faced and frowning, as he taps furiously at his iPhone screen. When he's not busy with his phone, he stares at his clasped hands. Sometimes he stares at me with eyes so dark you could get lost in them, and I want to die all over again.

You'd think after the humiliation I've put myself through tonight that I'd want him to leave me so I can suffer alone, but I don't. It's comforting to me that this brooding man I've only known for a few hours has decided to keep an eye on me, even if he is only doing it to keep his conscience clear.

When my phone died and I had nothing to distract myself with, I asked him what he was doing and he responded with, "Believe it or not, Miss Jones, I have a busy life outside of rescuing damsels in distress." Any headway I'd achieved with him was erased after the vomit incident.

Now, I'm exhausted on every level and have a splitting headache, and everything feels so much worse.

"Any luck on the toothbrush situation?" I ask Liam hopefully. It was the first thing I'd asked for, desperate to get rid of my bad breath and cotton mouth. Unfortunately, he couldn't find one. Patrick had simply raised an elegant eyebrow, as if I deserved to suffer with vomit breath for my behaviour. Whether or not he is right is irrelevant.

Liam screws his face up. "Sorry, no luck yet." I do my best not to let tears spring to my eyes as I force myself to smile. I'm becoming more fragile the longer this night drags on. "Hope-fully you won't be here too much longer," Liam gives me a warm smile as he jots something on a clipboard. "Trust me, you're ranking high on my list of favourite patients, with or without brushing your teeth."

I return his smile with a sheepish one of my own, which falls away as I hear Patrick mutter something under his breath. He's analysing Liam with a look I can't quite recognise.

"What is your problem *now*?" I hiss, watching as his attention snaps to me.

"Nothing."

Pleasantries between the two of us dissipated some time ago. I can understand why *he's* so annoyed but I'm puzzled by my own behaviour. I'm no longer drunk and owe him for sticking it out with me. Call me crazy, but I feel like he doesn't *want* me to be nice to him. This whole evening has been bizarre.

Liam chuckles under his breath, his gaze flickering between the two of us. "I'll be back soon, Hazel." He gives me another smile and shakes his head as he walks off.

Patrick's defined jaw pulses.

"What? Just say whatever it is you want to say."

"I have nothing to say."

"Righto." I nod, and my irritation flares. "You don't have to stay."

"I know."

"Then what's the matter?"

"*Nothing* is the matter." He looks down at his phone. I glower at his profile for a few extra seconds before sighing and falling onto my pillow with a dramatic huff.

Why did I have to see Luke? Why did I have to freak out? Why did Patrick have to come across me in the alleyway and bring me here? I could've slept this off at home.

"Worried your new victim will be put off by your vomit breath?"

There it is.

I roll my eyes as I turn my attention towards Patrick, whose attention is still on his phone.

For someone who's had his night ruined, he's incredibly at ease. He's removed his jacket and rolled up the sleeves of his white shirt, so they cuff at the elbows, a glimmering gold watch on his left wrist. His right foot rests comfortably on his left knee, his posture relaxed, as if he's waiting in the foyer of a hotel for his car to arrive. Something I imagine he does a lot.

"Are you jealous?"

"Of your vomit breath or your new suck-up boyfriend?" Patrick lifts his face so his dark gaze settles on me, and I ignore the involuntary shudder that crosses my shoulders.

"How is he a suck-up? He's a nice guy who's doing his job."

Patrick sniggers. "Sure."

If I didn't know better, I'd say he *is* jealous. He's like an old man when he's grumpy. I wonder if I'll be that cross when I'm approaching forty, sleep deprived and dealing with drunk strangers.

Whipping the blanket off, I swing my legs over the side of the bed, shuffling my feet into the hospital slippers. If I can't get away from him, a mini trip to put some distance between us will have to do.

"Where are you going?" Patrick asks.

"Japan. Where do you think?" The nurse who did my initial assessment has come by every hour ordering me to pee. She said it's to ensure I can get in and out of bed and still function after hitting my head, and that I remember where the toilet is and don't feel dizzy. On one of my trips, when Patrick was out of earshot, I assured her all I felt was shame, regret and a killer hangover coming on. She gave me the faintest of smiles.

"Make sure you knock before you enter this time," Patrick says, his tone dripping with sarcasm. My face reddens as the memory of me walking in on an elderly male patient who forgot to lock the door springs to mind. Why did I even mention it to Patrick?

"At least that guy made me laugh. All you've done tonight is bitch and moan."

"For good reason."

"You offered to take me home! If we'd gone straight there instead of coming here, you'd be done with me by now." I exhale deeply. "Look, I appreciate everything you've done, but you don't need to hang around and continue guilting me."

Patrick shakes his head. "You have an odd way of thanking people who have your best interests at heart."

"Why the hell would you have my best interests at heart?"

Patrick peers up at me, as if deciding his next words carefully. I wonder what it would be like if I didn't have vomit breath, so I could straddle his lap and kiss him.

Jesus. I need some sleep.

"I don't want your friend to come home and find you dead in bed tomorrow morning, because you were too stubborn to get your head examined."

Patrick returns his gaze to his phone. The break in eye contact helps me relax. My gaze travels to one of his shirt buttons that's come undone, exposing a hint of sculpted pec. The sight of his flesh elicits a tingle from my lady parts. Patrick, sensing my contemplation, looks up. "Yes, they're real."

I give him a flat smile. "Sorry, I was too stunned by your wayward chest hair to look at anything else." I shrug and continue my walk to the bathroom, biting my lip at the look of mild surprise on Patrick's face, and thinking about how a fine dusting of chest hair on a man is so incredibly sexy.

When my eyes open from another restless sleep, I don't feel as rough and I'm no longer surprised to wake up in a hospital bed.

What I *am* surprised at is the collection of items on the table next to me that weren't there before. A soft sigh of relief escapes my lips.

"Your boyfriend dropped those off for you," Patrick mutters from his corner.

I don't even look at him as I spring out of bed, scooping up the cleansing wipes, toothbrush, and tube of paste.

"Bloody hell, an entire pack of wipes." I gasp.

"Told you. Suck-up."

I race to the bathroom and spend way too long scrubbing my teeth and tongue, followed by wiping my face, armpits and, ultimately, every inch of skin with the wipes.

When I finally make my way back to my bed, I'm buzzing at my newfound cleanliness. Patrick's gaze follows me as I shimmy under the blanket.

"Happy now?" he asks.

"Very." Cocky with my improved oral hygiene, I throw Patrick an exaggerated open-mouthed smile. Patrick's eyes narrow slightly, and I can't tell if it's the stare of someone who's turned on, or murderous.

Deb, my initial assessment nurse, walks to my bed, distracting me from my analysis of Patrick's expressions. Patrick stands as she crosses to my side. "You'll be free to go shortly, Hazel."

"Yes!"

"A couple of things before you get too excited." She peers at me over her thick spectacle frames and hands me a piece of paper filled with text. "This sheet has all the information you need to know about dealing with a mild concussion. Whilst we've treated your injury as minor, I want you to treat this situation seriously. Pretend you *did* knock yourself out for five minutes." She turns to Patrick as my face falls. I don't want her to think I'm rude, but this is overkill.

"Do not let her drive for at least twenty-four hours," she

continues. My head snaps up, my eyes boring into the side of Patrick's face as he politely listens to her orders. "Do not leave her alone for the next twenty-four hours. She'll need to be woken up every hour once she falls asleep tonight, and don't just nudge her, get her to walk to the bathroom or get a glass of water. Make her do something that involves her using her brain."

Patrick's gaze locks with mine, and my stomach flip-flops. His expression is unreadable as heat creeps up my neck. This woman thinks Patrick's going to be lying next to me tonight, waking me up. I warn him with my eyes to keep his mouth shut. If we have to stay here any longer, my lid will flip.

Deb turns back to me. "You can have paracetamol for the pain and use an ice pack if you need to on your head. It's going to be tender for a few days, but it'll be okay. Everything's on the sheet. Liam will be by with a medical certificate and you're not to return to work until you're rested and healed."

"But I feel fine—"

"And no alcohol for the next twenty-four hours."

A snort escapes me, but I bite my lip at her frown. "You don't need to worry about that." A flicker of amusement dances in Patrick's eyes.

"I should hope not." Deb narrows her eyes before nodding at Patrick. "You did the right thing bringing her in."

A smile threatens to break out on his stupid face. He's won the whole night.

"Thanks Deb," I grumble, pushing the blanket off me. I may not have won the night, but I'll be victorious when I climb into my own bed.

As I collect my clothes and lay them in front of me, the scent of stale beer and vomit reaches my nostrils. This shit will be set on fire when I get home. At the sound of the curtains moving, I lift my head and see Patrick stepping away.

"I'll give you some privacy," he says softly, closing off the space.

"Hang on a sec." He halts as I step towards him. "Could you untie the back of this?" Patrick groans. "Think of it as one more favour to hang over my head," I snap, spinning so he can untie the gown. "I'm not asking you to undress me, for God's sake."

I hear Patrick's breath catch in his throat, but I'm too busy clutching the gown to my body and keeping my own breathing steady to care. He loosens the straps before grunting, "I'll wait for you outside."

When I push the curtain open a few minutes later, Liam stands at the desk, holding my medical certificate. "Your ticket to some days off, and," he holds out a sandwich in plastic casing and a small orange juice, "Some snacks for the road. I figured you'd be starving."

I want to kiss this man. I accept the food and the certificate, knowing full-well I'll devour the sustenance in minutes and never use the medical document. Lisa would have a fit if I took any days off other than for being dead. Even that wouldn't be a good enough reason.

"Thanks, and thank you so much for getting me this stuff." I hold up the toiletries in the plastic bag hooked on my arm. "Honestly, the wipes were a lifesaver."

Liam raises his eyebrows in surprise. "I'd love to take the credit, but your boyfriend got those for you while you were sleeping." Liam's comment catches me off guard and I can't help but drop my gaze to the toiletries, too stunned to correct Liam about Patrick being my boyfriend.

I smile my thanks to Liam, shuffle towards the exit and wonder if Patrick isn't as cold-hearted as I'd thought.

8

"WHAT TIME IS IT?"

My teeth chatter between mouthfuls of turkey sandwich as Patrick and I across the almost empty car park.

"Nearly three." He points his keys at his car and the head-lights flash.

My pace slows and my chewing stops as I near the vehicle until I stop dead in my tracks. "That's a different car." I didn't hit my head that hard, did I? The Mercedes has been replaced with a black SUV.

Patrick keeps walking. "Good observation, Miss Jones."

"What happened to the Merc?"

"It's being cleaned," he replies. "You emptied the contents of your stomach all over the carpet, remember?"

I'm too tired to feel embarrassed. "I remember. How did you get a new car?"

Patrick walks to the passenger side and opens the door. "I sorted it while you slept. Now, if you don't mind, I'd like to get going."

Frozen to the spot, I swallow the rest of the food in my mouth, my eyes scanning the exterior of the car. "Is this a

Maserati?" I may not be a car buff, but I've seen enough episodes of *Entourage* to recognise that symbol anywhere.

"Really?" Patrick asks with a sigh. "We've been here for five hours and you're asking about the car?"

I lift my chin. "Yes, I'm asking about the car."

"Yes, it's a Maserati," he growls.

"You own a Mercedes and a Maserati?"

"Yes."

A few tense beats hang between us. "What did you say you do for work again?"

"I didn't," he replies, his raspy voice causing the hair at the back of my neck to stand up. "And frankly, this night has been way too long to get into a deep and meaningful conversation about what I do for a living."

I wince at his words and the overwhelming sensation of shame from my behaviour during this entire night engulfs me.

"Hazel—"

"I'm sorry. I'll get in the car." I shuffle towards him, my face tingling with shame.

"Thank you." He sounds over it; over dealing with someone acting like a drunk teenager. My brain and eyeballs hurt, and I realise I want to thank him, and apologise, and yell at him for everything. Everything that isn't his fault.

Patrick cranks the heat as soon as we're on the road and after a few minutes of driving silently toward my house, he clears his throat. "I run my own business."

I peer over at him, watching as streetlights pass over his profile. "What sort of business?"

Patrick's mouth twists, his scar silver in the darkness. "Consultancy work, mostly."

"Sounds vague."

Patrick chuckles. "I'm a property accountant."

"Ah, so you help rich people get richer."

Patrick nods. "Sometimes."

"That explains all the bling." I wave my fingers across his fancy watch-adorned wrist and then gesture to the interior of the luxury car.

Patrick flashes me a grin, his tired eyes creasing in the corners. "I know it's not to everyone's taste, but I like nice things. The older you get, the more you realise life's too short to not treat yourself."

"Sounds like dangerous advice coming from someone who tells people how to save and spend their money."

A chortle escapes Patrick's lips and I beam. "I swear, I give excellent advice."

"Sure. I'll remember that if I ever need any property or *business*-related insight."

"You said earlier you had a business idea of your own?" Patrick prompts, his large hands smoothing over his steering wheel with ease. "What is it?"

I roll my eyes. "I'm not about to tell that to a legitimate businessman."

"But you've been so chatty all night."

I bite the inside of my cheek. "I wanted to be a graphic artist and thought of starting my own design business, focusing on designing book covers. I had a few clients lined up at one point."

"What happened?"

I shrug. "Shit happened."

Patrick nods in thought. "Maybe you should re-visit that some time. See how it feels. Trust me, I'm a legitimate businessman."

It could be delirium brought on by utter exhaustion, or something else, but we smile at each other and remain quiet for the rest of the drive.

When I see my street approaching, I almost cry out in relief. Bed is so, so close. Before the car has even switched off, I let myself out and close the door, praying Kali isn't home, so I don't have to answer a million questions. With any luck she's passed out drunk inside, or better yet, passed out drunk at Alex's house.

"I'm not leaving until I know with certainty, you're inside that house." Patrick walks past me towards the porch. "Don't argue with me!" he calls over his shoulder.

I don't argue with him. Exhaustion and shame have won the evening. I traipse up the driveway after him, fumbling to find my keys. Of course, as I reach the porch, I drop them, and a groan escapes my lips. Patrick bends down and scoops them up, peering at me with the softest expression I've seen him wear all evening. "Let me."

I step back, too tired to argue, and let him open the door. "Thanks for your help tonight." I glance at his tired face and am delighted to see the hint of a smile once again.

"You're welcome."

My breath catches as Patrick takes in my features; his gaze drifting to hover near my mouth. My fingertips itch to reach up and touch his stubble.

Five solid seconds pass as we stare at each other. My heartbeat picks up, my breathing becomes louder. I don't understand the dynamic, and I don't care. The electricity pulsating between us is something I'm enjoying.

Patrick looks away. "You should get inside. It's cold out here." Disappointment and confusion wash across me as I stare at his profile, willing him to turn back, but he doesn't.

"Thanks again," I say as I open the door. "Sorry for ruining your night." I close the door swiftly without allowing myself another chance to imprint his beautiful face in my mind, and head for my bedroom. Kali's open door signifies she's not home, and hopefully stays out for the *right* reasons. Unlike me.

As I enter my room, I flick on the light, tear the ankle boots off my feet and rip the outfit from my skin. What a fucking disaster this night turned out to be I want to forget it ever happened.

I entertain the idea of a shower, but I know I'd pass out in it. Instead, I pull on the comfiest pants and baggiest shirt I can find with such aggression I nearly fall over.

Why am I so angry? And embarrassed? Did I imagine something with Patrick outside or was he thinking the same thing I was? That he wanted to touch my face, that he wanted to *memorise* my face before we parted ways?

I want to cry with relief as I sink to my bed and flop onto my back with my eyes closed. The tension in my body is at risk of bursting my seams. I'm delusional, but it's nothing a solid sleep can't fix.

"For someone fixated on serial killers and true crime," a voice startles me, and I jerk upright, "You do little to deter potential predators. You didn't lock the front door." With my bag of toiletries and medical certificate in his outstretched hand, leaning casually against the door frame, is Patrick. "You forgot these."

"Uh, thanks." I cross my arms over my body like a shield. "You can drop them there."

Wait ... how quickly did he follow me in? Did he see me change? *Oh Jesus.*

Patrick continues to hold the bag as his gaze wanders around my bedroom, taking in my colour-coded bookcase and empty calendar, and the clothes and makeup strewn across the floor.

I swallow back my nerves. "Getting a good look there?"

"Do you have a spare blanket in here?"

"For what? To wrap my dead body in?"

Patrick's mouth curves into a knowing smile. "You heard what the nurse said. You need to be woken every hour."

I wait for his face to give me a sign he's joking. "You think you're the one to wake me?"

Patrick looks around again, his dark eyes dancing with amusement. "Do you see anyone else?"

"I'll set my alarm," I lie.

"As if you'll get out of bed."

"I will."

"Great," Patrick says, dropping the bag. "I'll be on the couch and see you when you wake up. Every hour, on the hour." He turns without another word, leaving the door ajar behind him.

What. The. Fuck?

Is this really happening? He must be joking. He *must* be.

I creep to the door and peer into the living room. He's not joking. Patrick has kicked off his shoes and is holding one of the blankets Kali and I use for our Friday wine nights.

He's going to sleep on my fucking couch.

I find my dead phone to charge it up and set my alarms, wondering whether I have enough energy in me to message Kali and give her an update. I decide against it, given she's either having sex or has passed out. If she has time for my update, she'll come straight home out of fear of me being kidnapped.

So, I don't call or message her.

I don't contact anyone.

I keep the door ajar and flick my light off, peeking once more into the lounge where Patrick is now settled under *my* fleece blanket.

I get into bed and allow its comfort to wash over me.

I'll never fall asleep knowing he's out there.

The alarm from hell wakes me.

I force myself to walk to the bathroom. I pee.

On the way back, I can't help but peek into the living room to see his body asleep on the couch.

I go back to bed, a small smile on my face.

An hour later I jolt awake, gasping for breath, sweating and with a dry throat.

It's dark outside as I pad across the floor to the kitchen. I fill a drink bottle with water and gulp it down, tipping my head back quickly and instantly regretting it. My head feels like it's filled with lead.

As I tip-toe back towards my room, I look across at the couch. Patrick is on the sofa, his open eyes glistening in the darkness.

I slow my pace, the energy from his eyes slamming through me and into my chest. I freeze.

I don't want to go back to my room.

9

HAVE you ever woken up with a killer hangover? I have, and plenty of them.

I've woken up in foreign places next to strange men and once with a strange woman. I've woken up reeking of stale booze and body odour, filled with regret, shame and utter wonderment as to how and why I acted the way I did the night before. I've woken up filled with promises to myself that I will never, *ever* be so fucking stupid again.

Yet here I am.

To be fair, at least I can blame part of this shitty feeling on what I *think* was a mild concussion. I remember that part. I also remember lots of beer and shots and Luke. Luke with *her* and a goddamn diamond ring. Why couldn't my mind have erased *that* memory?

And there was Patrick, right? Did I imagine that dark mop of hair, those dark eyes and defined jawline? Possibly. I wish the vomiting in his car was my imagination, but that's too vivid. *Oh God, kill me now.* I know he took me to the hospital, and at one stage I was ready to give him a good slap whilst also wanting to know what it'd be like to jump his bones.

I remember the rush of heat that flooded my core the minute my gaze landed on his lips. I remember the tension on my front porch, and again when I got up in the middle of the night.

He stayed on the couch!

Fuck.

A wild surge of butterflies batters my ribcage as I tiptoe across my room, grabbing my dressing gown off its spot on the back of the door. After several controlled breaths, I duck my head out and peer into the living room, wrapping the robe around me tightly.

Patrick is gone.

My navy-blue fleece blanket is folded neatly on the couch, and my laptop sits closed on the coffee table, a piece of paper perched on top of it. With a shaky hand I pick up the note and read:

Yes, you vomited in my car. Yes, you have a mild concussion. Take it easy for the next few days.
P.

I want to slap my face with the amount of cringe coursing through my veins.

I find the *how to treat a concussion* information sheet on the floor of my bedroom and return to the comfort of my bed to read through it a few times, noting the part about how short-term amnesia can occur in the hours and days after knocking your head. *Good.* Hopefully that means my fuzzy memories from last night will become clearer as time goes on. Having blanks in my brain is unnerving.

There are several messages on my phone: three from Kali talking about Alex's penis, and a photo from Mum of her and Dad sitting on their yacht somewhere sunny up north. No other messages. A flitter of disappointment passes through me.

I check my Instagram account to see if I've ruined my life. Too many times I've woken to videos I've posted on my story that have made me want to die. Me, drunkenly talking to the camera. Me, yelling abuse at my friends. Me, thinking I can sing when being driven home from a night out. Once I talked to the camera in bed and a nipple slipped into shot. Yes, one of *my* nipples and it had been up for twelve hours before I noticed and deleted it. I've been anti social media mostly since then.

Last night I appeared to be too busy drinking, getting into a stranger's car, and vomiting in it, to get my phone out. I have friend requests from Meg and Rachel and make appearances on both of their Instagram stories, but I seem relatively pulled together in them. Another crisis averted.

Rather than replying to my messages, I scroll through my contact list for any sign of a new entry, preferably one beginning with 'P', but come up empty. There are no messages or missed calls from Patrick or any unknown numbers.

I can't say I blame him for not leaving his details. It's for the best. I don't think he relished babysitting a woman ten years younger than him who had no regard for her own safety. Still, I'd appreciate the opportunity to thank him. Despite the vomit and the bickering, I know there was decent conversation, and now that my head isn't swimming with booze, I realise Patrick went above and beyond to help me last night. I was immature and talking shit, undoubtedly taking my pain about Luke out on him.

The thought of Luke elicits a long groan from deep in my belly, and I slide myself into an upright position, resting my head against the headboard. I battle the urge to cry, my chest aching as I let my head fall into my hands. Here I am, hungover and smelling of vomit, with tears in my eyes, because of the man who ruined *everything*.

I can't believe he cheated on me. I can't believe he's slapped a giant rock on *the* woman. They've only had a few months of an honest relationship and he's already proposed? I deserve to be smacked in the face for being so gullible.

Maybe Patrick was a guardian angel sent to save me from myself. Maybe if he hadn't helped me, I would've gone back inside and made a complete fool of myself in front of Luke and done God knows what else.

I might never know what could've happened, but what I *do* know is that I won't be seeing that handsome, moody stranger anytime soon.

And, I am never drinking again.

By lunch time I've showered, changed my bed sheets, and tidied up the kitchen. It took every ounce of strength I had. I'm curled up on the couch, about to watch *Home Alone,* when Kali bursts through the front door.

"Oh, it's good to be alive!" she cries, dropping her bags at her feet.

"Keep the noise down you fool, I have a headache," I grumble, but smile as she bounds across to me and joins me under my blanket, which still smells of Patrick. "Last night was good?"

"I think I'll keep him around for a while," she says with a grin.

Kali's effortless ability to jump from man to man, and relationship to relationship, with unapologetic honesty has always been something I've admired. She loves exploring sex with multiple partners and she loves her independence. She tells this to every man she meets and it generally leads to them falling head over heels in love with her.

"What happened to you last night? You should've told me you wanted to leave; I would've come with you. Why does this blanket smell like hot man?"

She's perplexed, her eyes widening as she takes in my

expression. Before she can say another word, I give her the run-down of what I remember, which ends around the time I got into bed, confused about the strange, great-smelling man on the couch.

"This is why you should always tell me *before* you leave somewhere on your own," she scolds. "Seriously, this man could've killed you! He slept on our couch? With *this* blanket?"

"Yah."

She quirks an eyebrow at me. "Did you at least fondle him?"

"No, Kali." My head lolls backwards onto the couch.

She sits up. "You had what sounds like the best kind of man, sexy and angry, on our couch, and you're telling me you did nothing?"

"Did you not hear the part about me being a drunken pest and bringing up *all* of the vomit?"

"There's no way he would have refused you, even if you were falling over and destroying his car. You looked bangin' last night." I scrunch my brow up in confusion, trying to pinpoint a niggle at those words. "What did the doctor say about your concussion?"

"He said I was fine. I'm alive, aren't I?"

She ignores me and pulls out her phone, launching into a Google search about concussions. "Did this guy at least wake you every hour?"

"Sort of."

"Hazel! You could've died in your sleep."

"But I didn't, so let's move on with our lives," I reply, reaching for the remote control. Kali smacks my hand while she continues to scroll through her phone, and I grumble under my breath about her being a pain in my ass.

"I can't believe Luke was there. I didn't even see him," she continues.

"To be fair, your eyes were rarely anywhere but on Alex."

"Good point." She smiles to herself, then falters. "I'm sorry I wasn't a better friend last night. If I'd seen Luke or known he was going to be there I would have—"

"Knock it off, you did nothing wrong." I lean in and kiss her cheek. "It was late in the night. Security was probably letting anyone in at that stage."

She frowns to herself. "And you're sure she had a ring on *that* finger?"

I sigh, dropping my head to rest on her shoulder. "Yes, she did."

Kali and I sit in silence, our synchronised breaths drowning out the whirring of thoughts in my head.

"He had two cars." It takes a second to realise I said the words out loud.

"What?"

I straighten up, squinting in an effort to remember my vague memories from the night before. "Patrick. He drove me to the hospital in a Mercedes. After I vomited in it, he switched it out for a Maserati."

Kali nods, impressed. "Sexy, angry *and* loaded, and you didn't attempt a move on him. I can't even look at you right now." She stands up. "I am, however, in an amazing mood, so I'm going to make my poor concussed bestie some soup."

I grab her wrist. "I don't need soup. I'm fine."

"I'll get a fresh loaf from the corner store."

I release her arm, surrendering at the mention of delicious, warm carbs from our favourite seven-day bakery. "Potato and leek would be great."

As Kali heads for the kitchen, my phone vibrates and my stomach leaps in hope.

Luke Taylor.

My stomach bottoms out and I bring the phone closer to be sure of what I'm seeing. Luke. *My* Luke. The wave of anxiety and fury is surprising, even to me.

This time yesterday, I was fine. Thoughts of Luke were

squashed into the depths of my subconscious, where they would stay for eternity. And now? I'm a bloody train-wreck. *Why* did I agree to go out?

An unexpected tear trickles down my cheek as I unlock my phone and read a message filled with everything I've been craving to hear.

LUKE

> I know you don't want to hear from me. PLEASE read this before you delete it. I saw you last night, and I know you saw me. And I can't stop thinking about you. You looked amazing as always, and seeing you reminded me of how much I screwed up. Please meet me for coffee or something. I miss you.

My heart pounds as I drop my phone and close my eyes to stop the surge of tears spilling from them.

My hangover hurts.

The pain in my chest is crushing.

My head throbs.

This is why I wanted to stay as Robot Hazel.

10

As I WAIT for the elevator to reach me on Monday morning, I squint at my tired expression in the mirrored doors.

I have creases in my cheeks from not moving during last night's twelve-hour sleep. A solid lump has grown exponentially on the back of my head since Saturday night and my muscles feel as though someone pumped lead into them. Walking feels like wading through mud.

That could also be because my mind feels heavy too. It constantly cycles through a smiling Luke, his petite fiancée, and a frowning Patrick. When I'm not busy stewing with guilt about how rude I was to Patrick, I'm picturing Luke, still waiting for a response to his text message. I didn't know what to say. I still don't, but I read the text he sent over and over and over. I read it so many times it's imprinted in my brain word for word.

Kali, who is a loud and proud feminist, would never obsess like I am. Even if she was falling to pieces, she would've deleted that message. She would've told Luke to go fuck himself and already moved on to better things. She knows her self-worth and knows there are better things out there for her. She does the things we tell our friends to do when a man has crushed them. Me? I'm strong, but I'm not that strong.

I should've called in sick.

I know that would've been fruitless. I could do with some more sleep and the Issei Sagawa documentary is calling my name, but I know my brain would've led me to sulk around the house, cleaning until my nails went raw, whilst simultaneously worrying about Lisa firing me for taking a day away from the office.

The elevator doors spring open and I step inside, Marketing Marcus greeting me with a big, cocky grin. "Morning, Hazel, how's the lioness treating you?"

"Better than she's treating you, I'll bet." I hit the number sixteen and offer him a smirk.

He chuckles. "That's a fair call."

Marcus and I have always had good banter, especially with working for a woman who, despite being good at her job, treats everyone around her like five-year-olds.

Last week, Lisa and Marcus got into it in the middle of the 'creative space.' What started as Lisa asking the team to keep the noise down, eventuated into a war of words. Lisa told Marcus his team was incompetent, and Marcus told Lisa to grow up. Considering neither of them is a fan of apologising, they haven't spoken since.

"I hope she hasn't been too difficult to deal with recently," he says somewhat sheepishly. Marcus is a big guy with a stocky build and scruffy facial hair. He's in his forties and self-assured, so seeing him look apologetic is a rarity.

I smile. "Nothing I can't handle."

Marcus nods as if agreeing with me. "I've never seen anyone deal with Lisa as calmly and beautifully as you. She wouldn't survive without you."

The laugh that escapes my lips is genuine. "I don't know about that."

"You obviously have a great relationship under all the politics," he replies. "No wonder you didn't apply for the junior marketing role. A bloody shame, but I understand. She must take care of you as much as you take care of her."

My entire body locks up at those words, my ears prickling as if I've misheard him. "Sorry ... junior marketing role?"

"Yeah, you know, when Pottsy moved back home to look after his dad? Not sure if you ever met him. Nice kid. Terrible circumstances with him leaving, but because we only advertised internally, we got a replacement pretty quick. Chris is a great asset and it's only been a month ..."

I'm not sure if time is slowing down or not, but I'm not listening to what Marcus is saying. There was a junior marketing role advertised to internal applicants, and I missed it? No. No way.

"When was this advertised?" I ask, cutting off Marcus from whatever he's saying.

Marcus frowns, stroking his chin. "Hmm ... we went out in May? God, has it been that long? That's right. We offered the job to Chris at the end of June."

A tiny maniacal laugh escapes my lips as I feel the colour drain from my face. A position opened to internal applicants? The head of marketing knew I was interested in that area, and I didn't know about it. Even though my mind drifts to excuses like Lisa not giving me the heads up or the organisation not advertising it for long enough, I know neither of those are true. I missed it because it happened right after Luke and I split. When I was drinking too much, not looking after myself, and was an all-around mess. It's the only time in my five-year period of employment here where I slacked a little.

The elevator doors spring open and Marcus steps out. "Don't worry Hazel, I don't take it personally that you didn't apply, but I would've loved you on my team based on some of the input I've seen from you over the years." He waves his arm as if it's merely an inconvenience, a small slip-up that means nothing. "Have a good day."

I'm too busy fighting more tears, the back of my head throbbing, to say goodbye. My opportunity to get away from Lisa came and went, and I missed it because of some fuckboy.

When I arrive at my floor, I take a deep breath and roll my shoulders back. My whole life seems to be filled with taking deep breaths and trying to keep my shit together. I'm not scattered, I'm not a mess. *Pull yourself together, woman.*

After I set up Lisa's office, I head to my desk and sink into my chair. My head is aching again and the conversation with Marcus causes it to throb more.

Once I power up my computer, I open my emails and notice one from Rachel with the subject line: *Please tell me you did ;)*

Puzzled, I double click the email to be greeted by dark features, an angular jaw, and a smouldering expression, staring at me. It takes a few seconds to remember Rachel snapped a photo of Patrick on the weekend. It appears her impulsive photo-taking on Saturday night paid off. Patrick really is as beautiful as I remember, even in the darkness of a dingy alleyway.

The words beneath Patrick's face read: *Let's meet for lunch today so you can tell me alllllll about this guy* and I can't help but grin. If only Rachel knew the full absurdity that was Saturday night.

I find myself mesmerised by Patrick's steely gaze for far too long. How is it someone can look so beautiful when surprised by a drunk girl snapping a photo of him? My vague recollection is becoming more vivid now I can see his face. I'm also mortified Patrick saw me vomit in his car, and left my house without leaving a single detail.

I exit the email when I see Lisa marching along the hallway. She's donned a low-cut top and tight-fitted skirt for today and seems particularly obnoxious already. I'll have to get in earlier to prepare myself for the day if she keeps showing up minutes after I do.

"Hazel, I need you to go downstairs and get me some coffees."

"Coffees?" I know I'm an errand-girl around here sometimes, but I'm pretty sure I graduated from coffee runs twelve months ago.

"Yes." She adjusts her high-waisted skirt in the reflection of her half-glass window. "Get me a skinny soy latte and a long black, would you? I just got off the phone with my eight a.m. and he likes his coffee hot, so, no dawdling."

Consumed as I was by the weekend, like an idiot, I didn't go over today's appointments before I arrived. I've no idea who's coming in today, what should be prepared or what needs to be done.

"Let's get moving, Jonesy!" she shrills with a clap, and I push myself up, grab my purse, and head for the elevator.

I should have called in sick.

When I return ten minutes later, Lisa sits across from a dark-haired man whose face I can't see. I want to smack the back of his head for arriving early and making Lisa even more on edge. She spots me and waves through the glass, signalling for me to hurry. The impatient expression on her face re-ignites the fury within me for missing the marketing role. It's going to take every ounce of strength not to pour this coffee over her head.

"Finally, Jonesy!" Lisa sings in her fake, angelic voice, bracelets jingling as she ushers me inside from her high-backed chair. "Bring those in. We've got work to do." I plaster my trade-mark professional expression on my face and turn to nod to the man in the chair opposite Lisa.

I gasp. The tray of coffees slips from my hand.

Patrick looks stunned.

11

"OH, SHIT!"

Lisa's cry brings me back into the room, heat rushing up my neck as I realise the mess I've made. I scoop up the cups, fumbling to clean up the spill of hot coffee on her glass desk. Patrick is on his feet, grabbing tissues from the box on the desk to help wipe up.

"I'm so sorry," I hear myself say. *Who did I murder in a past life to have this happen?*

"She still doesn't know how to walk in heels," Lisa jokes, trying to keep her guest at ease, whilst aiming her laser-like stare at my face.

My head shakes in apology as I turn my face towards the mess in front of me.

"Big weekend, ma'am?"

Startled, I glance up at Patrick whose expression is jarring. His lips pressed into a firm line and the tic in his jaw show annoyance, but something dancing behind his eyes causes my knees to buckle.

"I'm so sorry," I say again.

Patrick wordlessly holds my gaze for a couple more beats,

and then, just like when we were at the hospital, his demeanour changes as if he's flipped a switch.

"Would you mind getting a bin?" he asks, his tone clipped. He's holding wet tissues in his hand.

"Uh … of course," I stammer, grabbing the waste basket from under the desk and holding it out so he can throw in his rubbish. I chuck in mine, snapping back into reality and wiping the table again with more tissues. "I'm sorry."

"It's fine," he says curtly, turning to Lisa. "Let's get back to business, shall we?"

My lips threaten to quiver with the continuous disappoint-ment and shock that has been this morning. Any sign that Patrick might've been pleased to see me has been shot to hell in a split second. Whilst I have visions of me reaching down and shoving the soaked tissues down his throat, all I do is hunch over like a berated child, too shellshocked to do much else.

"Could you get us some fresh coffees please Hazel?" Lisa orders, sitting back down in her chair and inviting him to do the same.

"That won't be necessary," says Patrick gruffly, taking his seat. "I'm not staying long."

"Oh." Lisa is taken aback, and I dread the lecture I'm going to get later if I ruin any prospects for her. "Jonesy, the paper-work for the two o'clock meeting is on the bench. Take it with you and leave us."

I grab the paperwork as instructed and beeline for the door without a backwards glance, closing the door behind me.

When I get back to my desk, I sink into my chair, my face hot with humiliation.

What the hell is he doing here?

Discreetly, I peer around my monitor, watching as Lisa listens intently to something Patrick says. I lean back in my chair and close my eyes, trying to rationalise my thoughts. Patrick is *here*, at my office. Thinking back to Saturday night, he told me he works as a financial consultant, working in property development. It makes sense he's meeting with the head of property at a large corporation. But *here?* I don't think I told him anything about my work … but I can't be sure.

Oh, for God's sake Hazel, he's not here because he wanted to bump into you.

My eyes snap open and I click my mouse, first pulling up Lisa's calendar and finding today. There it is. *8am, private appointment with P.* By the look of things, Lisa put it in herself. It's rare. The woman has had me set up Tinder dates and bikini waxes with specific design details before, so she's not shy on most things. Plus, there's no way I'd put something on her calendar and leave out that much detail. I'm organised, anally retentive and take pride in my obsession of not missing a beat at work.

Except for today, it would appear. I shudder as flashes of spilling coffee and Patrick's cold eyes glaring *through* me flash into my mind.

No, this must be something she doesn't want me knowing about. Like the time she scheduled "meetings" with a married man from the fifth floor. I eventually found out about it, as did his wife. The former because I'm a good at my job and the latter because Lisa's terrible at having affairs.

When I'm brave enough to look again, Lisa is flicking her blonde, voluminous hair over her shoulder. I can make out Patrick's profile, and he looks at ease. He's smiling. *She's* smiling. It's too much smiling for my liking.

About twenty minutes later, Lisa's laugh catches my attention and I realise she's opened the door, walking her guest and my Saturday night saviour to the elevator. They shake hands as they finish up their conversation and as she heads towards the restroom, a golden opportunity arises.

I've got to be sensible. This is my place of employ and I've worked too hard for someone to come and unsettle that. *Don't overreact.*

I rise from my seat, watching as Patrick takes his last few steps across the luxurious waiting room to stand outside the elevator. *Don't overreact*, I remind myself.

It takes a split second to decide.

I take off, quickening my pace as the elevator doors spring open. I arrive at the elevator before they close, Patrick's posture tense as his eyes lock with mine.

"What the actual fuck?" I slam my hands against the elevator doors to keep them from closing. Not my most eloquent choice of words, but it's the first thing that tumbles out of my mouth.

Patrick stares at me, his expression hard. "Hazel."

It takes me a second to find my voice again, my eyes getting lost somewhere over his pink mouth, perfectly cocooned by his immaculate facial hair. "What are you doing here?"

"I had a meeting," Patrick replies, his golden-brown eyes glistening with humour. "With your boss it would seem."

"Yes, it *would* seem. About what?"

Patrick's eyes flash, the humour vanishing. "That's a private matter."

The elevator beeps, signalling I need to either get in or get out of the way. Instead, I lower and raise my arms, resetting the sensors to keep the doors open. "Are you serious? You're really not going to tell me what you're doing here?"

Patrick's face registers my concern, and he looks like he might reassure me, or give me one of his small smiles or hell, even throw me a sarcastic comment, but he doesn't.

"No. How's your head?" Patrick asks. The tenderness in his deep voice sets off vibrations in my chest.

My rage simmers a little. "Sore."

"You should've called in sick." Patrick's eyes dart to the foyer behind me, and I wonder if he's worried about people seeing us talk.

"And you should stop popping up in my life and telling me what to do," I snap.

Patrick's mouth twists as though he's suppressing a grin. "Yes, ma'am." He moves his head to direct me to step away, but I'm not ready to let him go yet.

"Would my boss be bothered you were in my house on Saturday night?" I ask innocently. "Lisa can be quite territorial."

Patrick sighs. "You really want to play that game? You vomited in my car, *Jonesy.*"

The way he mimics my boss's voice irritates me and I reach forward, shove him in the shoulder and physically assault a man who could have me assassinated in under twenty-four hours.

Patrick's lips part in surprise and my bravery dissipates. "I'm sorry—"

"I *helped* you," he growls, and the hairs on the back of my neck stand on end. "I got you to the hospital to see if you had a concussion, which you did, but not before you *vomited* in my car—"

"Shh!" I hush him, stepping inside the elevator, shortening the distance between us, glaring up at him as the doors close with a soft thud behind me.

"I know. I'm sorry!" A huff escapes my lips. "I'm having a really shitty morning, okay?"

He licks his lips as though stewing on his next comment. "I'm sure things seem bad right now after your weekend, but give it time. You're still recovering."

I want to explain. I want to sit him down and tell him he got the wrong impression of me, that one night (or several nights) of too many drinks doesn't define a person, doesn't define me. The reality is, everything that happened Saturday night was my fault. I got myself into a dangerous situation and I only have myself to blame. I know I should thank him, but I can't help but feel fired up.

"You're not going to tell anyone, right?" The thought of Patrick slipping in a funny tale to my boss when he's sweet-talking her brings on a hint of nausea.

Patrick tilts his head to look at me, a mischievous glint in his eye. "Don't want your boss knowing about your relationship with tequila?"

"I do a good job of keeping my personal and work lives apart," I retort, folding my arms. "I don't know why you're here, but you shouldn't be. Promise me you won't say anything to anyone. Ever."

Patrick steps towards me, the move catching me by surprise. Our faces are inches apart and I swallow the lump in my throat, doing my best to stand my ground.

"Or what?" His deep voice reverberates through my chest and confrontational Ballsy Hazel has second thoughts and no response to his question. "What are you going to do? Vomit *on* me this time?"

I tilt my chin up in defiance. "I'm up for the challenge. Bonus points if it's in your Maserati."

I swear a grin is threatening to break through, but it vanishes before I can be sure. Patrick edges nearer, his pink lips dangerously close, and I have to fight the urge to slap him ... or lean into him. His thick lashes frame his hypnotic golden-brown eyes and I have to concentrate on not falling under their spell.

"Trust me when I say you won't be coming anywhere near either of my cars again."

"*Promise* me you won't say anything," I demand. Patrick's fierce glare softens as he ever-so-slightly chews the inside of his bottom lip. I swallow again. Anger brews inside my chest. I know I'm not imagining the intoxicating energy between the two of us. I can't breathe properly.

Butterflies erupt in my stomach, my heart races, my palms sweat. He's acting like a jerk and yet there's a yearning sensation coursing through me, like I want to shove him up against the wall and wrap my legs around him.

"Patrick." My voice sounds unlike myself as I drop the tough-girl persona in a last-ditch attempt to get him to leave my personal life out of my work life. "This job is the only thing I have in my life right now. This, and a concussion."

At my change of tone, his face relaxes a little, the darkness in his eyes replaced by sincerity. "I promise I won't say anything," he replies, breaking the tension and stepping back, hands in his pockets.

The elevator doors open before I have time to say anything further and we're forced to the back as a group of people pour in, chatting animatedly. *How many people can we possibly fit in here?* I ask myself, squinting to double check the capacity on the opposite wall.

Without warning, Patrick's left arm loops around my waist, pulling me to him to make more space as the doors close. My back presses against his rock-hard chest, and his muscular arm curls around my waist, his large hand tucked into the side of my ribs. Patrick's chest rises and falls behind me, his warm breath tickling the space by my ear, the smell of pine and coffee engulfing my lungs.

When we reach the ground floor and the doors open, Patrick uncurls his arm from me, breaking the hum of electricity charging through my body. Steadying myself subtly against the railing, Patrick strides out the doors behind everyone else, unaffected.

"Until next time, Jonesy," he purrs, a hint of a smile at the corner of his mouth. He swiftly walks away and the elevator doors close, leaving me breathless, confused, and focusing way too much on the fact he said we'd be seeing each other again.

When I get back to my desk, Lisa calls me into her office. Sometimes I think she waits for me to sit before yelling out, just to be annoying.

"Yes, Lisa?" I ask, scanning her desk for any traces of coffee. I know there's a ream of abuse heading my way and I deserve it.

"Could you send me through the notes from the webinar?" she asks, peering at me over her glasses. It takes me a second to process my surprise at her lack of annoyance. "Michael Miller's emailed around asking for feedback. Ordinarily, I'd let you reply, but it's for the executive report."

Dumbfounded, I stand unmoving. For the second time today, I'm blindsided by the actions of my past self.

"I, uh ..."

"You did watch the webinar yesterday, didn't you? Or were you too hungover from your big night out?" Lisa's tone is light, yet her words cut right through me. My cheeks flame. I'm officially an inch tall.

Lisa's manicured eyebrows arch in surprise. "Something tells me my jokes about your weekend antics might not be that far off." The jingling of her bracelets breaks through the distress radiating off my body. "Have the notes to me by the end of the day."

One part of my brain screams at me to explain my concussion; to show her the medical certificate to get me off the hook, but I don't. I've never been one to make excuses for my work slacking, mainly because I've never had to before today. I never slipped up. Even during the worst days of my break-up or during the partying stint, I didn't slip up. I might have missed a job advertisement because of distraction and yes, on the overall scale, my careers goals and love life are in shambles, but when I have a job, I do it well.

I say nothing and leave her office, with the equivalent of my tail between my legs.

12

THE WEEK PASSED IN A BLUR.

When I wasn't busy beating myself up for losing an opportunity to get out from under Lisa, I kissed her ass to make up for my giant cock-up earlier in the week. The coffee-spilling and forgetting to watch the webinar made for a challenging experience. Not only that, but I found myself thinking about Patrick. A *lot*. The irony of having my life slip so far out of my grasp over one man, only to keep thinking about another, is not lost on me. It's not as if I'm *into* him or anything. I'm just intrigued. Plus, there was the moment in the elevator ... I guess he was making space, but he didn't have to be so *physical*, surely.

On Friday evening, I rehash these thoughts to Kali as we commit to our usual routine of ordering too many pizzas and cracking open a bottle of red. When I finally finish my word-vomit about the Patrick situation, she's grinning at me with sparkling eyes.

"He's gotten under your skin, hasn't he?" she teases.

"No!" I shout, too quickly, and Kali chuckles. "I just don't get this guy, showing up in my life twice in two days, acting like some mysterious James Bond character."

"Maybe he's been paid to assassinate you," she muses. "Although he could be a little more discreet. Perhaps he's a federal agent … or a hire-a-husband for your boss. Ooh, a sex worker!"

"Ew." Shaking my head, I top up both our glasses generously.

"Sex work is a legitimate job."

"That was more a reaction to me imagining him and Lisa having sex."

"Fair call," Kali agrees. "I'm a fan of a conspiracy theory as much as the next person, but you're desperately searching for a reason to keep talking about him, because you think he's sexy and you want to see him again."

I bury my face in my goblet.

"Your silence is very reassuring," she says, with a smirk. "Honestly, it's so good to see you get worked up over something again. Even if it is another asshole."

I peer at her over my wine glass. "What?"

"I don't care what you say about this guy. This is the first time in months I've seen you heated about something. Hell, it's the first time I've seen you express any sort of emotion other than Robot Hazel."

Kali's words surprise me.

"You're not offended by that are you?" she groans.

"No." And I'm not. "I just hadn't realised how little I'd thought about Luke this week." Kali and I burst into victorious giggles and I revel in the warmth from my friendship with her (and the wine), but mostly the friendship.

We spend the next little while coming up with a range of conspiracy theories involving what Patrick's job could be: secret agent, assassin, SAS, mafia.

"The mafia would be kind of sexy." Kali giggles again.

"Something tells me it's not quite as hot as the movies make it out to be," I reply, downing the last of my wine. My cheeks are hot and my eyelids heavy; a solid sign I've had enough to drink for tonight. "But it would be cool if he came here to kidnap me and forced me to be his sex slave." I snort as I finish my sentence and Kali laughs again.

"Yes, she's back to thinking about penis!"

"There's no chance in hell of me having anything to do with Patrick's penis. The guy's grumpy as all hell."

"He's in the mafia. Can you blame him?" Kali asks. "Plus, remember what I said the other day about sexy and angry guys in the sack? Keep that at the forefront of your mind for when you next run into him."

"Hopefully, there won't be a next time."

"Liar." Kali nudges me with her foot and giggles.

Rolling my eyes, I change the subject. "Is Alex the angry type?"

Kali grins and lets her head fall back on the couch behind her. "Fuck yes, he's furious."

Tipsy giggles erupt from the two of us once again, and for the first time in months, my life is slipping into the sunlight.

Lying in bed, my face warm from the wine and my good mood, I stare up at my bright phone screen, already on Luke's Instagram feed. It's remained unchanged since I last visited. There's no mention of him seeing anyone, but that makes sense, considering he posted nothing of me when we were together. He kept his feed filled with photos of his adventures with his mates more than anything. I scarcely made an appearance and never saw it as a red flag until now.

Before I can talk myself out of it, I tap at the screen and unfollow him, blocking him immediately after. A smile inches across my face at finally taking some control.

High with the power of it, my fingers tap away to some of

the artist accounts I used to visit daily, their feeds bursting with breathtaking paintings, illustrations, and photographs. Creative Hazel soars with happiness at their successes: booked out with commissions, gallery exhibitions, rave reviews.

Hope fills my lungs, and passion surges through my veins. This is what I've been missing. The rush of adrenaline as ideas and possibilities start to come to life, an undeniable tingling in my fingers, itching to pick up a pen and draw. This is what it felt like when I was at school creating graphic novels, and at university, when I'd make website pages for fake clients. It's an overwhelming surge of endorphins just waiting to be released.

I'm lucky to have found a passion in life that I can make a career out of. It's the one thing that when I'm doing it, it feels *right*. I know it's what I'm meant to be doing, and I've gone for months without it. I've been starving my soul of what it loves to do, instead of using it to comfort me.

I drop my phone next to me and jump out of bed, sliding the bottom drawer of my desk open. Packed away months ago when I could do nothing but despair and watch my life fall apart, is my design tablet wrapped in bubble paper, sitting on top of some sketch pads.

Unwrapping it, I collect the cord and plug it in to charge it. The screen comes to life. Next to the open drawer, I sit on the floor, lean against the wall, curl my fingers around the pen, and draw.

13

"HOW THE HELL did you convince me to come here?"

Kali smiles her thanks to the server who drops off our chilled beers. "Because you're easy to manipulate."

"Gee thanks."

My Saturday afternoon plans of listening to a true crime podcast whilst doodling on my design tablet are shot to hell, with Kali somehow talking me into having drinks and tapas in the outdoor bar at the casino. Whilst gambling and over-priced cocktails are not high on my list of wants or needs, Kali's plea of accompanying her so she could enjoy a drink in the sunshine before she goes on her date won me over.

"Think of this as a favour to me, for bailing on the week-end," Kali offers.

"You didn't notice I'd left," I argue. "Alex was your flavour of the night, remember? I really thought that would last longer than it did."

"I'm seeing him tomorrow," she explains. "We're not exclusive. He's seeing some chick called Bree tonight."

"Your life exhausts me."

Kali smiles, lifting her glass up. "Thank you, and here's to you, for joining me back in the land of the living. No more Robot Hazel." Lifting my glass to tap hers, I swallow a large gulp of the refreshing amber liquid, mulling over her words.

Despite my recent vow never to drink again already broken, I can't deny I've turned a corner. My attitude today, compared to a week ago, has drastically improved. Something changed last night. For the first time in months, the familiar cloud of existential dread doesn't loom over me.

The Garden Bar at the *Star Casino* spans a large space on the ground floor. Green AstroTurf, complimented by an array of flowers, surrounds our table on the back deck, giving us the perfect vantage of the entire area. Sitting in the sun, with my best friend, and a clearer head I've had in months, is almost surreal.

Kali and I sip our beers, laughing about the previous weekend, and discussing potential plans for her birthday in a couple of months. Summer approaching is enough to get the two of us excited. I may be pasty, but I'd pick hot, sweaty days under the Australian sun over the cold, *any* day.

Kali hails the server to order more beers as my gaze roams the wide, open space again. There's a group of guys in smart dress pants and shoes, donning brightly coloured Hawaiian shirts for what could only be a bucks' weekend. Inside, ladies laugh over lunch, whilst their young children run riot across the lawn.

Two men stand chatting at a wine barrel nearby and I nearly fall off my stool. Dressed in a dark suit, brown locks mussed on top of his head, is Patrick.

Kali, who's texting on her phone, glimpses my stunned expression and whips her head around, before whipping it back. "What? What is it?"

I don't answer her. Instead, I watch as he smiles; the smile that's seared in my memory from the few times I've seen it. It's wide and filled with straight white teeth, reaching up to his eyes and crinkling his olive skin. His joyous expression sets off my erratic heartbeat.

My gaze travels down to the light shirt poking out from under his jacket, and I wonder what Patrick might look like shirtless. My brief encounter back at the hospital was all olive skin, muscle, and a smattering of chest hair. My mouth salivates. Kali's right. I do need to have sex.

Across from him is an older man with a neat grey beard, dressed as stylishly as Patrick. You'd be forgiven for thinking they discussed their outfits before arriving to ensure they'd be the best-dressed people in the entire establishment.

Kali whistles, following my line of sight. "He's the assassin, isn't he? No wonder he got under your skin."

As if he can sense us gaping at him, Patrick's eyes flick up. Kali and I whip away, acting overly nonchalant. Fuck.

Please don't have seen us. Please.

"Is he still looking?" Kali hisses after an uncomfortable moment of sitting stiffly.

"I don't know, I can't fucking look, can I?" I snap, covering my mouth in case Patrick can read lips, one of the many conspiracy theories Kali and I came up with last night.

"Maybe he *is* following you." Unlikely, but the alternative is the universe playing tricks on me by having us bump into each other multiple times in one week, with me always unprepared.

Kali peers over her shoulder and I smack her hand resting on the table. "*Stop* looking at him."

She gives me one of her trademark grins. "No wonder you constantly talk about him. He's ridiculous. I've half a mind to walk over and smell him; maybe even lick his face."

"Sure, that wouldn't be weird at all."

Kali doesn't react to my comment. At least, not in the way I thought she might. Instead, she hops off her stool and marches to the bar, leaning across to whisper to the server. The sinking sensation in my stomach is an unequivocal indicator of what's coming next.

Several minutes later, after I've cursed Kali with the fire of a thousand suns, our server delivers two shot glasses to Patrick's table. I can't help but cover my face with my hand as Kali watches the madness unfold.

"I hate you so much. I hope you trip right before your birthday and smash your teeth into your face in front of a crowd of people." Kali simply laughs. "Now he's going to know we were talking about him."

"Have I ever steered you wrong?"

At those words, I whip my head back and glare at her. "Is that a serious question?"

"Trust me, Hazy." Kali smiles before we sneak a look at Patrick and his friend.

His companion raises a shot glass and flashes a kind smile at the two of us, before tipping it down his throat. I try my best not to look at Patrick's face, but a magnetic force drags my gaze to his. When our eyes meet, I'm feverish. A memory of him staring at me intently on my front porch races to the forefront of my mind and my lips tingle.

Patrick hasn't taken his shot; his gaze is still on me. My heart is about to burst out of my eardrums. The seconds drag by as I wait to see what he'll do.

He breaks his gaze when his friend says something to him, and he takes the shot. Kali glances at me and winks. "We're in."

Twenty minutes later, I'm pinching myself as to how I let Kali get me into these situations.

Kali and John, Patrick's fifty-something flamboyant companion from Melbourne, are chatting like they're long-lost besties. John dragged Patrick to join us, where he's been perched on the edge of his stool ever since.

It turns out John is a high-roller and travels around the world, living a lavish lifestyle filled with private jets, limousines, and more money than I'd know what to do with. Thank God he's happy to share his over-the-top stories with us, otherwise I imagine the four of us would sit in silence.

Maybe Kali hoped using the cover of shouting a drink to the man who 'saved her best friend's life' would cause conversation to flow freely. Or perhaps if she kept John busy with conversation, Patrick and I might exchange words and end up realising we're soulmates. Neither of those things has happened.

I've spent most of the time doodling innate patterns on napkins with the pen that arrived with the bill. Patrick switched to water the minute he got here and I wonder if he did that because he thinks I can't control my drink and might need to be rescued again. It makes me slow down on the beer intake.

"You should come and visit me in Melbourne," John says clapping his hands together. "I could take you to some of the best restaurants in Australia. Maybe for your birthday, Patrick?"

Patrick barely grunts in response as he takes another swig of water. You'd never know he was laughing under the sunshine half an hour ago.

When a server drops off another round of drinks for us, purchased by John, Patrick says, "You've got a rash on your neck."

It takes me a second to realise Patrick has spoken. To *me*. Kali and John are deep in their own conversation about being foodies, not having noticed we're finally speaking.

Patricks nods to me when I say nothing, and my neck gets hotter. The redness on my neck and chest has always been my tell when I'm nervous, anxious, or excited. Any sudden surge of blood to my face displays on my body for the world to see and I regularly curse my genetics for giving me something so obvious.

"I get this when I drink," I reply, sipping my beer.

Patrick tilts his head, and I squirm under his gaze. "I don't remember seeing any rashes on Saturday night," he muses. "Maybe it's only when you've had one, not when you've had fifty?"

A noise escapes Kali's nose, signalling she heard that comment and she's holding back a laugh.

The truth of the matter is, he is one hundred percent correct. I get a rash when alcohol first touches my lips, but it fades after the first couple. Based on my state on Saturday night, I'm willing to bet my neck was rash-free.

I'm jittery. I never used to have trouble sinking my claws into a battle of wits with men. When I dated Luke, I had the confidence of a woman in a secure relationship. Now, it seems a few months of avoiding genuine male interaction has negatively influenced my skills and with Patrick, I can't unscramble the words from my brain to my mouth.

"Must be," I reply, doing my best to seem bored. "How's the serial killing coming along? I've got to admit, I'm a little insulted you didn't add me to your tally."

"You're not my type," he quips.

"Is Lisa your type?"

Patrick stills his hand on his glass, a scowl forming on his face. "No."

"Oh, come on Patrick!" I cry. "You guys are close in age. She's successful and sassy, like you. You guys are perfect for each other." I flash him another smile. I'm not even sure what game we're playing right now, but it makes me giddy when his nostrils flare slightly, and his jaw does that pulsating tic thing.

"I don't know if I should take dating advice from a woman who spent three years of her life with an unfaithful man who said *cheerio*." He sips his water, his unblinking gaze not leaving my face, which is on fire.

My empty glass slams a little too loudly on the wooden table.

"Let me guess. You've never made mistakes in your dating life? Your last girlfriend was a size zero model who helped the needy and had a master's degree in engineering? I'll bet she had to be perfect in every way for your impossibly high standards."

"My standards are quite basic and mainly involve a sense of humour and human decency."

"That's it? She was a decent human being with no flaws? She didn't chew with her mouth open or laugh obnoxiously or, I don't know, leave her dirty laundry on the floor *next* to the basket?"

Patrick's gaze drifts to the side, as if he's reflecting on a fond memory. "She was perfect."

Those three words strip away the buzz of humour and banter between us violently, the air thick with unspoken emotion. Patrick's hardened expression crumbles, his Adam's apple bobbing as he casts his gaze downwards. Guilt and shame flare in my stomach as I realise I've inadvertently upset him. Pain is written all over his face.

"You deserve better than Luke. Never forget that." He finishes his tumbler of water and stands. "I have to go. Excuse me."

Patrick moves away from the table, my gaze following him as he stalks across the expansive dining area, and out of sight. Kali puts an arm around my shoulder, sensing it's time to finish up.

"We should get going anyway," she says politely to John, giving me a quizzical look.

John clears his throat before standing, a kind smile on his face. "I can see why he can't stop talking about you, Hazel."

14

HALF AN HOUR LATER, our taxi pulls up outside our house. Kali farewells our driver cheerily. I'm sure he was stoked to hear me asking inane questions about what could've happened to Patrick's ex-girlfriend and questioning whether he really had been talking about me. I'm sure he was also delighted to hear about Kali's sex life and my lack thereof.

As we edge towards the house, I triple-check my bag, like I always do when I've had a couple of drinks – to check my life is still in there.

Phone—yes.

Cards—yes.

Lip gloss—

"Oh, Christ almighty."

I snap my head up at the sound of Kali's groan and look past her head to see Luke sitting on the steps to our house. *My* Luke.

My heart stops.

The air is thick, and my feet slow as if weights are strapped to my ankles.

The bags under Luke's eyes and the slight look of apprehension on his face are clear. He has a light smattering of stubble and his usually precision styled hair looks dishevelled. We make eye contact, but I look away. I don't know what will happen if he looks at me for too long. Will I beg him to take me back? God, I hope I don't look as desperate as I feel.

"Kali," he says, with a nod to my best friend, standing as we get closer.

"Eat a dick," she snaps, pushing past him and up to the door. She turns and looks at me. "Yell if you need me."

Kali knows me too well. Any other self-respecting human would tell this guy to piss off so they could move onto bigger and better things, but naturally, she knows I don't have the strength to do that yet. I'm curious to hear what he has to say after seeing me on Saturday. After cheating. After getting engaged to someone else.

Oh, that's right. He's engaged.

"Hi."

"What are you doing here?" I want to slap myself for the weakness that saturates my voice.

He shrugs somewhat sheepishly. "You never wrote back to my message."

So you've decided to ambush me? There's no denying the surge of satisfaction crashing through my body, knowing my lack of response bothered him enough to show up on my doorstep.

"You can't show up at my house because I haven't replied to a message, Luke." I wrap my arms around my body and hold on to my elbows, sober. I know Luke's gaze is on me, as if he's trying to will me to look at him.

"I needed to see you." Luke shifts his stance, stepping closer. "I meant every word I said in that message."

My throat is the driest it's ever been. I need water. Why is there no water?

"Hazy ..."

"Luke don't–" I take a tiny step backwards. He stops where he is, but when I look at him, his eyes are alight with fire as he

searches my face. It's hard to control the way air traps in my
throat, as my mind flips through memories of Luke I'd tried so
desperately to quash.

"You look good, Hazy." He sounds sincere, and even hopeful.
My bottom lip might draw blood if I bite down on it any harder.

"You shouldn't be here," I say.

"Why not?"

"Where would you like me to start?" Blinding fury blurs my
vision and I dig deep to scream, "You cheated on me and you're
engaged!"

Luke's expression twists uncomfortably, and my fury is
almost enough to distract me from the hollow sensation in my
chest.

Tilting my head to the side, I ask, "How soon after did you
propose to her?"

Luke tugs at his ear with obvious discomfort. "When we
went to Bali in June. It was an impulsive sort of thing."

"I see." I definitely *do not* see.

Several seconds of silence hang between us. I can't think of
anything else to say. Getting confirmation of what I already
knew hurt more than I thought it would. And yet I remain in
front of him, because he came to see me, and I need to
know why.

"Why are you really here, Luke?" I close my eyes, embarrassed, as tears pool. I gasp when Luke's calloused thumb gently
wipes a tear from my face.

"Please don't cry, Hazy," he whispers.

I cry more. "What do you want?" I force my blurry eyes open
to see Luke's pained face close to mine.

"I don't know." Luke keeps his hand on my cheek, moving
his thumb backwards and forwards in an attempt to comfort me.

The energy crackles between the two of us and my hurt and
rage slip out of my grasp, replaced by something familiar. I want

to lean into him. I want him to hold me and tell me how sorry he is for what he did. That he made a mistake.

The screech of a car horn blaring startles me and I step back, shaking myself from my daze. Luke looks like someone slapped him.

"You should go," I mutter.

"I'm ... I don't even ..." He runs his hands over his face. "Can I message you?"

"That's not a good idea."

"I know, but ... I've obviously got some shit to figure out. Please, don't cut me off yet." I can't bring myself to say yes or no, or nod or shake my head. This man destroyed my life, and I can't find the words to tell him to piss off.

Luke senses my turmoil and backs away from me. "I'm gonna go, but I'm going to message you again and I hope you reply."

As I open my mouth to respond, the sensation of someone watching us comes over me and I break eye contact with Luke to survey the street behind him, seeing a sleek black car pulling away.

15

THE NEXT WEEK AT WORK, I'm run off my feet.

Lisa has me working on her upcoming trips interstate to check out several potential storefronts and meet with company directors. She's got me back to running her personal errands, including picking up dry cleaning, helping her organise cleaners for her house, and being a general all-around pain in my ass. I'm willing to bet this version of Lisa, who is even more unbearable than usual, is partly this way because of my nightmare week last week. She's making me grovel and she knows it.

I can't really complain though. Being this busy and working hard not to make *any* mistakes is taking up so much energy I barely have time to think about Luke. He's messaged me a couple of times. I'm proud of myself for replying to only one of them and I didn't even include emojis.

Patrick, on the other hand, *has* been on my mind. His upsetting reaction to his ex-girlfriend has plagued my imagination. So have John's comments about Patrick talking about me. What has he been saying? Was it about how I vomited, or something more positive? I have no way of finding out either way. He hasn't shown his face back in the office or appeared in Lisa's calendar again.

On Thursday afternoon, Lisa calls me into her office as she's collecting her things to head off. "Jonesy, I need a favour."

"Of course."

"I've got to go to Melbourne this weekend." Lisa slides her arms into her long grey jacket. "Unexpected, but it can't be avoided."

"Did you want a flight this afternoon or tomorrow morning?" I ask, getting my phone out to search for flights.

"No, no, I've got it covered," she says. My hand pauses above my screen as I watch how she flits about the office. She's flustered and that's another reason I book her trips, even the personal ones. She's got too much going on in her brain to sort her own life out.

"I need you to go in my place to the Henchman Charity Gala on Saturday." The surprise must be clear on my face, but she doesn't acknowledge it as she grabs her belongings.

The Henchman Charity Gala. The biggest charity event of the social calendar, filled with silent auctions, flowing booze, and a heap of important people. The glitzy and glamour-filled event Lisa said just last week, she wouldn't miss, even if she had to sit next to Julian all night.

I've never attended the gala. Mostly, it's the executives from Green and Acre who attend, alongside representatives from other conglomerates who've donated to the Henchman Charity Fund; millionaires and people I have nothing in common with. It's always covered by the press and each year the stories get more and more wild. Last year, a famous cricketer and an Instagram model got photographed having sex in a separate function room. It was very scandalous, and Lisa didn't stop talking about it for weeks afterwards. That she's considered *me* to replace her at such a tantalising event is an enormous surprise.

"I want someone to represent the property branch," she insists. "If anyone knows this branch as well as I do, it's you."

It's the best compliment I'm ever received from Lisa. She knows I know the team, and that's something I can agree with, with confidence.

"I've sent my personal apologies to George," she says, picking up her handbag and pushing past me towards the door. "And I've let him know you're coming in my place. You should have all the details." True enough, as I'd booked everything for her.

As I follow her out of the office, agitation rolling off her body, I pray she's not on the brink of ruining another marriage. She impatiently presses the button for the elevator and checks her watch. "Get yourself a dress. You can take my place at the makeup and hair appointments."

My eyebrows have sprung to my hairline. "Wow. Thank you, Lisa."

She doesn't acknowledge me as she swipes through her phone, exhaling as the doors open. "Don't let me down, Hazel. Make a good impression."

The minute the doors shut, the smile I'd been suppressing takes over my face and a tiny squeal escapes my lips. I pull myself together, looking around to make sure no one else saw me.

Back at my desk, I text Kali the good news.

KALI

HFI I YEAH! Wine at 4.30pm sharp. Stoked for you my girl x

I know I should get back to work, but I spend the rest of the afternoon browsing dresses online.

"Kali ... this is a bit *much.*"

"No such thing." Kali fusses over me as if she's dressing someone for their wedding, smoothing out creases that don't exist and ensuring my boobs pop an appropriate amount for a work function. "This is your chance to charm the pants off everybody. It doesn't hurt to take advantage of your assets while doing so either."

As soon as I finished work, Kali had me meet her at one of her favourite boutique clothing stores to find me a "jaws-on-the-floor-dress" for the gala. I can't deny that the gown Kali picked out for me, satin, olive-green floor-length, with a split up to the thigh, is beautiful. Stunning in fact. It's a flattering contrast against my creamy skin and brings out the darker green in my eyes. My hips are subtly accentuated. And my boobs? Not so subtly.

"It's a work function," I remind her, turning so I can see most of my exposed back. The twice a day gym sessions are paying off.

"Whatever. It's the Henchman Charity Gala. Did you see what some women wore last year? Jesus, Mimi would have a fit if she saw the photos."

I laugh when I imagine Kali's grandmother's face if she saw some of the dresses from previous events. Her eighty-some-thing-year-old heart wouldn't cope.

"My point is, you need to stand out," Kali says firmly, assessing me in the mirror's reflection. "And this is going to make you the star."

"I don't want to be the star." Yet as I say the words, I know this is the dress. This is what I'll be wearing to the gala and if it gets me a bit of extra attention, which could lead to striking up conversations with some important people, I'm all for it.

Last year, every important person from Green and Acre was there, including the heads of the overseas locations and design and marketing executives. Not to mention minor celebrities, social media influencers, sporting stars, fashion designers and advertisers. If I could somehow end up in a conversation with any of them and share my interest in branching off into another area of the company, I'd be happy.

Kali literally screams when I agree to buy the dress and she proceeds to select my accessories, and heels I can walk in, all while boosting my confidence. By the time we get home, I'm starting to believe some of what she's telling me.

16

THE GALA IS TAKING place in one of those over-the-top convention centres that can house more people than I can count. By the time I make my way indoors, the pre-drinks have started, and I can see why this is one of the most talked about events on the social calendar.

Beautiful executives mingle around the Plaza Ballroom, with its dazzling bright lights and decorations. Despite being out of my depth, a smile spreads across my face as I enter the bustling hall and crane my neck up at the multiple crystal chandeliers hanging from the ceiling.

The sheer number of people laughing and talking at the tables is startling. Most of them already have drinks in their hands, some of them two. An enormous number of them are lining up to get professional photographs taken on a mini-red carpet set-up, whilst others squeal with delight as they see their friends.

I beeline for the front of the room where I know my table is, weaving through the endless array of large circular tables, covered in white tablecloths, adorned with ostentatious centre pieces, and bows hangings from the chairs. I catch the attention of several people I walk by and it's another reminder of how women should indulge in hair and makeup appointments more often.

Lisa's hair stylist arrived at my door minutes after I arrived at the hotel, treating my hair to a rigorous regime of brushing, pulling, and braiding, tutting throughout the entire appointment. At one point I was sure she was going to lift my hair up from the roots. The result is a perfectly styled low bun, and layers cut so that a few soft ribbons fall gently around my face.

As she applied her finishing touches, my flamboyant makeup artist Ezekiel arrived, launching straight into conversation about growing up as a gay Indian male in Melbourne, who stole his mother's makeup whenever he could. He painted with such gusto I spent the first ten minutes panicking at what he was doing to my face. True to his word though, Ezekiel went for a more natural look, focusing on making my eyes look big and bright.

I look fucking amazing.

I remind myself of that as I arrive at my table at the front of the room. No one is seated, but several people are standing around talking to each other like old friends. They halt their conversations to look at me silently as I slow my pace. I may as well have *Newbie* in neon lights on my forehead.

A short stocky man with a neat grey beard and balding head makes his way over to me, a slight limp in his step. This man has never taken notice of me before, but I know his name is George Wilson, the founder and Chief Executive Officer of Green and Acre.

"Mr Wilson," I croak out. "I'm Hazel –"

"Yes, yes, of course!" he bellows. A nervous chuckle escapes my lips as he shakes my hand vigorously. "Lovely to finally meet you. I'm so glad you could come. These nights are always such fun."

"If you find hours of executives kissing each other's asses

fun." A tall, suited-up man reaches his hand out to mine, a playful smile on his lips as he winks at George. "Ain't that right George?"

"Julian, you're full of it," George grumbles, although I can tell he's joking. "Hazel, this is Julian Bell. He heads up finance in Sydney."

Ah, the *weasel* in the flesh.

"We've exchanged a few calls and emails over the years," I say, shaking his hand.

"I'm willing to bet everything I own, you're Lisa's much-needed filter. I know Lisa and her emails are always way too nice."

"Julian," George warns. "None of that when she's not here to defend herself." Julian holds his hands up in a surrender and George nods, before being approached by more people and turning away.

"Apologies, Hazel Jones. I shouldn't badmouth your boss. I was all geared up for a battle of wits this evening and am disappointed I won't get to spend my evening riling her up." Julian sips his beer and shrugs and I decide I like him. His light and fluffy demeanour has me thinking that Lisa's distaste for him is more to do with his ability to take her down a peg each time they speak, and maybe a bit of jealousy over his bond with George.

"You must have been with the company for some time now?" Julian asks.

"Five years." I help myself to a glass of champagne from a passing server. "I don't know where the time has gone."

"You'd think working under Lisa would make it drag."

I smile. "I thought George said you couldn't do that while she wasn't here to defend herself?"

"You're loyal and I like that, Hazel Jones. Have you got any plans? Got your sights set on rising to the top? Working at a sister-site overseas? Saving money for a gap year?"

"I'm twenty-seven. A gap year is long gone," I reply.

"Never." Julian shakes his head. "It's all about stage, not age. I'm eight years older than my wife and I remind her of that every time she tells me to grow up."

"Something tells me she has to tell you that a lot." I sip my champagne as Julian laughs. "Is she here tonight?"

"I wish. She's back in Sydney looking after our two boys." Pride lights up Julian's face. "She's an interior designer and the best mum in the world. Thankfully, my boys inherited her good looks and my sharp wit."

"Thankfully," I agree, and Julian laughs again.

"You're a firecracker like Lisa under all that loyalty, aren't you?"

"Not quite. I could take some more lessons on going after what I want."

Julian nods in understanding. "It's a good skill to have, but contrary to what your boss believes, you don't have to be an asshole to everyone to do that well." I stifle a giggle and sip my champagne. "Take George, for instance. Gentle, kind, nice as pie to everyone. Listens to what you have to say respectfully, knows how to take a joke, and is still one of the most powerful and respected people in this room."

"You don't think that has anything to do with the fact that he's a man and maybe his authority isn't seen as bossy or threatening because he has a penis?" The words slip from my mouth effortlessly and I raise my eyebrows in anticipation of Julian's response.

He eyes me with a grin. I've surprised him.

"Well played, Hazel Jones," he says, and I laugh.

"For the record, I've always known George to have a wonderful reputation," I explain, watching as he bellows out a laugh in a small circle of people. "Lisa can be … difficult sometimes, but I wonder, if she were a man, how differently she'd be treated. She might be tough, but she's got to compete in a male-dominated industry, in a male-dominated world. Sometimes you've got to be mean." I shrug at my own ramblings and turn back to Julian, who is surveying me thoughtfully.

"Very insightful." He sips his beer, his brow furrowed. "I guess I never really thought about it that much."

"Nothing like a feminist rant to kick off your evening, hey?"

"I enjoyed it." Julian clinks his bottle against my glass. "She's lucky to have you, but you should be your own boss. I hope you have that on your radar."

"Does being a self-employed, self-sufficient graphic illustrator of book covers count as being my own boss?" My champagne flute is nearly empty. Whoops.

"Damn straight that counts!" Julian cheers, grabbing my glass and placing our empties on the table. A server with a fresh load of drinks offers his tray to us and we each take a new one. "How far have you gotten with that?"

"I'll be honest with you, Julian, things have stalled of late."

"Well, Hazel Jones, we need to work on how to kick things back into gear."

"You know, you don't have to call me by my full name every time," I point out.

"Yes, but it sounds so important, *Hazel Jones!*" he bellows. "Future illustrative artist extraordinaire. I like it. There are plenty of important people in here. Who knows? Tonight could be your lucky night, Hazel Jones."

The champagne causes me to smile hopefully.

———

Wedged between Julian and George for the evening, the two of them alternate between pleasant conversation with me and exchanging witty banter with each other. They make settling into the event much easier than I anticipated and I laugh along with everybody else at the table as if I belong there.

George tells me his wife died five years earlier, leaving him to eat too much and work too hard in what should be his retirement years. I'd say both those statements are dangerously true. His belly is so curved he looks like he might topple over at any moment, but he's sweet and his laugh is booming and jolly, like Santa.

Julian is the charming class clown of the table, having everyone in fits of laughter at his own expense. Every time the emcee comes on stage to invite a new speaker up, or tell a joke, Julian yells out something which has hundreds of people howling.

After an hour of eating and downing a couple of drinks, I have a pleasant buzz, but am mindful of not repeating Kygo. I drink two large glasses of water for every half glass of champagne, which is more than I can say for the rest of my table.

The other directors and upper management get louder and more boisterous by the minute. One of them even shouts across the table about how much more she prefers my company to Lisa's, and I have to suck in my bottom lip to keep from snorting.

"What do you think of all this pomp and ceremony, Hazel?" George asks me, exhaling as he finishes his third course.

"I'm having a good time, but I've eaten too much," I admit. George chortles and leans back in his chair, rubbing his belly in agreement.

"Better take some deep breaths, old man, you need to get up there shortly." Julian waves a fork in the direction of the stage where the emcee is preparing for his next announcement. "Somehow, this retired geezer still manages to be the bloody star of every event he's invited to."

"Maybe that's because I made the largest donation of anyone this year," George argues.

"It's because Healey treats you like you're his sweet old

grandad and doesn't know how to say no to you." Julian winks at me, popping a slice of lamb into his mouth.

"You talk some shit, Julian," George says with a grin on his lips. "Where the hell is Healey, anyway? I haven't seen him all night."

"Who knows? Probably up to table twenty by now."

"Julian ..."

"I'm not saying there's anything wrong with being a ladies' man," Julian says earnestly. "I don't even know him, but from all accounts, he's a superstar with every woman that he comes across. You single, Hazel? George could be your adopted grandad."

I shake my head. "I don't need any more ladies' men in my life, thanks."

"Smart woman. George, give this girl a raise, or the contact details of one of your design friends in Sydney." Julian's comment catches me unawares and I laugh awkwardly.

"Hazel, my dear, are you interested in design?" George asks. His wrinkled cheeks are pink from his red wine, but his focus seems genuine and sober.

"You're welcome," Julian whispers, leaning away to chat to the man next to him.

I nod as I turn towards George. "I've always wanted to work in marketing or design. I enjoy being creative. I had this idea of creating book covers for authors a while ago ... it's something I'm interested in."

George's face lights up at these words. "That is wonderful, Hazel. Are you any good?" His grin is cheeky and not at all challenging.

"I think so." I give him what I hope is a confident smile.

"When I get back to the office, I'll send you the details of my friend in Sydney. She heads up a design team at a big publishing house down there. I know it's competitive and I don't want to lose you from the company, but maybe she can point you in the right direction to get your own art out there?"

Hope erupts from my chest, but I do my best to wind it in. I don't want to get too ahead of myself. "Thank you, George, that would be fantastic."

The emcee gets people's attention, signalling the last round of speeches and awards are to take place before the band comes out and the 'party comes to life'. I'm so euphoric from how this evening is turning out that I laugh at the emcee's cringeworthy jokes under my breath. I don't understand how some people are howling with laughter, including a guy called Brad who sits directly across the table from me.

"This guy's so funny!" he yells out to anyone who will listen.

George leans in towards me. "He's terrible." I don't bother to stifle my giggle as I listen to people being called out for recognition of donations of money and time to the charity. In between presenting guests with acknowledgements, information is shared about the charity and the children they've helped since its inception. That's when George is called up. A whole segment is dedicated to thanking him for his work over the years, highlighting some of the ways his donations have helped children in care. He might be humble, but the man enjoys speaking. He's got a natural gift of engaging an audience.

When George finishes, I cheer along with the entire room. The applause lasts for a solid thirty seconds, while George waves bashfully to the crowd and hobbles down the steps.

"And lastly …" The emcee is back on stage, trying to settle the crowd who are growing more intoxicated and itching to burn off some energy on the dance floor. "I know he's a man of few words, so I won't make him say any. I've learnt my lesson. No, no, I'm joking, of course. But I will ask him to stand as we all give him, our founder and benefactor, a round of applause for all his hard work. Ladies and gentleman, Mr Patrick Healey."

17

A SPOTLIGHT SHINES on a man in a suit reluctantly rising from a seat, two tables down from mine. I almost spit my champagne across my leftover lamb as applause erupts around me. I've seen that man in a suit enough times to know there is no mistaking him.

Patrick, six foot two of brooding man, gives a wave of thanks to the room, grateful, but not happy in the spotlight.

"Huh, he is here, what do you know?" Julian says, as he joins in on the clapping.

What is happening? And why can't I breathe properly?

That must have been why Lisa and Patrick were meeting. It's plausible it had to do with the gala and Patrick hit her up for a donation. That makes way more sense than him being a spy or con man. It also means he's probably kind, generous and an all-round decent human, because not only did he save my ass, but he started a charity to help underprivileged kids too.

Applause and cheers for Patrick thunder through the hall, with some people rising from their chairs to show their appreciation. As Patrick re-takes his seat, I curse myself for the irrationality of my imagination.

Maybe he recognised my name from a memo between him and Lisa and he felt the need to get me home safely that night. He didn't tell me about his job and Lisa because he tried to keep things professional between us.

I am mortified.

The emcee wraps up the presentations once Patrick leaves the stage, and the room erupts with chatter and music. Guests head to the dance floor as the jazz band kicks off with a funky remix of a latest hit.

Julian asks if I want to dance, and I wince as he stands up. "I'll be over here if you change your mind. Ladies?" He holds his hands out to the two women at our table, and they accept the offer, giggling like schoolgirls.

George, who has remained quiet, almost as if asleep since he sat back down, smiles at me. "Not much of a dancer, Hazel?"

"Not so much in public."

George chuckles, his smile broadening to someone approaching behind me. "Patrick my boy!"

I freeze and my heart rate accelerates with the thought of Patrick near me.

I turn my head and see Patrick towering above the two of us. It seems I've forgotten how to speak. Whether from his dominant presence or the fact every time I'm around him, I can't think straight, I'm not sure.

"Don't get up, George," Patrick says as George starts to stand. He returns to his seat gratefully.

"Another successful gala, eh Patrick?" George bellows. "You getting ready to head back already?"

"Would you mind if I stole Miss Jones away for a dance?" My body flinches in surprise as Patrick throws his signature charming smile at George, who beams.

"Not at all!" George booms, throwing me a smile. "I know you said you're not much of a dancer, but you can't say no to a dance with Patrick."

"Uh–"

"Great, let's go," Patrick interjects, pulling me out of my seat by my elbow and towards the dancefloor. I barely have time to register what's happening before I'm standing amongst a throng of people whose inhibitions are evaporating.

Patrick pulls me flush to his body, one hand resting on my exposed lower back, the other holding my hand. Even though the tempo is upbeat, Patrick leads us into a slow dance, and I do my best to not fall over my own feet, whilst simultaneously trying not to swoon from his touch. My skin crackles.

"So ... you're the founder of the Henchman Charity?" I ask.

Patrick stares out at the crowd over my shoulder. "Yes."

"And a benefactor."

"Yes."

"You never mentioned that."

"You never asked."

I suppress a sigh. It's like pulling teeth. "So, you get rich people to donate to your cause?"

"That's part of it."

It all falls into place. Lisa. George. John from the casino. He uses his connections to hit people up for his charity. The charity *he* started.

"Do you live in Brisbane?" I ask.

"Based in Sydney."

I had more luck getting answers out of this guy when I was completely smashed. Although come to think of it, maybe I imagined he engaged in conversation with me.

"Are you always this chatty when you ask ladies to dance?"

Patrick frowns. "I rarely *chat* when I'm dancing."

"I hate to break it to you, but what we're doing would marginally pass for *swaying*."

"You'll still be the most talked about guest at this party for all the right reasons for *swaying* with me. That's got to look good to the boss, right?" Even though the words seem arrogant, they don't come across that way. As I look around, I notice a few sideways glances at the two of us. Patrick, a real life Adonis and founder of the charity, and me, the newbie in a revealing dress.

Julian, who's moonwalking across the dance floor, catches my gaze and gives me a know-it-all look that says, *I thought you were done with ladies' men?*

"I don't want to be the most talked about guest at this party," I say, eyeing Patrick. "Despite what you might believe, I don't relish attention."

His heated gaze drops to my lips. "Is that why you wore this dress tonight?" The edge to Patrick's tone causes my body to betray me. My fingertips curl and grip his flesh a little tighter.

I'm turned on.

"I don't want to be the most talked about guest at this party," I repeat. "And I don't need gossip spreading about me and the Henchman Gala's number one ladies' man."

Patrick offers a crooked smile. "Ladies' man?"

"Don't play dumb." I *knew* a man as handsome as Patrick would woo every attractive woman in sight.

Patrick nods in understanding. "Ah, yes. The rumour mill is already in full swing. What's the latest? I've slept with every exec in the room? George and I are a couple?" Patrick smiles again, unbothered by the topic.

"I didn't get the details," I reply, suddenly wishing I'd never said anything.

"They're rumours, Hazel," Patrick assures me as he continues to lead us in a swaying rhythm. "People can't help themselves. They never see me with a woman, so they presume I'm having a sordid affair behind-the-scenes or I'm in a secret gay relationship. A scandalous, playboy story is far more exciting than the lonely, old bachelor trope."

Puzzled, I mull over his words. It makes little sense to me why Patrick would be lonely. Whilst we've had our fair share of choice words, I can tell he's not a *bad* man. Plus, he's wealthy, he helps children in need, and he knows how to dance. People in this room *like* him.

"What are you thinking about?" Patrick adjusts his hand on my back, his fingers flexing over my exposed flesh.

"I'm wondering what happened for you to become the lonely, old bachelor type," I reply truthfully. My gaze falls to the scar on his cheek.

Patrick regards me, his expression thoughtful as he steers us around in a slow circle. "Isn't it always the same thing? Pain. Heartache. The fear of getting hurt again. Sometimes, you think you're never going to get over them, that you'll never meet anyone who could make you feel anything again. And then, you do."

We're in that place again: the front porch, the elevator, the Garden Bar. His gaze is fierce as he waits for me to say something. But my throat is thick with emotion and I've forgotten how to speak. *Is he talking about me?*

Our dancing stops, but the two of us still touch, still hold hands, unmoving. I wait for him to say something else, to explain himself. His jaw tics. His breathing becomes deliberate. I can tell, I *know*, he is battling something internal.

A wayward dancer bumps into Patrick and we separate, the connection vanishing. Patrick helps to steady the giggling, apologetic woman who carries on across the floor. When Patrick looks back at me, his expression has clouded, like we weren't just having a suspenseful moment that set my soul on fire.

"What do you mean?" I breathe.

Patrick's expression is blank. "By what?"

"By what you just said."

Patrick gives me a flat smile and I can sense the disappointing response before he opens his mouth. "My point is, you'll get over Luke. It'll hurt for a little while, but the pain will subside, and you'll get over him."

Yep, the electricity has vanished, replaced with an uncomfortable tension.

"Wow, what insightful advice," I gush with sarcasm. "That's not at all patronising. You really have opened my eyes to *brand new* information."

Patrick rolls his eyes. "You're so sarcastic, it's exhausting."

"You're so *moody*, it's exhausting," I snap. "Heaven forbid you cut the cryptic bullshit and act like a grown-up for one minute."

"Says the reckless woman who threatened me in her workplace elevator."

"You better be careful," I warn him mockingly. "People here might think something is going on between the completely perfect benefactor and the careless errand girl in a shiny dress."

"Yeah, like anyone would believe that."

My body stills. He didn't mean it the way it came out, did he? I'm too upset to think anything other than the worst.

Patrick's face fills with regret. "I didn't–"

"Forget it," I say, stepping away from him.

"Hazel, that's not what I meant," he insists.

As I turn to leave, I shoot him a look which I hope comes across as *I'm sick of your shit*. "Do you *ever* say what you mean?"

Not wanting anyone to see the tears threatening to spill, I move past my table and snatch up my clutch. George, immersed in conversation, doesn't notice me storm past.

I'm determined not to cause a scene in front of my colleagues. I'm not sure whether Patrick is following me, but quicken my pace in case, pushing the door open and into the fresh air.

The crisp chill hits my skin harshly as I move away from the well-lit building, around the corner into the semi-darkness, and lean my head against a wall.

It was a brief comment. It was barely hurtful. We always banter with one another, so why did that one affect me so much? Probably because he's right. No one could ever believe something other than lukewarm courtesy could happen between the two of us, even if I thought maybe something *was*. We're too different. He's made that clear to me since the second we crossed paths. So, why seek me out tonight? What was the *point?*

A noise from the darkness to my left startles me and a man dressed in a suit appears, holding a bottle of beer in one hand, a cigarette in the other.

"Evening, love." His English accent is slurred. "Needed some fresh air, too?" His leering gaze travels up my legs to hover on my chest for an uncomfortably long time.

My fight-or-flight receptors kick in, alarm bells ringing. I'm close to the main entrance, but out of sight of other guests.

"I was about to go back inside." I start to head back the way I came, but he moves abruptly, blocking my path. Faster than I'd give a drunk credit for. I swallow the lump in my throat as panic settles in my belly.

"Why don't we finish this beer together before you go? You smoke?"

"No, thank you." I step back. "My husband's waiting for me." Maybe it'll give me the edge I need to get past him, but he doesn't move. His eyes search my face, a sneer on his lips as he assesses me, and bile rises in my throat. He tosses his beer bottle and cigarette onto the ground to free his hands.

"I don't think your husband's waiting for you," he snarls and nods at my hand. "No ring."

Ordinarily, I'd come up with a clever response about my ring getting re-sized, or not going with the outfit, or how I'm allergic, but I'm paralysed by fear, in a dead-end corner, with no way out, behind a man who's twice my size and reeking of alcohol and cigarettes.

He steps towards me and I scream.

18

THE MAN'S hands grab at my chest. I try to push him off, but he's much stronger than me, despite my regular gym workouts. My defiance angers him, and he shoves me hard. I stumble back on my heels and hit the brick wall behind me, hot with panic and fear.

Someone will hear me yell, someone will help. But what if they don't? It's late. People aren't near this area and most sounds are drowned out by the buzz of the centre.

"Stop being a fucking tease," he spits, edging towards me.

"Get away from me!" I hold an arm out and he stumbles. I squeeze my eyes shut as I smell the disgusting scent of cigarettes near my mouth, his rough hand grabbing at my breast again.

A loud grunt followed by a crash of bodies forces my eyes open. The man is on the ground, and Patrick straddles him with ease, bringing his fist down to collide with the man's cheek.

The sound of punches is sickening, but not enough to shake me out of my daze until I hear it several times. Patrick hits the man again and again, tiny specks of blood flying from the place of impact.

"Patrick! Stop!"

Patrick doesn't seem to hear me. Another punch connects with the man beneath him who groans. Patrick repositions himself above him, and holding the man's collar with both hands, lifts his head and slams him back onto the ground.

"Stop! Patrick, no, stop! Don't do that!"

Patrick freezes, his hands still curled around the collar of the man, who's groaning incoherently underneath him. Through ragged breaths, Patrick pats the man down, stopping at one of his pockets and fishing out his wallet. Patrick locates his driver's licence, scans it, before he leans down and speaks into the man's ear. He does a great job of murmuring something I can't hear, because the man's face freezes in fear and he nods silently.

Patrick releases his grip, dropping the man's possessions on to his chest with disgust. The man fumbles to collect his things as he scurries back from Patrick's feet, before standing and tearing off out of sight.

Barely having time to process what's happened, my gaze desperately moves to Patrick's reddened, clenched fists for signs of damage. "Are you hurt?" I whisper.

Patrick closes the distance between us without hesitation. "Forget that. Are *you* hurt?" He places his large hands on both of my cheeks, his face close to mine and his eyes scanning my face frantically.

I swallow, but I don't answer. Patrick's erratic breathing slows as he surveys my body for injury or marks. His hands pull away, but I surprise myself by reaching out and grabbing one of them.

"I'm not going anywhere." In a swift movement, he pulls me into him, wrapping his arms around me; my face pressed against his chest. I sink into him, digging my nails into his skin through the front of his shirt, warm tears falling down my face in quiet sobs.

I don't know how long Patrick holds me for, but his grip

never waivers as he whispers comforting shushing noises into my ear. I try desperately not to relive what just happened, but can't help the wave of nausea and fear crashing over me as I realise I'd been in a very ugly situation.

My breathing slows, and my tears stop. When I peel myself away from Patrick's safe embrace, half my makeup is now on the front of his white shirt.

"I'm sorry." My voice comes out thick and blubbery as I gracefully wipe my nose with the back of my hand.

Patrick's eyes crinkle with humour. "Don't worry about it." He reaches his right hand up to tuck a strand of hair behind my ear. He's surveying me, gauging my reaction. My eyes catch a flash of red and I grab his hand, pulling it in front of both of us.

"You're bleeding." My thumb traces across his raw, scratched knuckles, blood glistening under the luminous streetlight.

"It's nothing." He glances at his hand but doesn't move it from my grasp and I hold tight to him.

Music bursting from somewhere nearby breaks our bubble and I drop his hand and the electricity humming through my body dies.

"Do you want to go back inside?" Patrick asks, still watching me.

I shake my head. "Not really."

"Let's get out of here then." Patrick tenderly places his hand on the small of my back and steers me away from the convention centre, the loud noises of the partying guests fading away as we walk in silence.

I hug myself as I walk, my mind replaying the scene. I felt helpless and powerless at the hands of someone else, and it was terrifying. Every piece of advice I'd learnt through true crime podcasts or survivor stories was erased from my mind right when I needed it.

Patrick stays close the entire way back to the hotel. He doesn't say much, but he doesn't leave my side. When we travel the elevator to my floor, he remains silent, and accompanies me to my room. I'm grateful to get inside. Exhaustion hits me at the thought of relaxing. When I turn to Patrick, he's hovering outside the door.

"You can come in." My throat is dry, and my voice is croaky. Patrick steps inside and closes the door behind him, letting his eyes wander around the enormous suite. He lets out a low whistle as he slides his hands into his pockets.

"Someone hit the jackpot."

"And as the *founder* of the Henchman Charity, you didn't?" I ask, sinking down onto the plush living room couch. I drop my clutch onto the table, accidentally turning my tablet on.

Patrick grins. "I have the penthouse reserved for me on the top floor of this building."

"Of course, you do."

Patrick's gaze drifts to the light beaming from my tablet, his head tilting at the image on the screen staring up at him. My cheeks redden because I know exactly what it's open to; a rough sketch of me in this green gown I drew on the train ride up here. "You really can draw, Jonesy."

"Thanks," I say dismissively, reaching down and turning the tablet off.

Patrick moves to sit across from me, his face somewhat pained. "How are you?"

"Much better now I'm back here," I reply and sigh, closing my eyes. "I would kill to be in my own bed tonight."

"Pack your things. I'll come and get you in ten."

I snap my eyes open. Patrick's face is anything but mocking as he backs out of the room. "No, Patrick I—"

He leaves the room without waiting for me to finish, closing the door with a loud thud behind him. *Is he serious right now?* I haven't time to wonder as I've got a lot of crap to shove into my suitcase before he gets back.

True to his word, a light knock sounds ten minutes later, and I open the door to find Patrick waiting for me. He's changed out of his suit into more casual black pants and a black shirt, like an off-duty Calvin Klein model.

I ignore the way my lips tingle as I take him in. "You changed."

"You didn't." Patrick's dark gaze travels up my body and it takes every ounce of courage not to fold my arms to cover myself. I *want* Patrick to look at me.

"You don't need to drive me back."

"It's no problem," he assures me, grabbing the handle of my suitcase. "I've only had two drinks all night and as much as I enjoy the penthouse, I'd also like to wake up in my own bed tomorrow morning."

I wonder what Patrick's bed looks like. What would he look like sprawled out on it … naked? The thought alone is making saliva pool in my mouth at a ridiculously fast rate.

After Patrick and I check out at reception, the valet brings Patrick's car around. I climb into the Mercedes and savour the scent of the leather, the smell taking me screaming back to the first night I met him. What I can remember of it.

Patrick joins me, his cologne drifting under my nostrils. It's so familiar. As Patrick's car comes to life, he glances at me watching him.

"I promise I won't lock the doors," he insists. A grin breaks my cheeks and Patrick matches it as he turns the car on.

"Did you really only have two drinks tonight?" I ask.

"I wouldn't lie about that, Jonesy." He grins as I roll my eyes at the use of my nickname. "I promise, I'm all good to drive. Unlike yourself, I'm not much of a drinker."

"I have a memory of you taking a tequila shot that says you're lying," I argue.

Patrick smiles and pulls out of the hotel driveway. "I'm not saying I don't enjoy drinking now and then, but when I'm working or need to bring my A-game ... it's best if I stay clear-headed."

He switched to water after taking that shot at the casino. Did he need to 'bring his A-game' with *me*? The thought makes me smile.

"Are you cold?" Patrick's hand reaches for the air-conditioner dial before I answer. The goosebumps on my arms are a dead giveaway. "Here ..." He reaches into the back and retrieves his suit jacket, draping it over my lap. "It's not much, but the car should heat up shortly."

I lift his jacket to my chin, subtly inhaling the scent the clothing is coated in.

"What's the smile for?" he asks, cautiously.

"I'm not used to you being so pleasant."

Patrick shakes his head, a smile at the corner of his mouth. He gets us to the motorway effortlessly and we're coasting away from the city lights in a matter of minutes.

"Did you have fun, you know, before?" Patrick breaks the silence that has fallen over us. I love that he's trying to talk for once.

"I did. Surprisingly."

Patrick chuckles. "Galas not really your thing either?"

"It was the first one I've ever been to, but based on the amount of effort getting ready took, I'd say I'm more a Netflix and Chill kind of girl." I blush at my choice of words, hoping Patrick doesn't know the real meaning of the phrase, or that I'm thinking of what it'd be like to do that with him.

I don't have much time to muse on it though. The long, boring road and straight line of lights and trees, and the scent of Patrick's jacket, hypnotise me and I drift off to sleep.

"Hazel, we're here."

My eyes open to the sound of Patrick's gentle voice as his sleek car pulls into the driveway of my townhouse. I manage a subtle stretch before getting out of the car. Patrick retrieves my bags from the boot and meets me at the front door.

"Kali's not here, so you don't have to worry about waking her," I tell him as we step over the threshold. Kali messaged me earlier to say she was headed to some guy called Eaton's house, and I'm grateful she's not home.

It's déjà vu, both of us arriving at my house in the early hours of the morning, after I've gotten myself into a dangerous situation. I'm not sure whether being sober for this occasion will be a good thing or not.

Patrick, without instruction, walks into my bedroom and places my bags on my bed. As he exits, he catches my gaze. "I'll be in the living room."

I only nod as I close the bedroom door behind him. Am I still asleep? Dreaming? I stare at Patrick's jacket in my hands and hug it closer, inhaling his scent like an actual stage five clinger.

The attempt to reach the clasp at the back of my gown is feeble at best, remembering Ezekiel fastened it for me before I left the hotel. I can't reach it and I don't think I'd be able to undo it if I could.

After a deep breath, I open my bedroom door and walk straight into the living room. Patrick's taken a seat on the couch, his right foot crossed and resting on his left knee, his shoulders relaxed and a book in his hand, as if he's settling in for the night. He looks right at home and I admire him sitting in my living room, amongst my things.

"I need your help. I can't undo the stupid clasp at the back …" I wave my hand in the general direction over my butt and my cheeks flush. His gaze snaps to the area above my ass and I want to die a little.

Patrick visibly swallows and pauses, surveying me. My

stomach flip-flops. The entire night has been a bit of blur; arriving at the charity gala, conversing with the CEO, leaving in tears, arriving home with the man who drives me insane. It's laughable, and the look that man is giving me sends shivers to the base of my spine.

I wave my hands as if it'll erase the fact I spoke. "Don't worry about it. I'm sure I can—"

"It's no problem." Patrick stands from the couch and strides to me, the look in his eyes less intense, but still there as I spin around, exposing my back to him.

"If you can undo the tiny clasp at the top, I can take it from there," I say, attempting a casual shrug. It's the hospital gown situation all over again.

My breath catches in my throat and I tense as Patrick's fingers brush against my lower back. I sense the heat of his body close to mine. He gently unfastens the clasp that sits above my butt crack. I hear it click open, but Patrick's hand doesn't move. His warm fingertips remain on my back and I remain frozen.

I turn so I can look at him. Patrick hasn't moved, his eyes black with intensity.

My underwear is wet.

19

LUKEWARM WATER RUNS down my face as I sit on the floor of the shower, my head against the wall. It's heaven. I brush my teeth for the third time, aware of how much garlic was on the lamb, reliving the night in a rush of fuzzy images.

The sequence of events that led me here ends with me thinking again of Patrick's strong face, olive skin and dark eyes; the way he tackled that man to the ground, the power and fury behind his punches, the way he scooped me into his arms.

The way he undid my dress ...

I wonder if he's still here. I don't know how much time has passed. The hot water faded a few minutes ago.

I stand and shut the taps off, wrapping a soft, fluffy towel around me. When I step out of the shower and see my reflection, I don't even contemplate doing anything about it. Patrick's seen me with smeared makeup, snot, vomit, and saliva all over my face. I don't think there's much point in pretending now. If he *is* still here.

He is.

As I swing my bedroom door open, he looks up at me with

his beautiful face and suddenly, I'm re-thinking the sausage dog pyjamas I threw on. "I thought you might have gone."

"I wanted to be sure you didn't drown in the shower." He lowers the book he's reading, his gaze subtly scanning my body. The simple look re-ignites the spark in my belly. These reactions are to do with the whole hero/saviour complex thing, right?

"I like your pjs."

"These are *Peter Alexander*, thank you very much."

"I said I liked them." Patrick puts the book on the coffee table and stands, walking towards me. "How are you feeling?"

"Better." I give him my best attempt at a hopeful smile, but butterflies are in my stomach again.

"Do you want to call Kali? It might be a good idea for you to have someone here tonight."

I shake my head. "I'll save Kali's update for tomorrow."

A silence hangs between the two of us, before he closes his eyes and runs a hand through his tousled hair. "I really am sorry for what I said to you on the dancefloor. It came out wrong."

"I overreacted." I grab a lock of my wet hair and twirl it. "Thank you for bringing me home and ... for everything."

"I can stay for a little while. My conscience would feel better." Patrick coughs, averting his gaze as he waits for my response.

I grin. "Are you hungry?"

Patrick's lips twist as if he's suppressing a smile, and I take that as my cue. I head into the kitchen, flicking on the lights and pulling ingredients out to make ham, cheese, and tomato toasted sandwiches.

"You're really quite domesticated, aren't you?" Patrick pulls out a stool and sits down, watching.

"Toasties and pasta are my specialities."

"Ah, the MasterChef."

"Anything involving fewer than five steps, five ingredients *and* includes carbs, I'm your girl."

Any remnants of champagne in my system have disappeared and I've realised Patrick and I are going through a transition, from bickering acquaintances to two people who eat toasted sandwiches in my kitchen. Having him around tonight brings a sense of calm and I can't help but wonder if I've softened on him a bit more after he punched a guy in the face for me.

"Thank you again," I say. I brave a look at him. Patrick is resting his chin in his hands, a small smile on his face, his eyes glistening, watching Hazel the MasterChef at work.

"You're welcome."

My gaze drops to his bloodied hands, and I wonder how he's not in more pain. "You need ice on those."

Without waiting for a response, I grab an icepack from the freezer and wrap it in a clean tea towel, handing it out to him. Patrick takes it gratefully, pressing it onto the knuckles of his right hand. "I'm actually allergic to tomatoes," he adds.

"How awful."

Patrick lets out a pleasant rumble, sending a bolt of electricity through my body. "You sound devastated."

"I am!" I move the sliced tomato away from Patrick's sandwich and hesitate. "Are you going to have a seizure if tomato touches any part of your sandwich?"

Patrick chuckles. "No, I'll survive."

"Does that mean you can't eat pizzas with tomato bases?" I query, piecing the sandwich back together. "Or tomato-based pasta or bruschetta? Tomatoes are pure, edible joy."

Patrick pauses, biting his lip. "I don't like warm, soggy tomatoes in sandwiches."

My mouth drops open and I fling a piece of tomato at him, which he deflects with his free hand. "Why would you lie about that?"

"I didn't want to hurt your feelings."

"Well, that's a new development." We fall quiet and my

blood warms as I busy myself with the sandwich press to distract myself from this change in dynamic.

"How's your hand?" I ask, nodding to the icepack.

Patrick stretches and contracts it with a wince. "I'll live."

"Maybe we should take you to the hospital and get an x-ray on it."

"I don't think so."

"So, I have to go to the hospital, but you don't?"

"You knocked your *head*. Plus, I'd be able to tell if it was broken. And I'm older than you."

My lips twist as I suppress another smile.

When the sandwiches are ready, I serve them up, grabbing us both a glass of icy water to accompany the meal. Joining Patrick at the breakfast bench, we chew in comfortable silence.

"So, what do you think?" I ask.

"The best toasted sandwich I've had all day," Patrick replies, his eyes twinkling.

I can't help the genuine smile from spreading across my face, taking a too-large bite to hide it.

Patrick and I end up talking about an array of topics without an ounce of awkwardness. I can't believe he doesn't have any social media accounts and he can't believe I watch Christmas movies all year around.

I tell him my favourite flower is a white tulip, because the colour and shape somehow remind me of the *Aladdin* Disney animation I watched on repeat as a child. Patrick tells me he loves cars and confirms he has European heritage. Italian, specifically. His given name is Patrizio, thanks to his Italian mother, who insisted on giving her sons Italian names if she had to take their father's 'boring' Australian surname. To avoid schoolyard bullying, he started introducing himself as Patrick when he was ten.

Shamelessly, I tell Patrick about my obsession with true

crime, and how it leads to me accusing people of being serial killers or coming up with conspiracies about people.

"You mean like me?" he asks with a knowing smile. Patrick has relaxed, his body turned towards me, one of his feet resting on the footrest of my stool.

"I don't know what you're talking about." My chin falls into my hand as I return his smile with exaggerated innocence.

Despite being the early hours of the morning, and Patrick undoubtedly as exhausted as I am, his face is stunning. He must have beautiful parents who have passed down their wonderful Australian-Italian genes.

"Do you look like your parents?" I ask.

"My mother's Italian genes definitely beat out most of my dad's," he replies. "Thank God I got his height. My mother is barely five foot." I laugh softly, imagining a short, dark-haired, and loud Italian woman fussing over her tall boys.

"What about your brother?"

Patrick lets out a snicker and rolls his eyes. "We look nothing alike, but he's, what did you call it? A ladies' man."

"Maybe it runs in the family," I offer.

Patrick shakes his head. "What about you? Do you look like your parents?"

"People say I resemble my mum. I've got her eyes and mouth." I pretend I don't notice Patrick's eyes dip to my lips. "Mum says I got my stubbornness and ability to eye roll from Dad."

Patrick chuckles. "He must be unbearable if he's like you."

I snatch my phone off the countertop. "I'm going to tell him you said that."

"Don't you dare," Patrick warns, with a grin on his face. He leans in to pry my phone from my hands.

"Dad might be retired, but he used to box when he was younger," I tell him, attempting to hold my phone out of reach. "I reckon he could give you a run for your money."

"I don't doubt it." One of Patrick's large hands encases mine, and my strength dissipates from the spark of electricity. We still. His expression softens. We maintain eye contact for one beat, two beats, three beats longer than necessary.

Patrick's smile fades and his full lips part, his prolonged eye contact igniting pleasure aches in my joints.

"I know you got those supplies for me at the hospital," I whisper, holding his gaze. "Thank you."

Patrick smiles briefly, uncurling his hand from my wrist. "You're welcome." He pauses, his focus on his hands in his lap. "When I saw you at the casino ... I came back to apologise to you for walking off so abruptly. I drove here to apologise, but then, I didn't."

Images of me spotting a black car peeling away at the top of my street flash before my eyes. It *was* him.

"I *knew* I saw your car!" I cry, shoving him playfully in the shoulder.

Patrick's lip twitches. "I don't know what you're talking about," he says, repeating my words from earlier.

Lord save me.

My breath is erratic, my chest is heaving. His mouth is attracting my attention, and I wonder if his breathing is sharper, or if I'm imagining it.

We stare at each other silently for what feels like ten *actual* seconds. I hold my breath and watch as Patrick's gaze drops to my lips, his body edging closer.

"Hazel, I—"

Patrick's pocket rings, startling both of us, and I lean back as he retrieves his phone. He glances at the screen and sighs.

"No one's died, I hope?" I ask quietly.

He gives me a half-smile. "Overseas client. Excuse me, I need to take this." He stands and leaves the room to take his call.

A warmth washes over my skin as reality sinks in. Patrick and I almost kissed and I wanted it to happen. Whatever animosity I might have felt towards him has gone, replaced by desire and need.

I want him.

Patrick walks into the kitchen several minutes later. "I should get going. It's late and I'll bet your bed is calling you."

I smile, trying to mask my disappointment. *Yeah, with you in it.*

"Thank you for dinner. Or breakfast." He grabs his keys with one hand as he pats down his pockets with the other.

"You're welcome," I reply. "Before you go, are you going to tell me what you said to that man, when you whispered in his ear?"

Patrick tilts his head in thought. "It was something I used to say to my brother when I beat him in a fight."

"Which was?"

Patrick offers a half smile. "Let's save that for another day."

20

My legs are stuck in mud. I'm trying to run. The man edges closer to me, his breath putrid, his speech slurred and incoherent. Patrick stands nearby, but he's turned away. My screams go unheard as the vile man edges closer. If Patrick would turn around, if he could hear me, he could help.

Boom. Boom. Boom. The rumble comes from somewhere nearby, an earthquake? The man reaches his hand out towards my chest and I close my eyes.

Boom. Boom. Boom.

I snap my eyes open. It takes me a few seconds to pull myself out of my deep, disturbing sleep, and I exhale deliberately to calm my racing heart. I'm drenched in sweat.

The *boom boom boom* of someone pounding the front door echoes through the house and I whip the sheets off my clammy body, head pounding but grateful to no longer be reliving last night's disturbing events.

I swing the door open, still half asleep, and wonder if I'm still dreaming.

Luke. With his hands shoved into the pockets of his jeans, on my front porch.

"Lazy Hazy. Did you just wake up?"

Yep, I'm still dreaming. Or having a nightmare. My ribs grow tight and my stomach clenches as it hops between unease and hope. *What is he doing here?*

"I'm not even sure if I'm awake yet to be honest," I croak, mindful I must look a state. "Had a work thing last night," I add, as if needing to defend myself.

Luke nods. "That would explain it."

"Would explain what?"

He gives me a lopsided grin. "I tried calling you last night, but you never answered, and then your phone was off. I wanted to check on you."

My teeth grind together. My usual response of stomach flutters and swooning over Luke is replaced by annoyance. Luke's pandering is a turnoff, and he doesn't look as sexy as he once did.

"Thanks for checking in. I'm all good. My phone died during the night and I haven't bothered to charge it back up yet. Sorry you came all the way up here."

"Don't be sorry." His icy blue gaze travels up my exposed legs. He's not even bothering to be subtle. "Do you want to grab a coffee?"

A month ago, I would've jumped at the chance, but now I'm confused. Is it because Patrick and I had something last night or because it's a bad idea? That I don't want to re-open the door to the man who broke my heart?

"It's only coffee, Hazy, I swear." His face is hopeful as he closes the space between us, his grin never wavering. "I know how much you love your coffee."

True. I'm willing to bet I'm grumpy and annoyed because I haven't had my caffeine fix yet. "I need a minute to change."

"I'd be happy if you didn't change." His lips curl, and I curse my pale skin for the redness undoubtedly beaming from my cheeks. Stupid pasty skin.

"Don't say things like that," I warn.

"Like what?" His eyes widen with mock innocence and my stomach flips. We're flirting. So soon.

"You know exactly what I mean, Luke Taylor."

"I love it when you get cross," he says, stepping much closer. "It's adorable seeing you try to keep a straight face when all you want to do is laugh."

"That's not what's happening here," I say, as a smile turns up at the corners of my mouth.

"Are you sure?" he asks, stepping impossibly closer. "Are you sure there isn't a laugh bubbling under the surface, desperate to come out?"

"Luke, don't you dare—"

Before I can react, he reaches out and tickles the space under my ribcage, and I squeal. Within seconds, I'm half-laughing, half-crying as his hands run over my midsection, playfully pinching, and grabbing at my shirt.

"Stop, don't! Stop!" I screech. It's the first time I've had a positive interaction with him in months.

Luke switches his stance, pulling me closer so my back is against his chest. Effortlessly, he continues the torture, spinning me outwards to face the front yard.

My stomach lurches and my breath catches.

Patrick.

Patrick stands in fresh clothes on the pathway, two coffees balanced on a tray in one of his hands. My heart stops as we stare at each other. He is unmoving other than the ticking pulse in his set jaw.

Luke senses my change in mood and releases me, standing by my side while I struggle to form a sentence. Hell, even a word would do, but I can't think of what to say.

Patrick is here.

Unannounced, with not one, but two, take away coffees.

He came back to *my* house, with coffee.

For us.

Fuck.

"You must be Lukey-oh-one." Patrick offers Luke a close-lipped smile.

Luke puffs up his chest at his monstrous truck parked behind my car; big enough to hold two jet skis and a large dog in the tray. "Yeah, I've had that number plate since I was seventeen. It's a shame I couldn't come up with something more creative, hey?" Luke's gaze drops to the coffee tray, his brow furrowing. "Did I interrupt something?"

"Well—"

"Not at all," Patrick cuts in smoothly. "I dropped Hazel home last night after she attended an event of mine and I thought I'd swing by with coffee on my way to the office to say thanks for the hard work her company has been doing for my charity." He holds out the tray, his expression blank.

"Patrick—"

"I'm glad to see you're feeling better," he cuts in, placing the tray into Luke's hand with a slight nod. Luke, the idiot, smiles his thanks.

Patrick's gaze lingers on me.

"I need to go," he says, moving away. "Both of you have a pleasant day."

21

"I MIGHT GET to be in a commercial with Mick Fanning." Luke's blue eyes are wide with excitement as he continues telling me the story of how a friend of a famous surfer saw him out surfing and said he'd be in touch about a television ad. I've hardly been listening.

Ever since Patrick donated two coffees to me and my ex-boyfriend and disappeared out of my street, I've been thinking only about him. I've replayed last night and this morning over and over, with the urge to smack myself in the forehead becoming more and more real. If Patrick had returned two minutes earlier, or Luke had shown up two minutes later, things could've been totally different.

But is that what I want?

Until last night I'd been bickering with Patrick whilst fanta-sising about how sexy he was in the privacy of my own thoughts. I'd been wishing Luke was still in my life, but slowly coming to terms with the fact he's engaged to someone else.

Now, Luke sits next to me on my front steps, trying to win me over with an interesting story and I'm too busy thinking about how any headway Patrick and I made last night got wiped this morning.

And I care.

"Could you imagine if I got to surf on TV next to Fanning?" Luke asks, slurping his free coffee. I stare down at my still-full cup. The thought of drinking anything after watching Patrick leave this morning makes my stomach churn.

"That'd be amazing," I say.

And I *don't* care about this. Luke blabbing on about his hopes, dreams, and adventures non-stop used to be one of my favourite past times. Now? It's just irritating.

"I'll let you know if it happens. You'd get to see me shirtless."

I lean away instinctively. "What does your fiancée think of this amazing possibility?" I want to steer the conversation away from any sort of flirtation, despite what I may have been hinting at twenty minutes ago.

Luke looks surprised. "She thinks it's cool, but she's not into surfing as much you."

I'm not into surfing either. I tried to be because Luke loved it so much. There were so many things I faked interest in or listened to because that's what you do when you love someone. You take an interest in their hobbies; you listen intently, you support them.

"My CEO said he might be able to get me in touch with a design team at a publishing house," I say, offering up to Luke the best thing about last night. "It'd be pretty cool to be an in house book cover designer."

"That's awesome, Hazy." He seems pleased for me and I smile. "Don't get your hopes up though. Didn't you say it's hugely competitive? So many people are designing these days, it's next to impossible to get into the industry unless someone dies, right?"

Disappointment overwhelms me, not because Luke's voiced

out loud what I already know to be true, but because he went straight for cautioning me, rather than encouraging me or giving me a hint that maybe he might believe in me.

"I don't want to see you get hurt." Luke reaches for my hand resting on my knee and places a hand on mine, rubbing his thumb along the back of it. I stare at it for a few seconds. With a sharp jolt, I know it's wrong. The sizzle I used to succumb to under his touch has been replaced with something dirty, and I actually feel bad for the woman waiting at home for him.

I hastily pull my hands back and stand up. "I think you should go."

Luke looks up at me, surprise plastered on his face. "Seriously?"

"Yes. Seriously."

Luke looks blindsided as he stands up next to me. "Did I upset you?"

"Yes, actually, you did," I reply. "When you fucked someone else in our shower. Go home to your fiancée, Luke."

Without waiting for a response, I march back inside my house, slamming the door behind me, the image of Luke's flabbergasted face branded into my brain. When I get into my room, I flop onto my bed, open my laptop and do what I've been thinking of since I learned Patrick's last name: I type *Patrick Healey* into the browser on my laptop.

To my surprise, a couple of photos of Patrick come up in the search. Mostly professional headshots and some of him at events, shaking hands with people. One photo is of him in a tight t-shirt and jeans, laughing while he sits on a giant see-saw with an older woman and two small children at a charity fundraiser in a park. His face is unrecognisable. There's a smile on him I've never seen before.

To my disappointment, the website states what I already know. He grew up on the north shore of Sydney with his parents and younger brother. He works as an accountant, specialising in property development. He does consultancy work for corporations and high profile business people, which explains how he's in the know with people like John the high-roller and George, the CEO of the largest retailer in Australia. It explains his expensive suits and multiple cars and penthouse suites reserved in fancy hotels.

What it doesn't explain is anything about *who* Patrick is. Why he started the charity. What happened in his life between growing up to where he is now? What happened in his past?

I slam my laptop shut after another ten minutes of fruitless browsing. Patrick is a private person who tries to stay out of the limelight. I can't say I blame him. I hate extra unnecessary attention too, but I know it's more than that. There's a darkness to Patrick I can't pinpoint. He's elusive, he's moody, and he knows how to punch people. All things which pique my curiosity.

The memory of his face as he saw Luke and I kicks up another bout of guilt and shame. After last night, things were starting to shift.

Then Luke showed up and I was stupid enough to flirt with him.

I'm an idiot.

22

NEXT MORNING, I receive a frantic call from Lisa as I'm getting into my car.

"My flight's been cancelled. I need you to go to my house and get some cash out of the safe." It's not the first time I've had to run personal banking errands for Lisa. Her father is a mogul in law and the presence of physical cash on her person and in her house has been a constant to me.

"No problem."

"They're in bundles. Grab six and put them in one blank envelope. Patrick is coming by the office to pick it up."

Hearing Patrick's name triggers me and my hand freezes on the car handle. "Sorry, for who?"

"I don't have time for your incompetence today, Jonesy," she scolds. "Patrick. The man you spilt coffee all over, and from what I hear, is your new dance partner. Get the cash and keep it with you until Patrick comes by for it."

It seems someone's updated Lisa on our dancefloor antics, although she doesn't sound pleased about it. "Right, yes, sorry. Are these cash payments for the charity? Do you need me to fill in any paperwork?"

No response. I can tell Lisa's distracted. She's typing an email as she talks to me. I hate it when she does that.

"Lisa?"

"Hmm? No. No paperwork. The money's for Patrick."

I pause. "Patrick's working for you?"

"Yes."

"Doing what?"

"Making my life easier." Her haughty tone keeps me from biting back.

"Sorry, Lisa, I didn't realise."

"Yes, well ... just get the envelopes and keep this to yourself. I'll be back when I get on a bloody flight out of here." She hangs up before I get another word in.

My brain buzzes. Lisa doesn't share every aspect of her life with everyone, but she shares most things with me. The affair she had is the only secret I've known her keep from me and was a secret she kept poorly. This doesn't sit well.

No need to panic. Perhaps he's doing some private consultancy work for her ... and getting paid in bundles of cash kept in Lisa's safe.

Stay out of it, Hazel.

I don't need to know what's going on. I need to get the envelopes and hope if I get the chance to speak with him, he's not too pissed at me about the Luke situation.

At seven o'clock that night, I'm the last to leave my floor. Thanks to a storm cell in Melbourne, Lisa can't get a flight until tomorrow, which meant I got to use my time today catching up and not getting interrupted with stupid errands. Well, mostly.

A large envelope stuffed with cash is tucked into my hand-bag, which I'm holding onto for dear life, as I take the elevator to the ground floor. When Patrick didn't come by, Lisa told me to take the envelope with me. Why couldn't she do this tomorrow when she got back and leave me out of it?

As I swipe out at the main entrance and wave to the night-time security guard, I feel I'm doing something wrong. What if this, whatever Lisa is doing with Patrick, is dangerous or illegal? It would explain why she's been so off lately.

I fish my car keys out as I round the corner and slow my pace.

Patrick leans against my car; legs crossed at the ankles, dark hair mussed up with a couple of those cute locks falling into his eyes and still looking perfectly styled. The muscles of his chest and arms are cocooned in a custom-fit navy suit, leaving little to the imagination of the curves underneath it.

"Hey," I say, walking up to him.

"Hey, yourself." Patrick pushes himself off the car. "What are you doing here?"

"I work here," I reply.

Patrick offers me a small smile. "I meant, what are you doing here so late?"

"Seven o'clock isn't late when Lisa Fox is your boss." I strain under the weight of my handbag. "What are *you* doing here?"

"Lisa asked me to pick something up." Patrick's face remains impassive, and I'm again reminded of his usual reserved demeanour. He may have opened up a little on Saturday night, but that was a brief, if not very temporary, interaction. His lack of information-sharing could be a sign for me to stay away from him. That, and the visual of him pummelling someone's face in two days ago.

"Right. Is that why you're hanging out in a carpark after hours like some serial killer?" I ask.

Patrick meets my gaze, a smile on his pink lips. "What is it with you and serial killers?" There's a lightness to his tone and it helps me relax.

I shrug one shoulder. "We've all got our kinks."

Patrick smirks. "That we do."

The insinuation of his tone leads me to think that he's not annoyed about the Luke situation one bit. With heat flooding my cheeks, I fidget with the hem of my blouse.

"Here." I reach into my bag and grip the envelope, but before I pull it out, Patrick moves dangerously close to me, his hand gently on my wrist. "Not here, Hazel. Walk with me." He slides his hand up my wrist and curls his fingers into my hand, guiding me to walk with him, holding hands.

Now what the hell is going on?

As I fall into step with Patrick, my hand under his sweats. How well do I really know this man? *I don't.* What do my murder podcasts say? *Don't* walk off alone with strange men. Stay vigilant. Don't compromise your safety because you want to be polite.

#staysexydontgetmurdered

To be fair, my brain always thinks about those things. As a female who loves true crime, it comes with the territory. I've been in situations where my instincts have kicked in, alerting me to danger. But right now? My gut isn't screaming with fear or dread. It's adrenaline, sure, but it's also excitement. It's thrilling. The confusion and unpredictability of being around Patrick is intoxicating.

When we reach his Mercedes parked in a dimly lit area of the street, Patrick slows his pace. When I think he's going to unlock his fingers from mine, he spins me, so I'm pressed with my back against his car. He releases my hand and steps back, which I'm grateful for. I'm sure I was about to pass out.

"I'm sorry you've become something of a courier today," he says. "It was against my recommendation, for what it's worth." Patrick's face flashes with regret and I have to wonder if Lisa is just as difficult with him as she is with me.

"Do I even want to know what's going on with the two of

you?" I ask. Patrick surprises me by exhaling a loud, deliberate breath. He doesn't look angry. "Patrick," I whisper.

"It's business," he replies. "Working with one of the most powerful women in Australia prevents me from saying much more."

Of course. I had to sign a non-disclosure agreement when I started working for Lisa five years ago. I'm careful not to share anything with anyone, although if they wanted to grill Kali on what she knew, they'd have good cause to sue me.

"I'm going to lean really close to you now," Patrick says as his dark eyes drop to mine, as if waiting for permission.

"I'm sorry, you're what?"

Patrick closes the distance between us, so our bodies are touching. He leans down and breathes in my ear, "I'm reaching into your bag and taking out the envelope. Hold still."

Not a problem there. I'm rooted to the spot as Patrick's breath tickles my ear and his left hand rests gently on my hip, while the right one reaches into my bag. He gets what he needs effortlessly and slides it inside his jacket, keeping our bodies close the entire time.

"Is this in case someone is watching us?" I whisper.

"You're too smart for your own good, Jonesy." Patrick pulls back, allowing me to breathe. The sudden realisation I'm a pawn in their game angers me.

"Do you enjoy playing games with me?" I straighten up, so I'm no longer touching his car. Patrick looks stunned. "I don't know what's going on, but if you're so worried about not being seen, why couldn't we have gotten in your car? Or met somewhere else? You know where I live. You couldn't wait until I drove the twenty minutes home?" My chest is heaving as the words leave my body, my fingers curling into fists by my sides. Patrick stands, gauging me, eyes wide with surprise and confusion. "Look, I know Lisa can be difficult to work with, but do me a favour. Next time, flat out refuse to bring me into whatever the fuck it is you guys are doing."

I take a step to march away before Patrick blocks my path. "Wait."

Peering up at him anxiously, my eyes drift from his lips to his chocolate eyes, the flecks of gold around his pupils glinting in the darkness.

Patrick's mouth opens and closes as if he's struggling to find words.

My breathing is louder, more obvious.

My fingertips tingle, my stomach flips.

Patrick's face inches closer, and before I have time to process what is happening, he's pressing his lips against my own. It's light and gentle at first and I wonder if I'm imagining it, but I'm not. Patrick's mouth is on mine. I can taste heaven mixed with a trace of peppermint.

Total paralysis takes over.

Our eyes lock, and our lips are painfully still as both of us wait out to see if we're going through with this. We stand, breathing into each other's mouths, shaking with anticipation.

And then Patrick's lips part, moving tenderly against my own. My eyes close on instinct and my stiff body wilts beneath him. My handbag drops forgotten to the ground. Patrick places a hand on each of my hips and steers me until my back presses against the car door.

Heat pools in my stomach as we steadily become a force of tongues sliding against tongues, and my hands grab two fistfuls of shirt and pull him closer. A tiny moan escapes my lips as he pushes his large body against mine, his growing erection pressed against my stomach.

His hands run across my hips and back. When he curls a hand around my neck, my stomach bottoms out. Everywhere his hands touch causes fireworks to explode under my skin.

Our lips separate. Patrick's pupils are so big, a darkness to them that is hypnotising.

"I can't stay away from you," he growls, and before I can say anything, he's kissing me again. Hungry kisses that send volts of pleasure to my lady parts; kisses that make me forget where I am, and what I'm doing. I want to do this forever.

A passing car beeping its horn, followed by cheering from its occupants, breaks us apart and I fight to suppress my embarrassed smile. In the semi-darkness, Patrick's face is flushed.

"Time for us to go," he whispers, licking his lips, clearing his throat, and fussing with his shirt collar. Part of me wants to grab him and steal a few more seconds of this from him, but I don't.

"Let me." I reach up and straighten his tie before brazenly running my hands down his chest to smooth out the creases I caused.

Patrick's eyes are on me as I watch the roll of Adam's apple. "Thank you."

As I retrieve my handbag, I pretend not to notice as he subtly adjusts his groin area. Grinning to myself in the darkness, we head in silence along the street to my car.

When I'm safely in the driver's seat, I switch the engine on and roll the window down. "Thanks for walking me to my car," I say through still tingling lips.

Patrick gives me a heart-stopping stare that is somewhere between desire and hope, but it's so fleeting, I wonder if I really saw it. "You're welcome," he says with a half-smile.

He steps back and I reverse out of my park, eyeing him in my rear mirror until he's out of sight.

When I climb into bed, still high from my intense make out session with Patrick, I have two new emails. One from Lisa, who is, to my great surprise, thanking me for 'sorting things out with

Patrick.' It also appears George Wilson sang my praises, which led Lisa to sign off the email, with the words *'you can leave early on Friday,'* and she'll consider letting me attend future events if I *'keep it up'*. As far as Lisa goes, that's a compliment.

The second is from George's assistant:

Dear Hazel,

George wanted me to let you know he loved meeting you on Saturday and hopes you enjoyed yourself at the gala. Below are the details of Jess McNamara, who works at Bookish Publishing House in Melbourne. George has let her know you'll be in touch.

Kind regards,
Judith

My head spins.

Lisa *thanked* me.

George passed me the details of his publishing friend.

And I made out with Patrick in the darkness, leaning against his Mercedes, with his hard dick pressed against my body.

I don't know which one I'm most excited about.

23

"HAZY! DO YOU WANT A REFILL?" Reuben hollers across the café. Given it's only me and one other person left in the place, his booming voice echoes off the walls.

It's Friday evening and I'm buried in my favourite nook of the café, a wooden bench seat piled with cushions, by the window watching passers-by. The days are getting longer as summer approaches, and I'm grateful I no longer have to carry a sweater around with me everywhere I go.

I glance at my empty mug, my second since I got here two hours ago, and shake my head at Reuben. "No thanks, Ruby." Decaf or not, I've had enough coffee for today. Reuben nods as he starts to clean the coffee machine. He keeps the café open a little longer on Thursday and Friday nights in the warmer months, and right now I'm *very* grateful for that.

I've been hanging out in Reuben's café every evening since Monday night's press-up-against-the-car situation, because I keep a) thinking about what sort of work Patrick is doing for Lisa that he's keeping so tight-lipped about and b) thinking about kissing Patrick like a smitten teenager. Even trying to exhaust myself with exercise hasn't been helping like it usually would. The minute I stop my workouts, my mind races. My anxiety eases when I've got a golden retriever at my feet and my good friend bringing me free snacks, making the café the most successful option so far.

It's also forced me to sit down and tap into my creative side. When I contacted Jessica, George's friend at Bookish Publishing House, on Tuesday, something shifted. I have a brand-new shiny opportunity in my hands and it's up to me not to mess it up. I've got to keep my head in a good place and not let it get distracted by men and my boss's secrets and my ex and all the things that make it so easy to mess things up. I've got to focus on the things I *can* control, and that's sending Jessica a portfolio worthy of consideration by a renowned publishing house.

Easier said than done, however. As I stare at the blank screen in front of me, I wonder how I used to draw so easily. Cartoons, graphic-novel style comics, lifelike portraits. I'm coming up short on everything I try, and self-doubt trickles in every time I wipe the screen clean.

"You look like you're about to throw your tablet across the room." Reuben straddles a chair, folding his arms across its back to eyeball me. "Not going so well?"

"It's a slow process," I groan.

"Have you tried drawing with a bit of, you know, oomph?" Reuben asks.

"What do you mean?"

Reuben stands up. "I'll be right back."

He returns minutes later with a wine glass filled with red liquid. "This might help you relax. Didn't Picasso drink while he painted?"

"He was addicted to absinthe and it pretty much led to his death." I accept the glass from him. "But if it gets my creative juices flowing, it'll be worth it."

"That's the spirit."

Reuben leaves me to continue his closing process while I

attempt to come up with something that I don't think is garbage. Whether it's the red wine, my light buzz, my surroundings, or Rosie by my feet, I get some ideas out of my head and onto virtual paper. It's invigorating.

For the first time in months, the familiar warmth when an idea comes to life charges through my veins; shapes and faces becoming discernible as I scribble furiously on my digital art pad. Dark, mysterious figures with long coats and sexy eyes start coming to life. I use the drawing I did of myself in the green gown and transform it into something out of a gothic-looking fairy tale. The more I think about it, the more excited I get. Jess from Bookish Publishing might get some pieces of art she'll love.

After I collect a vegetarian pizza for Kali and me, Reuben drops me home. In my room, sorting through the latest pieces of clothing I've brought home from work, I find Kali. Her face is flawless with natural makeup and her hair is twisted in a fancy braid.

"Why does it look like you're not joining me for pizza night?" I open the box and help myself to a slice as Kali holds a lilac jumpsuit up to her body. "Ooh, cute."

"Hamish is taking me out," she says breathlessly, stripping her t-shirt off and pulling on the jumpsuit. "He's going to be here any second and I haven't decided what to wear."

I pause mid-chew. *"Who in the hell is Hamish?* See what I did there?"

"A new client in my Pilates class today." Kali reaches up to tie the threads behind her neck.

"Did you not hear my awesome true crime pun?" I ask.

"Yes, you're brilliant," she says. "Here's an idea. Maybe you could spend your Friday night hanging out with *real* people and not the hosts of some of your favourite podcasts?"

"That sounds terrible."

I move to the living room, setting up a comfy spot on the couch. *More pizza for me.* I decide to pass on more wine and instead opt for water. I've got to put some more work into my portfolio tomorrow, and I can't be dusty for it.

Hamish arrives minutes later and before Kali rushes out the door, she leans over the back of the couch and plants a kiss on my cheek. "Don't answer the door. Especially if creepy drunk men or Luke Taylor rock up. I give you permission to open the door if the assassin shows up with a briefcase full of cash though."

I smile as she traipses out the door. After I updated her on my terrifying ordeal last weekend and the events of the following days, she's kept an extra vigilant eye on me, which includes ordering me to lock myself inside when she's not here. She also wanted me to report the guy who harassed me, but after I assured her 'Patrick took care of it,' she dropped it.

Ten minutes after Kali leaves, the universe decides to fuck with me. A knock at the door causes the hair on my arms to stand on end. I click pause on the true crime documentary I started, every worst-case scenario flying through my head. Could the guy from last weekend know where I live? Could he have followed us home?

Three knocks sound again. I jump.

For God's sake, woman, get a grip.

Slowly, I edge towards the door to see who's there by peering through the side window.

"It's Patrick." Reflexively, I step back, my hands flying to my mouth in surprise. Kali's attempt at a joke before she left runs through my mind. Does he have a briefcase in his hands?

Cautiously, I open the door. Patrick stands on the front porch. There's no briefcase in sight, but he looks like an

Adonis. He's swapped out his usual business attire for his dark casual wear again. His long-sleeved black shirt sticks to the curves of his arms and chest, his dark fitted pants accentuate his muscular legs. As usual, several strands of his hair dangle in his eyes. The sight of him has me self-conscious, answering the door in an oversized grey shirt and booty shorts.

"Hi." I hear the pleasure in my tiny voice.

"Sorry to show up unannounced," he replies. "I was having dinner with friends around the corner and remembered I left my jacket here last weekend."

"Oh, right."

"Thought I'd kill two stones with one bird and grab it now, if I could." He puts his hands in his pockets and bounces lightly on the balls of his feet.

A grin spreads when Patrick realises what he's said. "I mean …"

"Have you been drinking?" I ask, surprised, and smile as Patrick tries to suppress one of his own. It's obvious now I take more time to survey him. The way Patrick's holding himself; it's slouched and careless and as he moves his arm to steady himself, I smell the faint whiff of alcohol.

"Yeah," he says, somewhat sheepishly. "My friend Maria is Spanish, and she makes this killer sangria. She also doesn't take no for an answer." The mention of him eating and drinking with a woman whom I can only assume is stunningly exotic sets off an unexpected pang of jealousy in my chest. "She's married," Patrick adds. "With two children."

There's a long pause as I silently thank Maria for feeding Patrick sangria and getting him to be more open this evening. "Sounds lovely. I'll get your jacket. You can come in if you like." I don't wait to see if he takes up the offer, hurrying to my room to collect his jacket hanging behind my door. I take the opportunity to calm my nerves before heading back. Patrick's stepped inside the door, his hands back in his pockets as he waits for me.

"Here you go." I pass the jacket to him as he peers into the living room.

"Pizza night?"

I scoff at the almost empty pizza box on the coffee table. "Yeah, for one. Kali ditched me again."

"Ah." Patrick shuffles from one foot to the other. It's the most restless I've ever seen him. "Look, I'm sorry about the other night. I hope I didn't upset you or make you uncomfortable."

If coming alive with sexual energy counts as uncomfortable, I forgive you.

I give him what I hope is a reassuring smile and say what a grown-up should say in this situation. "Not at all. No need to apologise."

Patrick nods to himself and looks down at the jacket on his arm. "Thanks again for getting this for me."

"No problem." I cross my arms to hug myself, squeezing my hands together under my arms to stop them from sweating. Patrick turns to leave but whips back.

"Did you invite Luke over on Sunday?"

"Uh … no." I stumble over my words, surprised by the question. Maybe he isn't as unbothered by that situation as I thought. "He just showed up. Like you have tonight. Not that this is anything like that, because I actually want you here. I mean, I don't *want* you here. Wait, that sounded wrong … I mean … him showing up last weekend was unexpected and unwanted."

Patrick's brown eyes are liquid and brilliant as they search my own with earnest. "Is me showing up, unexpected and unwanted?"

"No." The word flies from my mouth in desperation.

Patrick's breath hitches in his throat and it takes every ounce of willpower to hold his gaze.

Part of me wants to ask Patrick every question that's plaguing my mind. I want him to say whatever he's holding back. I want to know the darker, imperfect side of him and hear the truth come out of his mouth. I want to know why he's so reserved. I want to know why he's so hesitant to open up to me and what happened with his ex-girlfriend. I want to know what he's doing for Lisa and how he knows how to punch massive dudes into submission.

Sensible Hazel reminds Foolish Hazel of the old saying 'curiosity killed the cat'. Even if he answered every one of my questions, I don't know if I'm ready to let another man into my life.

"Do you want me to leave?" Patrick's gentle voice breaks my train of thought. His expression is soft and vulnerable.

I shake my head and walk to the front door, closing it. Patrick looks at me with what looks like relief, or hope, and places his jacket on the hall stand.

"I'll get you some water," I offer, heading towards the kitchen. He follows me and I do my best to steady my anxiety as I fix us both a glass. He downs his in several gulps, placing his glass down once he's finished, resting his palms on the bench behind him. I sip my water, not knowing what to say or what to think about the way he's watching me.

He clears his throat. "I have a confession to make."

My stomach flips again as I lower my glass and place it on the countertop.

"I didn't come here to get my jacket."

"No?"

"No." Patrick pushes himself away from the bench, edging forwards until he is standing inches from me. In the silence of the room, I'm sure he can hear the rapid beating of my heart. "I can't stop thinking about you."

Despite the growl in which they were delivered, the words send a bolt of pleasure through me. "Is that such a bad thing?"

Patrick offers me a half smile, shaking his head like he's remembered a private joke, but he doesn't answer my question. "There's a reason I don't consume excessive alcohol near you."

I tilt my head up to meet his gaze. "Why's that?"

He reaches his large left hand to my chin, and I gasp as his fingertips touch my skin, igniting a blazing fire down my body. "It makes keeping my hands to myself even more difficult."

The two of us stand breathing heavily as his words echo around us in the dimly lit room, his fingers drifting up my jawline. "Is this okay?" he asks, his voice hoarse.

I nod. His left hand slides around the side of my neck, his fingers splaying into my hair. His right hand bunches the material of my shirt up, and he hooks a couple of fingers into the waistline of my shorts, pulling my body flush to his. His hardness presses against me and an involuntary whimper escapes my mouth.

Patrick's brown eyes darken at the sound and before I back out or my brain tells me why this shouldn't happen, Patrick's lips crash into mine.

24

MY BODY IS ON FIRE.

My hands reach up and curl around the back of Patrick's head, my mouth finding his to fiercely return his kiss. He tastes like sangria and mint and it's the best flavour to ever dance across my lips. Patrick may be buzzed, but he's anything but sloppy as he swirls his tongue with mine, his experienced hands running over my back and waist greedily, before gripping my hips to steer me backwards. My butt hits the kitchen bench, and he wraps his hands behind the backs of my legs, hoisting me onto the countertop.

Patrick stands between my legs and our mouths separate, his lips wet and shiny, his warm breath caressing my face. There's an unexpected vulnerability in his eyes as he searches mine. Maybe for permission that this happening. Maybe to check that this is what I really want. Seeing the cautious and concerned side of this man only reinforces that this is *definitely* what I do want. I smile at him and lean forward, sucking on his bottom lip. A groan rumbles from his throat that sends a rush of adrenaline to every corner of my body, and we're kissing again.

The kisses are messy and perfect. Our teeth clash a little. We tease each other by using too much tongue and then pulling back to hover out of reach. He growls with desperation; I whimper with need. It's the best make out session I've ever had.

Patrick's fingers skim the hem of my t-shirt once again and my hands fumble at his waistline, desperate to break the physical barriers between us. Burning lust charges through me. I want to taste every inch of him. I want this man to devour me.

I wonder if he can sense my desperation, because he pulls my hips towards him so I can feel how hard he is. Yep. He's as desperate as I am.

"Bedroom?" he asks, with his mouth still on mine. The hot liquid pooling between my thighs intensifies and I slide off the bench wordlessly.

I'm forced to tear my mouth from Patrick's after nearly falling over a pair of Kali's shoes in the hallway. *How do they make it look so hot in the movies?* I grab Patrick's hand and lead him into my bedroom, thanking my neurotic self for always having things neat and tidy.

Once we're inside, Patrick kicks the door shut behind him and flicks on the light. The rapturous lust in his eyes turns me on until I'm certain my underwear is close to disintegration from how wet they are. After a beat, he whips his shirt over his head to reveal the body I had suspected was underneath.

Patrick's tan skin is painted in curves and ripples. He's not like the bulky, over-the-top types I'm used to. Patrick is sculpted and defined like an athlete. The 'V' shape of his abdomen is an actual pathway to his manhood, and I almost giggle aloud.

Patrick takes two quick strides to close the distance between us and helps me remove my top. Our hands find each other again, this time exploring each other's bodies without the barrier of clothing. His skin is smooth and firm under my hands, and I smile as I run my fingertips across his smattering of chest hair, remembering the joke I made to him in the hospital all those weeks ago.

One of Patrick's large hands cups one of my breasts. When he pinches a nipple, I gasp at the mix of pain and pleasure and he grins wickedly into my mouth. It's been too long since anyone took their time with me like this, squeezing, roaming, teasing, and massaging the touch points of my body in a way that's enjoyable for both of us.

Charged with confidence and desire, I slide my hand down over his abs and run it across the bulge in his pants. Patrick tilts his head back and groans before regarding me again.

"Wait," he pants, grabbing my wrist to still my hand. "I don't want to rush this."

With my hand paused on the strain in his pants, I look up at him. "Well, this is awkward."

Patrick's face breaks into a grin and I smile, my hand unmoving as I reach up and softly kiss his neck.

"You have no idea how much I've thought about this." I hear Patrick swallow and I lean back to see a new openness to his expression. Exposed, raw, completely defenceless.

"You've thought about this?"

Patrick smirks. "Yes, Hazel. I've thought about this. I've thought about this a lot."

My giddy smile almost breaks my cheeks. The softer side of Patrick is even more devastatingly sexy than the harder, elusive side. "What have you thought about?"

Patrick cocks his head to the side. "Lasting longer than two minutes."

A snort escapes my nose and I lean my forehead against his chest as he chuckles. Who would've thought the tension, the sniping remarks and the guessing games would lead to us standing half naked and laughing about Patrick's longevity? This is so easy.

Patrick tilts my chin up with his hand and looks at me with longing. "You are so beautiful."

My stomach bottoms out again. Even though I want to know

everything going on inside his head and what's been holding him back, I fight the urge to ask. Instead, I lick my lips and kiss him softly on the lips. "You're not half bad either," I say. "For a serial killer."

Patrick's eyes crinkle in the corners. "Again, with the serial killers. Am I about to find out you're one of those women who writes to convicted murderers?"

"Would that turn you off?" I tease.

Patrick pauses, his gaze roaming my face. "I don't think there's anything you could do that would turn me off." The realisation that Patrick has wanted me, thought about me, *fantasised* about me, causes the flesh in my panties to throb, and the humour of this situation is replaced by intense longing.

Both of Patrick's hands skate up my arms before stopping above my elbows, his fingers curling to grip my flesh.

"Get on the bed," he orders.

Obediently, I back away from him, my stomach somersaulting as my legs hit the bed, and I sit down. His hooded eyes never leave mine as he unbuttons his pants and drops them in a pool at his feet, and with them his underwear. A gasp slips from my lips as I take him in. I do my best not to stare below his waistline, but it's not easy. *Jesus.*

Patrick climbs onto the bed, so his body is hovering above mine, and starts kissing my neck. My eyes close to soak up every minute he's touching me. He covers me with his mouth, working his lips from my collarbone, down to my pebbled breasts. I grab his hair roughly as his mouth travels further and further south.

Patrick looks up as his mouth skims my waistband. Watching me, he hooks his fingers into my shorts and underwear and tugs them down. All the way down, exposing *all* of me to him. When he drops my clothes on the floor, he assesses me.

"Fuck me, Hazel. Look at you," he breathes.

Kill me now.

Patrick holds my gaze as he hovers above me again, this time sliding a hand to my dripping core. Painstakingly slowly, he drags a finger up and down my centre. Then two fingers. Up and down, up and down, never once breaking eye contact. A ragged whine escapes my throat, and his pupils dilate.

"Holy shit, you're wet."

"Yeah, I don't know if *I* can even last two minutes," I pant.

He chortles. "Fine by me." He stills his hand and carefully dips his fingers inside. It's just a tease, a tiny taster of what's to come, and I almost buck off the mattress.

Still laughing to himself, Patrick removes his hand and scoots backwards to settle down between my legs. He knows what he's doing; the way he patiently kisses up my inner thighs. He's an expert in teasing and pleasuring. When his mouth skims my bikini line and I feel the roughness of his facial hair on my flesh, my body quivers.

He squeezes my hips to hold me still, which earns him a grumble of frustration from me. From his mouth warm puffs of air skate across my entrance and I can only imagine the look of satisfaction on his face as he tortures me.

Animal-like groans purr from my throat when he finally runs his tongue up my slit and repeats the motion, up and down in experienced strokes, his fingers digging into the flesh around my thighs. I can hear how slick I am, but I'm enjoying this too much to care. *Too much.* I can't think straight. His tongue is *swirling,* fast, then slow, and fast again, every movement building towards my fiery climax.

As my gasping breaths grow into loud cries of anticipation, my vision nears the point of blindness. "Patrick I'm going to—"

I don't finish the sentence and Patrick doesn't stop as I tear over the edge, completely exposed and unabashed, as my hips jerk into his face. It's pure ecstasy.

As my heart rate slows and my grip in Patrick's hair loosens, my jelly legs straighten out onto the bed. Patrick sits back to admire me, and a laugh escapes me as I bask in my post-orgasm bliss.

"Told you I couldn't last two minutes."

Patrick doesn't chuckle at my joke this time and when my gaze falls to his hard length, tilted upwards and bursting with need, I can see why.

Patrick stands and moves away, returning seconds later, the sound of a foil package in his hands. I watch intently as he rolls a condom down his length and my body tenses at the thought of what's about to come. No pun intended. God, I can't even stop thinking for long enough to enjoy this. *Focus, Hazel!*

Patrick settles his body over mine, his chest heaving with anticipation. "That was the sexiest thing I've ever seen," he murmurs, running the tip of himself over my entrance. "I want to make you do that again." Patrick doesn't wait for my response as he pushes himself into me and I nearly choke.

Oh, Jesus save me.

Patrick trails gentle kisses up and down my jaw. He takes his time with me, slowly moving in and out as my body adjusts to his size. His ragged breaths heave into my neck, his hands guiding me, rocking us in sync. As my pleasure builds again, my breaths become sporadic and Patrick gazes down at me in awe, his lips parted.

I'd forgotten how good sex feels. How good *good* sex feels. I'd forgotten what it's like to be with a man who's focused and self-less. What it's like to have a strong man gaze at you with aston-ishment and wonder in his eyes.

The exhilaration of Patrick on top of me and inside me is overwhelming. My hands want to savour every inch of his body. I'm memorising the friction of mine and Patrick's skin rubbing together. I'm absorbing every messy kiss and every desperate breath. My hands run up and down his taut back and I watch as his own pleasure becomes clear on his face. His dark eyes are smouldering with lust, his mouth hanging open as his breath becomes raspy.

Patrick's thrusts become more urgent and the tension in my core builds at a rapid pace. Beads of sweat drip down his forehead, dampened curls falling into his eyes, but not once does he relent. He listens to every moan, responds to every signal. His eyes search mine with hunger, and as my pleasure closes in on its apex, I dig my fingernails into his back.

"Patrick ... Patrick." I struggle to get his name out as the heat grows, threatening to spill over and break me into a thousand pieces.

Patrick's eyes blacken as he locks his eyes with mine. "Come with me."

My orgasm tears through my body in violent tremors, my screams relentless as Patrick hits my spot over and over and over again. Seconds later, Patrick's body locks up above me, a strained strangle gasping from his throat as he meets his release, his forehead pressing against mine.

The heated haze cocooning my mind and body as I float back to Earth is euphoric. I don't know how I've lived this long without experiencing this. With him.

When I look into Patrick's eyes piercing my own, I know he's thinking the same.

25

I MUST BE DREAMING.

I've woken up content. No anxiety about work, no torrents of dread about Luke, no hangover and no wondering what Patrick is up to.

He's still in my bed and didn't leave in the middle of the night. He looks like a work of art, his long-lashed eyes closed and his bare chest rising and falling as he breathes softly. He seems so untroubled and peaceful, and I smile. He was exhausted. I don't think we passed out until the early hours of the morning. At one point, he finally asked for my phone number and added it to his phone, saying, 'I need this for the next time I want the sexiest woman on the planet to do *that* again.' My face had exploded with embarrassment.

My fingertips trace his chest and I allow myself a few more minutes of pure uninterrupted bliss before he and I have to face that we've crossed a line and can never go back. With Patrick being a constant confusion to me, I'm at a loss as to how he'll feel when he wakes up.

"I know you're staring at me," he mumbles, his eyes closed, his body unmoving. "Do I pass the test?"

"What test?"

"The *he looks acceptable with no clothes on during daylight hours* test." He opens one eye to watch me, a close-lipped grin forming on his mouth.

"Yes, you passed," I tell him. "What about me?" I hold my breath and my stomach sinks as he opens both eyes, straightens up and drags his gaze the entire length of my body. The silence is deafening.

His eyes lock on mine and he lifts himself so his body hovers over me. "I knew you'd pass that test the minute I laid eyes on you."

I blush as a mixture of a snort and giggle escapes me.

"You don't believe me?" he asks with a grin, leaning down and sucking at the skin under my ear. My body comes to life. How is it possible for someone to cause such an immediate and physical reaction?

"You're full of corny one-liners." I gasp as he nips my neck with his teeth.

"True. Are they working?"

I lift my hips and am greeted with his erection pressing against me, my wet skin causing him to growl. "What do you think?"

Patrick pulls back to give me a wicked smile before taking my mouth with his, our bodies rubbing together, our kisses becoming more ferocious with each grind.

Patrick's mobile phone blaring into the room slows our pace. "I'm really good at timing these calls, aren't I?" he groans, reaching to the bedside table and flicking the ring to silent.

"No rest for the wicked, hey?"

"Something like that." He leans down and picks up right where we left off, sliding his tongue into my mouth, and causing a rush of blood to shoot to my clit.

After fishing for a condom, we fall into something of an encore of last night, my body sizzling with pleasure, my mouth releasing groans which turn into shameless screams. Guttural sounds come from Patrick's throat as the tempo picks up and within minutes, we're both climaxing, and our sweaty bodies are exhausted once again.

Patrick rolls off me, subtly removing the condom before pulling me in for a hug, a gesture I'm so thankful he's still doing now he's woken, and the sangria has worn off.

"Do you have to work today?" I ask.

"I work every day, when I'm away from home," Patrick replies, stroking my arm. Those words jar me; reminding me that Patrick doesn't live in the same state as me.

"Where do you stay when you're here?" I ask.

Patrick chuckles. "I'm staying at an Airbnb in Main Beach. It has an actual man cave, an ugly purple brick wall out the front and a pin code to the front gate that spells 'ball sack'. It's not the Hilton, but it's a stone's-throw from the beach and away from the raucous buzz of this end of the Coast."

"When do you go back to Sydney?" I ask. Patrick's hand slows on my arm and his gaze travels to mine. My stomach clenches with unease, worried that I've ruined this post-sex bliss already by asking such a loaded question.

"When I finish up my work here," he murmurs.

Disappointment floods through me. "Right."

Patrick's hand moves to under my chin, so he can tilt my head to meet his eyes. "What are you thinking?"

I steady myself. I don't know where to start with my questions for him. I want him to fess up to every big and little secret. I want to ask him about his past and what he sees in his future.

"You're an enigma, Mr Healey. I have a lot of questions." I whisper the words; afraid I might upset the harmonious balance we have in this bed.

Patrick's thumb rubs back and forth on my chin, his eyes staring into my soul. "Ask me one."

I smirk. "One? I only get one?"

Patrick grins. "One question."

My fingers dance across his chest hair. His skin is warm under my hands, and I note the faint beat of his heart. I lift my hand to the scar on his left cheek and gently run a fingertip over it, Patrick's gaze fixated on me as he waits. "Why did you start the charity?"

Patrick's face breaks with relieved surprise, a glad smile settling on his face. I swallow down the guilt, mildly annoyed with myself for not asking a tougher question but buzzing from the joy on Patrick's face.

"I had a great upbringing," he explains. "But my brother, Anthony, had a rough go of things. He was in and out of foster care when he was young. My parents fostered him when he was around eight years old and eventually, he became a permanent part of the family."

"That's wonderful."

Patricks nods. "Anthony and I were best friends. I was two years older, so I felt a responsibility to show him how things worked in our neighbourhood, but he struggled. The foster system wasn't kind to him, and it took him a long time to adjust." I press myself into Patrick more.

"When I got myself into a good position in my career, I wanted to make things easier for kids that are in a similar position. I wanted to make their really shitty situations as good as possible." I try to imagine a younger Patrick, proudly doting on his younger, adopted brother; showing him how he could find some normality. It doesn't really surprise me though. It seems he's been self-assured and driven his entire life.

I wonder if the issues his brother faced left lasting scars on Patrick's psyche and he's fighting to make up for what happened to Anthony with the charity. It must weigh heavily on his mind.

"I'm sorry your brother went through that."

"Me too. I'm sorry any child has to go through that." He rests his mouth on the top of my head and inhales, kissing me firmly on the outward breath. It gives me butterflies. He trusts me enough to divulge something so personal about himself when, a week ago, we couldn't see eye to eye. A wave of anxiety washes over me as a realisation scares the absolute shit out of me.

I like him.

Oh, *shit*. I think I really like him. *Shit*.

"Alright, your turn." Patrick slides up to rest against the headboard, manoeuvring me to sit between his legs, my back leaning against his chest. "What's your story?"

"My story?"

"Come on, Jonesy. Don't make me force it out of you," he says darkly. His breath tickles the space behind my ear, and I struggle to find focus for a few seconds.

"My story ... only child—"

"No surprises there." I dig my nails into Patrick's rock-hard thigh, and he hisses. "As I was saying ... only child, lovely parents ..." I drift as I think back to my childhood, one that was entirely wonderful. "My parents were great. They *are* great. They've both retired and travel on their yacht for most of the year. They gave me every opportunity and endless amounts of support."

"But?"

A long exhale escapes my nostrils. "Sometimes I feel I let them down. They supported me and encouraged me to do whatever I wanted to do and what have I done? I quit dancing as a kid. I quit swimming. I went to university and instead of following my dreams, I'm *still* in a job I don't like, working for a woman I don't like. I was in a three-year relationship with someone who cheated on me. I put things on hold for him and I don't know why. It should've been a partnership, but it never was. Everything I wanted to do after school seemed to stall. I've only gotten back into art again, which I'm pretty sure was brought on by my concussion. Before that, it was as if I just gave up on everything. I'm the queen of excuses."

The words surprise me, and I sit in silence, processing. It's a release. So much of what I wanted to do hasn't happened because I sabotaged myself, or came up with an excuse, or put someone else before me. I'm not even sure when I started acting this way, but somewhere in my young adult life, I lost sight of what I wanted, and who I was.

Patrick squeezes me and I let my head fall back to rest on his shoulder. "I'm a mess. A twenty-seven-year-old mess. It's embarrassing."

"You shouldn't be embarrassed," Patrick says, wrapping his left arm across my waist and pulling me impossibly closer. "We all make decisions every day. Some pay off, and some don't. You should be proud that you've realised you're not where you want to be, not embarrassed. You've got a big heart, Hazel. You're clever and witty and, based on the one drawing I've seen, incredibly talented. Your parents are nothing but proud of you, I'm sure."

He presses his lips to the side of my head, and I melt, perplexed at this new side of Patrick. The walls he had up in the beginning have crumbled, exposing a sensitive, vulnerable, and thoughtful side to him, and it's turning me to mush. I should personally thank Maria for last night's sangria.

"Did George put you in touch with one of his contacts?"

"Yeah, the woman running the in-house design team at Bookish Publishing House in Melbourne," I reply, controlling my breathing as Patrick's hand slides down over my abdomen and under the covers. "She asked me to put together a portfolio for her to look at. I'm not sure if what I've come up with is any good though."

"Of course, you'd think that about your own work," he grumbles in my ear, his hand teetering between my legs. "Stop second-guessing yourself, Hazel. You owe it to yourself to jump all in with this opportunity. Take a risk."

I close my eyes, his hand dangerously close to where I'm throbbing for him. The irony of Patrick urging me to take a risk is almost too delightful. I wonder if he realises that, to me, *he* is a risk. A tantalising and secretive risk. My legs part on instinct, and I take a deep breath as Patrick's hand lingers.

On the bedside table, Patrick's phone vibrates again, startling both of us. He groans, and I sigh, as he reluctantly retrieves his hand and reaches for the damned thing.

"I've got to take this," he mutters, sliding me to the side so he can get out of bed. He kisses me softly on the lips before ducking into the ensuite.

I smile with giddiness, lying in the fog clouding my mind. Patrick and I spent hours having sex and are now canoodling in bed. Walls I never thought of attempting to break are falling with ease, and it warms me somewhere deep in my soul to know he feels safe sharing those stories with me.

I bask in the bliss of it before getting restless. I kick the sheets off and pull on my shirt, which ended in a crumpled heap on the floor after I tore it off last night. I grin to myself again. I don't remember the last time I felt this light-hearted.

On a whim, I decide I'm going to go get *us* coffees this time. I tiptoe to my bathroom door and raise my hand to rap on it, but I stop myself. The door is open a slither and I can hear Patrick's deep voice echoing through the bathroom.

"Yes. Everything's under control."

There's that curiosity killing the cat again. I shouldn't eavesdrop. I should walk away and get back into bed like nothing's out of place. Or get the coffees like I was planning to. Or at least start banging about so he knows I might overhear him.

But I don't.

"With all due respect, Anthony might be an idiot sometimes, but he knows what he's talking about." Patrick's voice is quiet and calm, before I hear him tut with annoyance. "He told you I was here?"

Those words stop me in my tracks. Silence, followed by a strange-sounding chortle, almost one filled with disgust, vibrates from Patrick's throat and into my chest. His voice quietens further, so I lean in closer. "She's ten years my junior. It's not like that, I can assure you."

I step away from the door.

He's talking about me.

My unwavering ability to jump to every possible worst-case scenario kicks into high gear. Who is he talking to and what concern would they have about him being here with me? His cold words remind me I barely know him. He might have been letting some walls down, but for all I know he was talking shit to get laid. Maybe the rumours about him being a bit of a player are true.

I stand several feet away, but I can't pretend I didn't hear something. My hands tremble and I'm sure my neck and chest are red with fury. How did I get myself into another situation with a liar?

The door swings open and I hold my stance next to the bed, folding my arms for stability and in an effort to look fierce. Patrick's expression is frustrated as he enters the room, his eyes widening in surprise when he sees me.

"Who was that?" My teeth ache with the pressure I'm exerting on them.

Patrick looks down at his phone. "A man I'm doing some work for. He's helping me with Lisa's ... account."

"Sounds like your brother threw you under the bus." Cocking my head to the side, I jut my chin out as I wait for his response.

Patrick's shoulder drop, closing his eyes as he takes a breath. "Hazel ..."

"I get it. I imagine banging someone who works for a client of yours is against the rules, so lying about it makes sense."

Patrick's eyes fly open. "I don't want to explain my personal affairs to the people I work with."

"That *ten years my junior* comment came to you pretty easily, if you ask me."

Patrick holds my gaze, his darkened eyes unblinking. "Please believe me when I say it's not like that."

"What exactly is it like, Patrick?" I demand. "For once, why don't you give me a straight answer?"

Patrick stands silently, his gazed bouncing erratically as he battles with his next words.

But they don't come.

A humourless laugh barks from my throat. "You should go."

Patrick's face falls, but again, he remains silent. He snatches up his pants, pulling them up his muscular legs, and runs a hand through his tousled locks. "I'm sorry, Hazel."

As Patrick pulls his shirt over his head; hot tears spring to my eyes before I can stop them. Embarrassment and confusion riddle my body. How ironic that moments after I allowed myself to slip into a blissful bubble with this man, he's bursting it without a second thought.

I watch as he gathers the rest of his belongings, his shoulders slumped. Any remnants of our euphoric night and morning have vanished from the room. As he heads towards the bedroom door, he turns back to regard me. Before he can speak, I turn my back and start busying myself by stripping the bedsheets.

"Don't contact me again," I say, angrily tugging a pillow free from its case.

I hear the front door close a minute later.

26

DON'T. Stop. Don't. Stop.

One minute to go. One more minute of pain and it's over.

Obnoxiously loud music blares in my eardrums, sweat pouring down my face and chest. One minute left of this workout. One minute and I can collapse on the floor in relief. The endorphins will take over and I'll be too tired to think about Patrick or the fact I sent my portfolio off to Bookish Publishing House and haven't heard a peep.

"Forty seconds left!" someone yells out near me.

"This is fucked!" Kali gasps next to me, dropping to her knees.

She's right. But I don't stop. This is one of the things I love about working out. The point of delirium you reach when you push yourself harder than you ever thought possible. When your muscles and lungs are screaming at you to stop, but you keep going. I keep my head down, my hands splayed on the rubber floor directly under my shoulders and my knees tucking in one at a time towards my chest.

"Twenty seconds to go! No stopping!"

Twenty seconds left. Pain shoots through my body, burning

in my abs and up to my shoulders. I'd better have a six-pack after this many mountain climbs. I'd better have an endorphin rush of longer than twenty minutes after slogging it out this hard today.

"Three, two, one, and you're done!"

I collapse onto the rubber mat beneath me, sinking back onto my feet and gasping for air. My sweat tastes salty and satisfying as it seeps into my mouth, and I can't help but mentally pat myself on the back for the effort I put in this morning.

Kali is lying on her back, starfish style, drenched in a shiny coat of perspiration. "This is why I don't come to these classes," she puffs.

"But how good do you feel now?"

"I'm dying," she groans. "I'm a Pilates instructor, not a fucking sadist."

Once we've peeled ourselves off the floor, we traipse out of the room, Kali perking up as we walk past the weights section of the gym. "Damn. Maybe I should come to this class more often."

"You're greedy," I say.

"I'm *generous*. I don't care if they date," Kali replies, nudging me.

"One day, a man is going to come along and you're not going to want to share him," I tell her.

Kali shrugs. "Possibly. But until that time, I'm happy dating *all the men*. Speaking of men, have you heard from Patrizio?"

I frown at her, the mention of his name threatening to kill my buzz. "No."

"Have you tried contacting him?"

"No."

It's been two weeks since Patrick walked out of my house. I haven't had any run-ins or unexpected drop-ins and he hasn't messaged or called me, as I requested. I wish I felt empowered for telling him to leave and never contact me again and I didn't feel used and disappointed, but that would be total bullshit.

After he left that morning, I was furious on multiple levels: with him for not being honest with me and with myself for being so gullible. Once the rage simmered down, I panicked. I had overreacted. Both of us would come under fire if our business were to get out. His comments about me being younger might have been an easy way for him to deflect and protect us both. Once I thought about contacting him again, I realised he hadn't contacted *me*, and my rage returned, the cycle continuing.

"Maybe you should make the first move?" Kali suggests, stepping outside into the sunshine and stretching her arms up.

I shake my head. "No way. It's been too long now. If he wanted to contact me, he would have."

"Didn't you tell him *not* to contact you?" Kali asks.

"Whose side are you on?"

Kali ignores me. "I think you should call him."

"I can't call him."

"You can," she argues. "Don't send a text message. *Call* him. Force him to answer, or not answer. A message can be lost, or he can sit on it for hours. You should call him right now."

I twirl my phone in my hands, wondering if I could be brave enough to contact Patrick at seven o'clock in the morning after our argument two weeks ago.

As I'm contemplating this, my screen lights up with a new email from Bookish Publishing, and I immediately open it.

Dear Hazel,

Thank you for the recent submission of your design portfolio. The team here is seriously impressed with your graphic art skills and illustrations, and we'd love to explore your gift.

Whilst we don't currently have any positions available in our teams, we have three places available in our twelve-week internship program in Melbourne, which starts in the New Year.

Applicants are required to submit a book cover design for one of the three book briefs attached in the application. We strongly encourage you to apply. Applications close on 30 November.

Looking forward to hearing from you.

Jess,

Creative Design Lead | Bookish Publishing House

"What's that face for?" Kali asks, leaning over my shoulder.

"Jess at Bookish suggests I apply for a place in their internship program," I reply, re-reading the email.

Kali squeals and grabs my arm, jumping up and down. "Fuck yes! That's amazing!"

"It's basically a rejection letter," I argue.

Kali halts her jumping. "What? No, it's not."

"They saw my artwork, didn't think it was good enough, and are gently letting me down by saying I can apply with a thousand other people to be an errand girl."

Kali's face twists in annoyance and she snatches my phone out of my hand to read the email. "That is *not* what this says. They loved your pieces. The lead of Creative Design contacted you personally. She could've had her assistant send this, but she didn't."

I whip my phone out of Kali's hand, unsure of how to take the email. It's not bad news, but it's not good news either. If they had *loved* my work, surely Jess would've called or made it clearer in her response. And what did I think was going to happen? That because I know George Wilson, they'd fall in love with my work and offer me a full-time role on the spot where I could work from home? I'm an idiot.

My endorphin-high didn't last five minutes.

"Even if I applied, and I scored a miracle place, it's in *Melbourne*. I can't go to Melbourne."

"Why the hell not?" Kali demands.

I head towards my parked car up the street. "I can't leave my job for an unpaid internship in a city where I don't know a soul."

"Please tell me you're joking." Kali races up beside me and slaps my arm. "You have savings, and I have my inheritance sitting there. Let *me* help you out."

"No way. Besides, it's for three *months*, Kali. I can't *move* to Melbourne. I hate the cold."

"It'll be the middle of summer!"

I swing my car door open and hop inside, slamming the door closed in frustration. Seconds later, Kali climbs in the passenger side. "Hazel, you are *crazy* if you don't at least apply. You have absolutely nothing to lose and *everything* to gain."

"I'd have to get a job to work around it. Living in a city is expensive."

Kali shakes her head in resignation as she closes her door. "You really are the queen of excuses."

Her reference to my conversation with Patrick elicits a wince from me as I fire up the car. "Please drop it, Kali."

I might not be a risk-taker, but I'm still making the best choices for my own life. Moving interstate by myself for an internship would be a huge risk. Here, I have a steady income, the beach close by and friends. I know people say you grow when you're outside your comfort zone, but even considering this is more reckless than brave.

"I'll drop it for now, but you don't know me at all if you think I'm letting this go." Kali turns up the volume on the radio and slides on her sunglasses. "Let's get caffeine."

As I pull away from the curb, my stomach churns. I ignore my gut telling me that despite all the reasons to stay, not one of them is good enough.

27

"YOU NEED to eat something before you fall over."

Meg pushes Rachel away from her with a laugh, stumbling as we head towards a spare table at the back of the food market.

"Quit tryin' to tell me how to live my life!" Meg yells, before giggling again. Some of her gin and tonic spills over the lip of her cup, but she doesn't notice.

"If you can't control her, we've got no hope," I say to Rachel. She sighs and storms after Meg, who's high-fiving strangers sitting down to dinner.

"Who would've thought Alex's cousin would be the one giving me a run for my money?" Kali muses, draping an arm around my shoulders. She sips her gin. "Party girl Kali has been replaced."

"Thank God, because I can't handle party girl Kali."

Kali kisses my forehead. "If anything happens to her, I'm telling Alex it was your fault."

"I figured."

Meg and Rachel invited Kali and I to spend our Friday night at Miami Marketta, a night-time food truck market with live music in the suburb next to ours. It's family-friendly, but also caters to those searching for a good time; like Meg, who hasn't stopped cutting in line at the bar to snag complimentary drinks from a hot bartender. I can't believe I once thought of her as innocent. She may put on a wide-eyed, good-girl façade during the day, but once she's had a couple of drinks, her inner brazen vixen comes to life. She's a great distraction for my brain tonight.

As I watch Rachel order Meg to sit down, I cast appreciative eyes across both of them. It's wonderful being out and social again. There's something about making new friends as an adult. It's not the easiest thing for me to do on a good day, so the fact that I can be myself around women I've only recently met is refreshing. If I were to apply for the internship in Melbourne, and bag a spot, I'd be starting back at square one with zero friends.

As good supportive friends do, the girls insisted I step up my game tonight and 'quit moping'. So, I treated myself to winged eyeliner and a low-cut top I haven't worn in a year. Rachel's vibrant red hair is pulled into a long braid that sits over one shoulder; her dewy skin is flawless under the luminescent lights. Meg's freshly cut bob is striking against her cheekbones; her leather mini skirt showing off her toned pins. The two of them look like they stepped out of a fashion magazine, no matter how tipsy one of them might be.

Kali leaves to grab Meg some pizza and I grab a couple of bottles of water before heading to their corner table. We've only been here an hour and Meg is dangerously close to legless.

"It's Miami Marketta, not Splendour in the Grass," I hear Rachel scold her. "Settle the fuck down."

"Oh, pfft. Would you lighten up? Hazel!" Meg smiles at me as I approach. "Tell Rachel to lighten up."

I shove a bottle of water into her hands. "Drink some of this and I will." Meg rolls her eyes again, but obediently unscrews the cap and takes a few gulps.

"Whatever happened with you and that guy from Kygo?" I ask.

Meg grins at me. "Frankie? We've hooked up a few times, but I don't think it'll go beyond that. He's too ... nice."

"Oh, for God's sake." Rachel tuts next to me and I laugh. "Heaven forbid you date someone who worships you and treats you well."

"There's nothing wrong with liking an element of danger," Meg argues. "Or a bit of mystery. Isn't that right, Hazel? Like that guy!"

I flinch. She's thinking back to that night she ran into me with Patrick. I don't know how much to share of what has happened with Patrick to anyone.

"I guess he had that mysterious vibe about him," I agree.

"No, no, no! I mean, that guy is *here*. He's here!" Meg squeals, cupping a hand to her mouth and giggling. I spin in my chair to look over my shoulder and sure enough, Patrick is walking through the crowd, a stunning brunette in a red dress by his side.

My stomach flips or sinks. I'm not sure what it's doing, but everything around me has become one monotonous hum. All I can see is Patrick's face smiling down at the petite woman next to him, laughing at something she's saying, laughing so wide the corners of his eyes crease. My heart skips a beat.

I spin back. "Shit."

"What's wrong?" Meg's eyes are wide as she takes another swig of water. Panic rises from my stomach and I drop my head into my hands. I can't handle seeing him, especially when he's fawning over some ridiculously beautiful woman who makes him *laugh* like he isn't hurting like I am.

"Hazel, are you alright?" Rachel rests a gentle hand on my shoulder. "Don't worry about him. Keep your head down. He's about to walk towards the other—"

"Oi, dickface! What did you do to my friend?"

I snap my head up to see Meg's tiny frame standing on the wooden seat, her arms aggressively waving over my head at the crowd behind me. The buzz of music and people talking drowns out her cries to most people, but a few nearby turn to look.

"Meg! For fuck's sake, get *down!*" Rachel hisses, reaching up to grab Meg's hand. Meg waves her off, her furious glare still directed behind me. A mixture of gratitude and fury bubble towards Meg. I love that she's standing up for me with no hesitation, but *Jesus Christ*, I want to die right now.

"Don't act like you don't know I'm talking to you, asshole! Yeah, you! You're a giant dick!"

"Meg, I swear to God I will cut your hair while you're sleeping if you don't get down right this second." Rachel slams her fist on the table.

"You might have a pretty face, but that doesn't hide the fact that you're a prick!" Meg takes a sip of her gin and plops back down on the bench, waving to a couple of guys a few tables down who cheered. "Fuck that asshole," she says to me.

I can't process what's happened. I'm certain his eyes are trying to penetrate my back. I must move. *Now.*

"I'll be back in a second." I stand up before Meg or Rachel can stop me. As I walk away, I hear Rachel chiding Meg again. With my head down, I squeeze through the tables, intent on finding Kali. *Don't look up. Don't look up. Keep moving.*

I apologise to several people I bump into before reaching the mouth of the pathway that leads to the food trucks, searching desperately for the Italian stall and any sign of Kali, when I bump into a hard torso.

"Oh, sorry—" I start, but stop as I find Patrick in front of me, expression stern, breathing unsteady as though he's been jogging. Jogging to get to *me.* His hand has firmly but gently grasped my arm to stop me from toppling.

"Hi." His dark eyes are wide. My body locks up. "Please, don't walk away from me."

I don't think I could if I tried. Patrick towers over me, his face filled with concern, panic even. It's the same expression I saw that night he saved me after the gala. I realise I'm mad at myself for being so angry with him instead of listening to what he had to say.

"Sorry about Meg. She's had a bit to drink."

Patrick's face relaxes as he releases my arm, glancing in Rachel's and Meg's direction. The two of them are watching us with obvious interest. "I deserve it. I should've made things clear the minute I stepped out of that bathroom."

"Why didn't you?"

Patrick's brown eyes are dark, but the golden flecks sparkle under the fairy lights. "I was afraid I'd scare you away. Ironic, isn't it?"

I'm busy trying to control my breathing when a tiny figure wraps itself around Patrick's right thigh. A young boy with jet black hair and amber eyes looks up at him adoringly, and my breathing's out of control again.

"Uncle Patrick! Mama is looking for you."

Patrick's tense posture relaxes as he cups the back of the boy's head. "I'll be a few minutes. Where is she?"

"At the table, silly." The boy giggles and looks at me, tightening his grip on Patrick's leg. "Are you coming to sit at our table?"

"Uhh … no. I've got to find my friend." I attempt a smile.

"Your friend can come too. We got a *big* table so there's lots of room." The young boy gives me a bright smile and I can't help but return it.

"There you are!" The stunning brunette woman in the red dress appears, flustered. "I turn my back for five seconds and you both slip out of my sight." She playfully slaps Patrick on the arm and smiles at me.

"Hello. I'm Maria," she says, extending a long slender arm to shake my hand.

Ah. Married Maria with the two children.

"You must be Hazel. Patrick's told me so much about you." I glance at him curiously, and he doesn't look away. He's regarding me, with what I would wager, is hope.

"I'm sure the reports are glowing," I say, shaking her hand. I wonder if she knows about the vomit in his car. "Lovely to meet you, Maria."

"And this is my son, Leonardo."

"It's *Leo,*" the boy groans, rolling his eyes.

"He's four going on forty," Maria says with a flat smile. "I need a wine. Have you seen David and Gabriella?" She turns to Patrick who shakes his head.

"Uncle Patrick, I want to go see the lights up there." Leo points towards the far end of the market, where a stall is covered with sticks of light, lava lamps and crystal balls.

"After dinner," Maria says.

"David is probably still waiting for the food," Patrick says in a hushed tone. "I can walk him up now to keep him busy."

Maria's eyes widen with gratitude before her gaze lands on the bar closest to us. Patrick smiles. "Go on, I'll take him."

Maria squeezes his arm and turns to me. "These opportunities don't come up often. It was lovely meeting you, Hazel." She's speeding towards the bar before I even have time to respond.

Patrick cups the back of Leo's head. "I better take this young man."

"Hazel, you're coming too, aren't you?" Leo asks.

An uncomfortable silence settles between us, despite the noise of the crowd. "I really should find my friends."

Leo's bottom lip pouts, his dark eyebrows furrowing. "Please, Hazel?"

Patrick's mouth twists to suppress a smile. "Please, Hazel?"

My eyes narrow into a mocking glare and Patrick's smile creeps up his face.

"Uncle Patrick can buy you a present," Leo adds. "He's going to buy me a present."

"Since when?" Patrick asks him with fake outrage, to which Leo giggles.

I lick my lips, watching as Patrick waits patiently for my response. His gaze drifts to them and back to my eyes. "Okay, but only if he buys me a present."

28

I'M hyperaware of Patrick so close to me.

He's dazzlingly handsome under the fairy lights. His white linen shirt contrasts pleasantly with his tanned skin, which is darker than the last time I saw him. It takes every bit of willpower not to continuously side-eye him as we head down the long walkway lined with food trucks and bustling with people. Leo insisted we each hold one of his hands, and Patrick agreed without hesitation. Watching him be so loving with Leo makes it hard to be angry with him. My ovaries hurt.

Patrick clears his throat after a few minutes of silence, turning his head to catch my gaze. "I'm really sorry. I acted like a complete di—" His gaze drops to Leo's head. "I was a complete douche. I was rude and I'm so sorry." His mouth presses into a firm line.

"What did you do, Uncle Patrick?" Leo asks, throwing his head back.

I bite back a grin.

"I wasn't very kind to Hazel."

"Mum says to always be kind," Leo says, his earnest brown eyes fixated on mine.

I smile down at Leo. "Your mum is right."

"Dad says mum is always right too," Leo agrees.

We approach the table lit up by colourful lights and Leo's face cracks with glee, letting go of both our hands as he gets closer.

"Eyes only Leo," Patrick warns. "Hands in our pockets, remember?"

Leo doesn't respond as he stands with his nose inches away from a bright orange globe shimmering with gold swirls.

"I'm sorry." Patrick's staring down at me with sincerity. The tic in his jaw shows he's nervous. "I didn't want people to think I was messing around on the job or for you to get into any trouble if it got back to Lisa." He reaches out and grabs Leo's wrist as he reaches for a giant star shooting lights up each of its arms.

"I get it," I assure him. "I'm sorry too. Going from an amazing night to hearing you dismiss me because of my age to someone ... it hurt. But I really do get it."

Patrick turns to me, regret in his eyes. "I didn't mean what I said."

I shrug. "It's true though. I *am* ten years younger than you. It's crazy, right?"

Patrick shakes his head. "That's what I'm saying. I don't think it's crazy."

My cheeks heat as he steers Leo away from the lights towards a display of squishy blobs glowing in the dark.

"I don't regret us, if that's what you're thinking," he continues. "I regret what I said to a colleague in the heat of the moment to keep him out of my business, and I've regretted not calling you every day since."

A heavy, Patrick-sized weight filled with doubt has lifted off my shoulders. Whilst I still have questions about his colleagues and his brother and who he was speaking to on the phone that day, Patrick's apology is more than I expected. I still like him, despite the mystery and uncertainty around him. I like him even though I don't know a lot about him yet. I like him even though he doesn't live in the same state as me, or that he plays his cards close to his chest.

"Thank you," I reply. "Let's forget it happened."

Patrick smiles with relief, the lines on his face creasing. The idea my forgiveness could bring him so much joy spikes my confidence.

"Did you hear from the publishing house?" he asks.

I twist away to hide my undoubtedly readable expression. I still haven't decided whether I'm going to apply for the internship. It's a step backwards. Throwing my energy into a mock design, only to have my hopes shattered, isn't something I'm ready to deal with.

"Still waiting to hear," I lie.

Patrick's eyes narrow, but he doesn't push the topic further.

"Kali's birthday is next week and the woman wants everything I can't afford," I deflect, admiring a large dreamcatcher on the wall, lit up by fairy lights. "Maybe I should get one of these. She's into that hippy shit."

"You shouldn't swear," Leo pipes up.

Patrick chuckles. "Hazel's allowed to say that. She's an adult."

"Not when I'm around," Leo fires back, reaching for a wand-like stick filled with purple fluorescent goo.

I laugh as Patrick jumps in to pry to Leo's hands away, doing his best to fight off laughter. I've got to hand it to this kid. He's got sass. "Sorry Leo." My eyes take in the stalls around us and fall on one filled with leather-bound notebooks and heavy-weighted pens a few feet away. "One sec," I say to Patrick and I walk over to it, my eyes bulging.

Some of the books have been designed to look and feel old, with stained yellow pages and burnt edges. One by one I pick up the empty books, flipping through the pages and smoothing them over with my hands. As much as I love my fancy design tablet, there's something about drawing with pen and paper that gets my creative juices flowing.

Charcoal pencils and spare sheets of parchment-like paper sit on the bench to invite people to test out the products. I pick up one of the charcoal pencils and run it between my fingers, testing the weight of it in my hand.

The woman behind the stall smiles at me. "Are you interested in any of our items?"

"All of them," I mumble. "These are beautiful."

"They're handmade by me and my husband." The woman beams at me as Patrick and Leo arrive at my side, Leo grasping the glowing purple wand. With his brows furrowed together, he watches me flip through the pages.

"Where are the pictures?" Leo asks.

"These are blank so you can fill it with your own." Placing the book down, I pick up a heavy dark brown leather-bound book, turning the pages and inhaling loudly. "It smells amazing."

Leo crinkles his nose as I hold the book down to him. "It smells old."

I laugh, placing the book back on the table. "Leather-bound, handmade stuff gets me every time. How much is this one?"

"Three hundred," the woman replies.

"Dollars?" I balk.

The woman laughs kindly and nods. "It's part of our hardcover series with the raised spines. Made from high quality cow leather, hand-painted and the pages are hand-stitched. It's our most expensive line."

I sigh wistfully, placing the book back down carefully. "I love it, but I think it's a bit much for me."

"You could get a wand too, Hazel," Leo says, waving it up at up. "Uncle Patrick got this one for cheaper because it said if you give hugs to your mum, you can have twenty dollars off. So, I have to give mum hugs when we go back."

Patrick, who's watching the exchange, smiles behind his hand and shakes his head.

"Hazel, do you want me to draw you a picture?" Leo asks, switching his wand into his right hand and picking up a pencil.

"I would love you to," I reply, bending down to his height. "I'll draw one for you too. What's your favourite animal?"

Leo screws up his face in thought, before shouting, "Lion!", followed by a roar.

"That's the best roar I've ever heard," I say, picking up a pencil.

Leo and I spend the next ten minutes drawing pictures. I focus on the one. Whereas he gets bored, drawing about fifteen different blobs and swirls across several pieces of paper. Filled with pride, he hands every one of them to me.

When I've finished my drawing, I spin the paper around, waiting for Leo's response. He takes a few seconds to absorb it, his frown pressed deeply into his forehead as he examines my sketch. The second his face breaks into a bright smile, my mood soars.

"It's me!"

"Leo the Lion," I say proudly, handing it to him. I drew Leo's face on the head of a lion, complete with a mane and tail.

"This is so cool!" he squeals.

When I smile in victory at Patrick, he's already staring at me with a primal expression. It's intense, his eyes wide with wonder, like he's revering me and thinking about devouring me at once.

Leo breaks Patrick's trance, tugging on his trousers to show him the drawing. Patrick dives right into fawning over it, promising Leo he'll hold on to it until they get back to his mum.

As we turn away from the stall, Kali appears out of the

crowd, her arms up in a *what-the-fuck-is-going-on?* pose. When she spots Patrick, she makes no attempt to hide her smug surprise.

"Patrick." Kali smiles at him before turning to me. "Hazel."

"Kali, it's lovely to see you again," says Patrick.

Her smile might break her face. "Patrizio. It's lovely to see *you* again."

I roll my eyes as she gives me an exaggerated wink.

"I hear you have some demands for your upcoming birthday?" Patricks asks.

"Yes!" she squeals, clapping her hands. "We've hired a house in Byron next weekend. Just a few of us, nothing major. We're going to hang out and de-stress and drink cocktails."

"She's not excited about it," I say. "She doesn't even have a gift list a mile long either."

"I enjoy getting presents," Kali replies. "More importantly, I *know* what I want. It's better than being someone who says, *oh, I don't need any gifts.*" Kali gives me a pointed look and I grin. I've never really cared about the whole birthday thing as much as her.

"Nothing wrong with knowing what you want," Patrick agrees.

Kali tilts her plastic cup at him in agreement. "Thank you, Patrizio."

"There is when everything you want has a five-hundred-dollar price tag," I argue, remembering a Dyson Air Dryer and Cartier bracelet were merely two of the items on her gift list.

"Not *everything.* You're so dramatic," Kali says.

"The house itself cost a small fortune," I point out, turning to Patrick. "She chose the one with eight bedrooms and an alpaca on site."

"I love animals! It's why I'm a vegetarian!" Kali cries.

"Naturally, you had to get the one with the alpaca," Patrick says.

Kali moves closer to Patrick, leaning a slender arm on his

shoulder. "See? A man who makes sense." She turns to Patrick. "Did you want to come, Patrizio? I'll make sure you two love-birds get the second-best room in the house so you can—"

"Kali." My warning tone is sharp as my line sight of sight flies to Leo, who's watching Kali with narrowed eyes.

She smiles at him, crouching down to his level. "Hello young sir, I didn't even see you there. What's your name?"

"Leo the Lion." Leo grabs for the paper in Patrick's hand, and shows Kali with enthusiasm. I have to fight the urge to do a fist pump.

"I'd love to come," Patrick says, smiling at me. "If it's alright with you?"

I'm stunned. Does he really want to come and mingle with my friends? Do I trust him enough for that? Am I even allowed to get involved with a man who's working with my boss? So many questions, and all they do is aggravate my anxiety.

"You don't have to come." I whisper the words out of fear of rejection.

Patrick's eyebrows knit together in a frown. "What do you mean?"

"Don't feel obliged to say yes."

"Do you not want me to?"

"No, I want you to. I mean, if you want to, I want you to. But if you don't, it's no big deal."

Patrick's face is gleeful as he regards me. I'm a schoolgirl getting hit on by the star quarterback in all those American movies.

"I would love to come, Hazel."

My grin nearly splits my face.

"Awesome." Kali claps again, her eyes glistening with glee. She and Leo hold hands and Patrick looks between the two of them curiously. "I run mums and bubs classes. Kids love me," she says with a shrug. She leans in closer. "We should rescue

Rachel. She called me and said Meg's vomiting on the street out front."

Patrick shakes his head. "You women and your alcohol."

"Don't start," I warn him, and he smiles. "We'd better go. It was great to meet you, Leo."

"Bye Hazel. Thank you for my drawing!"

"I'll call you," Patrick says, stepping closer to me. His gaze roams my face, and he leans down, planting a soft kiss on my cheek. A current runs up my spine and it takes all my self-control to not jump up and straddle him. I think Patrick can tell.

He gives me a wicked grin. "Good night, Hazel."

I watch as Patrick strides away with Leo's hands in his and shake my head at the dramatic change in events, and my feelings, towards the mysterious man in the suit.

29

"IF YOU CHECK your phone one more time, I'm making you do a shot."

I drop my phone down onto the sunbed at Kali's threat, scooping up my cocktail with aggression and taking a large gulp.

Kali's birthday weekend has kicked off at the mansion in Byron Bay. The spring gods are smiling down, blessing us with temperatures in the high twenties and sunshine for the foreseeable future. Kali, Meg, Rachel, and I spent the morning getting pedicures and manicures, and are now poolside, drinking cocktails Alex and his friends, Jack, and Ben, have been making on demand. It's Instagram perfect. Except I'm obsessing because Patrick's not here yet.

"He said he'd drive down once he finished work. I'm sure he's just running late," Meg assures me, adjusting her skimpy bikini so more flesh is exposed to the sunshine. "Being a sex god assassin is hard work."

Kali has updated Meg and Rachel on our theories about Patrick, whilst adding salacious extras of how amazing Patrick is in bed. That sleepover was the only time we've had sex. The past week we've both been slammed with work and barely had time to talk, although our sexting is definitely at boiling point.

He said he would be here around lunchtime. It's now after three and I haven't heard a peep.

"Do you think he lost interest?" I ask.

Kali groans. "Hazel."

"I messaged him last night saying my soaking pussy was waiting for him," I admit. Meg squeals, Kali cheers and Rachel's drink comes out of her nose. "What if I scared him off?"

"With wet pussy?" Kali cries. "I don't think so. That man wants to feed on you."

Meg sighs wistfully. "I wish I had a sex god assassin to feed on me."

"You have your choice of men lining up and find flaws in all of them," Rachel scolds.

"I do not," Meg argues, offended.

"Too nice, too ripped, not ripped enough, short eyelashes, even number of tattoos," Rachel lists.

"Hey, everyone gets a fair go with me," Meg says, before lowering her voice. "If they don't blow my mind in the sack the first time, they have to go. Life is short."

"Lots of people get nervous the first time," I say. "Guys have so much pressure put on them."

"Did Patrick buckle under the pressure Hazel?" Meg counters, sitting up to peer at me over her sunglasses. I grin at her and she pushes them back up her nose. "I rest my case."

"Your cousin didn't buckle under the pressure, if you were wondering," Kali pipes up. Meg gags dramatically, swiping to hit Kali playfully on the arm. "I think we woke the neighbours up with all the moaning and headboard banging—"

"Kali!" Meg shouts, covering her ears.

"Alex asked if I'd be interested in a three-way, and you know what, I might just—"

"Please make it stop!" Meg cries.

Rachel and I laugh as Kali launches into a detailed play-by-play of her first time with Alex and Meg squeals to drown out her words. "Rachel! Hazel! Help me!"

"You're on your own," Rachel says, sinking back to sip her cocktail.

"I would, but I have to pee." I head back towards the house, listening to Meg threaten to drag Kali into the pool if she doesn't shut up.

I navigate through the enormous eight-bedroom house to my room. Kali kept her word and assigned me the second-best room in the house, a massive one at the back of the property. Beautiful French doors open onto the large back yard, overlooking rolling hills of green. It looks more like an Italian postcard than a paradise an hour away from home.

After I pee, I take a second to focus, splashing cold water on my face. Tipsy Hazel wants to call or message Patrick, but we're also in the beginning of the seeing-each-other-so-let's-not-be-too-full-on stage.

Ugh. Dating is hard. You've got to be keen, but not too keen. Show interest, but not so much you come across as psychotic. It's been years since I've properly dated anyone, but I'm certain the rules are still the same.

As I duck out of the bathroom telling myself not to think about it anymore, I shout with surprise as I barrel into something hard.

Patrick, perfect in another pressed suit, stands in front of me, an overnight bag across his shoulder. I'm shaking with nerves, having not seen him physically in over a week and the memories of us exchanging filthy text messages plaguing my mind.

I want to jump him.

"Hi," I say, keeping it cool.

A smile forms on his face as he takes in my carefully chosen strappy black two-piece. "Hello, Jonesy." His voice is a warm coat of honey on my skin.

"Can you please stop calling me that?"

"Never." He grins, dropping his bag at his feet, his narrowed eyes on me. I'm self-conscious, but I don't cover my body. Instead, I hold my head high.

"Aren't you hot in that suit?" I ask. "It's nearly thirty degrees outside."

"Already thinking about de-robing me?" Patrick teases. I don't have time to roll my eyes as one of his large hands snakes its way around my hip.

"If you're not here for de-robing, this is going to be a severely disappointing weekend."

"I'm afraid I'm here in a professional capacity," Patrick says with mock sincerity. "Hence, the suit."

"Oh, well, if that's the case, I'll ask Kali if we can switch to separate rooms."

Patrick's eyes flash and he pulls me into his body so we're chest to chest. He tilts his head downwards and kisses me softly under my earlobe. My eyes close as his lips make contact with my skin, and a hot tingle dances to the roots of my hair. The slightest touch from Patrick brings me to life.

"Don't you dare," he purrs.

Thank God.

Thoughts of what he and I have become, and where we're headed, race through my mind at a frightening pace. His warm, kind smile and the intensity in his eyes – so far removed from his stern, cold frown when I first met him – take my breath away.

Patrick steps back to admire me. "I have something for you."

"What is it?"

Patrick smiles to himself as he bends down and reaches into his bag, pulling out a flat, rectangular item wrapped in brown paper and string.

"You do realise it's Kali's birthday and not mine, right?" I ask hesitantly, taking the heavy parcel from him. Patrick nods, motioning me to open the present.

My hands tremble with anticipation as I untie the delicate string ribbon and peel back the paper to reveal a solid block the colour of burnt coffee. I gasp.

It's the book from the leather-bound stall.

"Patrick ..." But words fail me as I turn the book over in my hands, running my fingers over the smooth cover, tracing down its thick spine. When I open the cover, a mixture of parchment and leather hits my nostrils.

"Patrick, I can't accept this."

"Of course you can. Think of it as an early Christmas present."

"This is expensive."

"It was worth it to see the look on your face."

I can't deal with this man. He's capturing my heart without even knowing the effect he's having on me. He bought this for me because he saw how much I admired it.

"It's a shame you don't have the place for a few more days. It'd be a beautiful spot to do some drawing."

I pretend to busy myself by flipping through the blank pages. The internship applications are due at the end of the month, which is only a couple of weeks away. I decided not to apply. Logistically, I don't know how I'd manage it and the disappointment of not getting a spot would be unbearable. I've had enough disappointment for one year.

Patrick's ringing phone breaks into my thoughts. He frowns at the screen and clicks it to silent. I don't miss the concern on his face.

"Busy at work?"

He nods, quickly replacing his frown with a smile. "No more than usual."

Patrick takes the book out of my hands and places it on the

dresser, turning back to me with a smoulder. "Seeing you in this makes me want to stay in and forget about whatever's planned for tonight."

We reach for each other and my insides heat as we kiss, and his large hands greedily roam my exposed body.

A quick knock sounds and the bedroom door bursts open. Kali, who has changed into her second bikini for the day, poses dramatically in the doorway, an enormous black floppy hat and matching black sunglasses covering most of her face.

"You guys can bang later!" she shouts, as Patrick and I jump apart. "Patrick, get changed. Now. We've got a beer pong championship to partake in." She leaves the room with a twirl, screaming to everyone else in the house to get outside or get their asses kicked.

"Beer pong's not fun," I say, reaching up and kissing him again. Patrick smiles into my mouth, pulling me closer, his length pressed against my stomach.

"I'd much rather stay in here than play beer pong," he murmurs.

"Let's stay then. Kali can wait." I sound like an addict scrambling for her next fix.

"I doubt Kali would knock next time she storms in here," Patrick says. "And there's no lock on the door. I already checked." I giggle, pulling back with resignation.

We'll have to wait to tear each other's clothes off.

"Thank fuck the CIA sent you here to track down Hazel."

Kali and Patrick are one winning shot away from becoming the beer pong champions, and the more Kali drinks, the more liberal she becomes. She's referred to every conspiracy she and I have mentioned during the past few months, and Patrick's taken it all in his stride.

"Focus, Patrick," she orders, her hands on her knees as he lines up his shot. "We need to knock this out of the park. There's dignity, pride and free shots on the line—"

Patrick tosses the ping-pong ball before waiting for her to finish, and we watch as it sails through the air and into the single cup at the opposite end of the table. Kali screams, chest bumping Patrick who stands there grinning like a loon. She screams again and gives Meg and Jack two middle fingers. Meg returns the gesture with a roll of her eyes, but they both down their drinks obediently.

"We still have one last shot, remember?" Jack shouts, bouncing on the balls of his feet.

"Yeah, good luck," Kali says, moving her arms around to distract him. Jack misses and Kali shrieks again.

"Impressed?" Patrick asks, wiggling his eyebrows at me.

"I've always wanted to rub shoulders with a world class, beer pong, doubles champion."

"This is where dreams are made, Hazy!" Kali shouts, high-fiving my hand before doing the same to Patrick. "Meg and Jack can suck my dick!"

Kali grabs Patrick's hand and demands he follow her as they do a victory lap of the pool area. Watching him laughing and mucking around with my best friend fills me with gratitude. This is how it's supposed to be. The closest Luke and Kali came to laughing together was never.

Patrick humours Kali by following her around the pool as she orders everyone to bow down to her. As usual, I end up distracted by the way the muscles in his back flex and contract as he moves. As he makes his way back to me, my stomach knots.

Patrick smiles, a genuine smile. Not a cheeky grin or an obnoxious smirk. He really smiles at me and I think it's my favourite look on him.

"What?" I ask, suddenly self-conscious as he approaches. "What's that look for?"

"You're beautiful."

My knees buckle and my want for him gets impossibly stronger. Long gone are the days of snippy remarks and defensive behaviour. This side of him ignites the fire in me more than I thought possible. It's intoxicating.

Kali demands, as beer pong champion, we go inside to get ready for dinner before we get too shitfaced. It's a good call, considering Jack did a power-chuck in the garden minutes after the beer pong game finished.

We file into our separate corners of the house. Someone blasts music through the sound system to keep the party vibes alive whilst Ben and Alex put Jack in the shower to sober him up.

I lead the way into our room, with Patrick trailing behind me. When the door closes with a resounding click, my skin breaks out in gooseflesh. We're alone and I'm a little nervous.

I busy myself by rummaging through my suitcase, doing my best to feign casual disinterest. "Do you want to shower first?" I ask, turning around.

Patrick's sitting on the edge of the bed, directly across from me. He's shirtless; still wearing a pair of shorts, watching me, as I cling to the pool towel wrapped around my body.

He says nothing.

I hover in front of him, letting his gaze travel up my body until it settles on my face.

Baboom. Baboom. Baboom.

I'm sure he can hear my heart beating out of my chest.

His warm hands reach out and find my thighs, pulling me to stand between his legs. He tugs at the towel. I let go of it and watch him as it falls away.

There's something incredibly empowering about standing in front of him. Patrick looks at me as if I'm a rare treasure he's never seen. The golden specks in his eyes dance as he takes me in, and his loud swallow fills in the room.

"You really are so beautiful," he whispers as his hands travel to my hips. "I haven't stopped thinking about doing this to you."

Patrick leans forward, and ever so gently kisses me through my bikini bottoms. A tiny gasp escapes my lips and I respond by sliding my hands through his hair. He kisses me again, this time moving his lips so I can feel his tongue through the material. My knees threaten to give way. How can a touch from this man bring me this close to collapsing?

When I look down, Patrick is gazing up, his eyes blazing with lust. His fingers tamper with the delicate strings of the bikini, unravelling the knots on either side with ease. I suck in a breath as the material falls away to the floor, and it takes every ounce of inner strength not to cower with shyness.

Patrick reaches up and tugs at my bikini top, the material loosening, and I help him remove it completely. I plant a soft kiss on his warm lips, and he reciprocates, the two of us slowly, gently, *lovingly*, falling into a rhythm. Patrick's hands grip the back of my legs and he shuffles up the bed, pulling me on top of him.

These kisses are different. He's so careful, so gentle, like he's savouring every kiss and every taste. When my hands find their way to his chest, I sense his racing heart beneath my palms, echoing my own.

Our lips break momentarily, Patrick's eyes filled with wonder as he looks up at me. There are a thousand things to be said between us, yet so much is spoken with this intense silence.

Patrick leans up and takes my mouth again. With my help, he pushes down his shorts and guides me so I'm straddling him.

My body is not my own, in the best way possible. I don't overthink it. I don't think about anything except becoming connected to Patrick. It's only a matter of seconds before we're rocking backwards and forwards in sync, our breaths becoming more ragged; the build in my belly becoming more intense. Although we could easily get messy and hasty, we don't. We're both enjoying the steady build, wanting to get there, but not wanting it to end.

When we eventually fall to pieces together, I can't suppress the surge of emotion that rises in my chest.

This man means more to me than I ever thought possible.

30

I SLIDE the lip gloss stick across my lips and pucker them at the mirror.

After Patrick sent me to oblivion, we had to race to get ready. I'm impressed with how quickly I showered and dried off my hair, whilst also sneaking peeks of Patrick's naked body as he manoeuvred around the room. It took every ounce of willpower not to ravage his bones again.

"You better not be dawdling in there Healey!" I yell.

Patrick ducks his grinning face around the door. "I've got to brush my teeth and put a shirt on. I'll be ready in a quarter of the time it's taken you."

"Yes, but see how good I look." I pretend to flip my hair over my shoulder, and he laughs.

Patrick's phone rings from the bathroom and the hair on the back of my neck prickles for the third time this evening, my smile vanishing. He ducks out of sight to answer it and closes the door, locking himself in.

Every time his phone shrilled the past hour, he's taken the call out of earshot. In the hallway, outside, and now the bathroom. It makes sense after what happened last time, when I overheard a phone call, but it still unsettles me.

My gaze falls to the book tucked inside my suitcase on the floor, reminding me Patrick went out of his way to get me something he knew I'd love. He might be private about his work, but he *is* opening up. I need to be patient.

I'd love to get him something as a thank you. *A new cologne?* No way. I love how he smells. *Maybe a new wallet?* I spot it sitting next to his car keys on the dresser and stand to inspect it closer. For someone who has such fancy things, it's a little worn, the brown leather peeling in the corners. It needs replacing. *Perfect.*

The thin white border of a small photo peeks out the top. Neon lights flashing the words *'curiosity killed the cat!'* dance in my mind's eye. I should put the wallet down and go see if Kali's ready.

My gaze darts to the bathroom door before I wriggle the photo out of the slot.

It's a Polaroid of Patrick. He looks younger, his skin smoother, his hair longer. He's laughing, standing in a kitchen with a red-headed woman. Her slender arm hooks around his neck tightly as she kisses his cheek. Sunshine radiates out of the photo. I flip it over. The words *Me and Chloe, Bondi Beach* are written in pen on the back.

Chloe.

Patrick opens the door, his phone call finished, and I turn to face him. I'm embarrassed, my face hot with humiliation. I've been acting the part of a smitten teenager all afternoon, and he's carrying around a photo of another woman who means something to him.

"Who is Chloe?" My voice cracks as I hold up the photo in between my fingers, gauging Patrick's reaction.

His expression transforms in seconds. His smile fades, his eyes tighten as he spots the photo. We remain silent, but the tension roars in my ears, my blood pumping with a mix of fear, dread, and anger.

"She's the perfect girlfriend, isn't she?" I prompt.

As if we're living in a goddamned made-for-TV drama, Kali bursts into the room, twirling to show off her party dress in dramatic fashion. "Are we ready to rumble ladies and gents?"

I tear my gaze from Patrick. "We just need to finish up our conversation. Can you give us a sec?"

Kali, not caring about the hostile vibe in the room, slings her arm around Patrick's shoulder. His gaze is still frozen on me. "Arguing about the internship? Talk some sense into her, would you?"

Patrick's brow furrows, our connection breaking. "Internship?"

Kali flickers her gaze towards me, and I run my tongue across my teeth in annoyance. She offers an apologetic smile. "This is an argument about something else entirely, isn't it?"

Patrick and I are silent as she backs out of the room. "You guys take your time; I'll make us some drinks."

As soon as Kali closes the door, Patrick whips his head to me. "What's this about an internship?"

I hold up the photo in my fingers. "I asked you first."

Patrick heaves a breath, running a hand through his hair. "It's a photo of me and my ex-girlfriend, Chloe."

Knew it.

Patrick steps forward, folding his arms. "Your turn. What's this about an internship?"

My jaw hurts. "Bookish said they liked some of my pieces and suggested I apply for their internship program."

"And you haven't applied because ...?"

I ignore him. "Why do you carry a photo of you and your ex in your wallet? You don't have photos of Chloe on your phone you can look at in your own time?"

"No." Patrick's nostrils flare, rage simmering in his breath. "Why haven't you applied?"

"Do you know how many people try to get into those programs?" I snap. "Hundreds, if not more. If they liked my work, they would've told me." I slam the photo down on the table and snatch up my clutch, heading for the door.

Patrick blocks my path and I nearly slam into his broad chest. "Did you ever think maybe they said you should apply because they have to follow protocols for applications, but they want you on their team?"

"Would it be easier for you if I *was* in Melbourne?" I ask, my tone scathing. "That way you don't have to worry about anyone up here seeing us together. Like Chloe, for instance? Does she live up here?"

"What? No! None of that is true! Why aren't you applying for the internship?"

"Because even if I got a place, it's for three months. Unpaid. In *Melbourne*. I'd have to quit my job and try to find somewhere to live in one of the most popular cities in the world. I don't know anyone in Melbourne!"

Patrick regards me, a puzzled look on his face. "You're not even going to try?"

"Why are you pushing this?"

"Because I want you to do something you love and stop working for a woman who makes you miserable!" Patrick shouts.

The irritating sound of Patrick's phone ringing in his pocket cuts through the tension in the air and I throw my hands up in frustration. "How convenient. Eight o'clock on a Saturday night and someone's having an accounting emergency. Better run where I can't hear you and answer that."

A bare-teethed wince breaks Patrick's hard expression as he fishes his phone out. When he glances at his screen, he gives a resentful sigh and slides his thumb across to answer.

"What?" he barks, not taking his eyes off me. I watch as he listens to the person on the other end, his body language morphing from tense to despondent. "Shit. Give me an hour."

Patrick ends his call, his eyes blazing. "I'm sorry. I've got to go. Can we talk about this tomorrow?"

Disappointment floods my chest and so does suspicion; jitters of rage shoot to my jaw. "Yeah sure. Tomorrow, next week. Whenever you've got your next lie figured out, right?"

I register the guilt on Patrick's face before he has time to hide it. "Hazel ..."

"I might not know what's going on, but I *know* you're not doing *consultancy work*," I hiss, making exaggerated quotations marks with my fingers. "My boss paid you cash in an inconspicuous envelope like some drug lord assassin. You don't take phone calls in front of me, you don't tell me *anything* about your job and you know how to punch people into submission. Don't stand there and tell me your late night bail this weekend is to do with *consultancy*."

Patrick's eyes are wide and his jaw tics a little, like it usually does when he's stressed or worked up. I'm gearing myself up for a barrage of fury, but it doesn't come.

Patrick keeps his voice low and steady. "I'm really sorry, but I have to go. Will you pass my apologies to Kali?"

"Are you serious?" White hot rage stirs deep within me. Patrick's closing off, acting like we didn't have the most amazing afternoon together. "Stop deflecting and be honest with me, for once."

"I need you to trust me," Patrick pleads.

"You're making it really difficult."

"Because I have to!" Patrick shouts. I step backwards, alarmed by his outburst.

"Have you ever considered I'm keeping things from you for a *good* reason?" he asks, his voice steady once again. "Or is everything I say and do immediately compared to that asshole who broke your heart?"

My eyes narrow with rage. "You're bringing up *my* ex when yours is still in your wallet?"

Patrick's pupils are so large, they blend into the darkness of his brown eyes, his pulse ticking under his eyebrow. "Stop acting like you're so innocent in all of this."

"What is that supposed to mean? I haven't done anything wrong."

"You're not as much of a victim as you think you are." I swallow down the sudden lump in my throat, but Patrick doesn't relent. "You're so crippled by what some dickhead did to you, you've basically given up on yourself. You've got a golden opportunity to take a risk and submit a killer application for a team of designers in the industry you *want* to work in and you're not even going to try! You walk around like the entire world is against you, like you're the first woman to have ever been betrayed. I hate to break it to you Hazel, but guess what? We've all been heartbroken."

Patrick finishes his tirade panting for breath, his face cracked with pain and angst and fury. His words hit my chest like bullets; pain and shame, rage bubbling under the surface of my skin.

"Do you know what I was thinking earlier tonight?" I ask, my voice shaky. "Things like, I have never felt this happy, *ever*, in my life before. That I couldn't wait to see what happened between the two of us. That after this weekend, we'd figure out whatever we're going to do because what we have is real."

Patrick falters, but I barely register it. Hate is seething out of me; I am on the precipice of launching myself at him. "But I'm delusional, and so are you. You're still in love with your ex and you can't admit it. You're lying to me and won't admit it. And I keep pretending like it's not a problem. Jesus, Patrick, you're a goddamned stranger to me."

As those words leave my lips, I realise how true they are, the weight of them sitting heavily on my shoulders. I know hardly anything about this man who I've let into my bed and my heart. Maybe I fabricated most of what I thought about him. Maybe I was living in the clouds. Maybe the entire time I've been falling for a stranger.

Patrick surveys me with an intensity I've only seen a couple of times on him. Once when he hit the man at the gala ball and earlier this evening, when he tugged the towel away from me. Two completely different scenarios, both giving me goosebumps.

A glimmer ripples across Patrick's face, a realisation. His face hardens, the intensity in his eyes fades to be replaced by coldness. He's flipped a switch.

Patrick's mouth contorts into a grimace. "Well, considering I'm a stranger, it won't be too hard for us to part ways then, will it?"

My stomach plummets as the tears spill out of my eyes, effortlessly streaming down my face. A hiccup escapes my throat, but I'm too upset to be embarrassed. "I guess not."

Patrick marches around the room, snatching up his belongings. I don't watch him. Instead, I turn away and rush out of the French doors into the balmy air, cursing him instead. I curse him for everything. For lying to me, for keeping secrets, for causing me pain, for causing such hatred to radiate from my skin.

I don't even look when I hear his car pull out of the driveway.

31

"IT'S TAKEN me nearly six days to recover, Hazel. *Six.*"

Kali, who has finally recovered from her birthday antics, is whining through the phone in my ear as I walk through the foyer of the Green and Acre building. She definitely felt the effects of her drinking last weekend, announcing every day this week that she is 'too old for this shit'. I didn't even see her before I left for work this morning – she organised for someone to cover her Pilates classes and took today off to lie in bed.

"Do we have jalapeños?" I ask her, pressing the button for the elevator. A couple of police officers are in a corner of the waiting area, speaking to a woman I recognise from Rachel's floor. My inner true crime nut does her best to subtly listen to what they're saying.

"Maybe we should make margaritas tonight," Kali muses, distracting me. "And no, we don't have jalapeños."

"What were you saying about your hangover from hell again?"

Kali has been the sounding board to my crazy this past week. After Patrick drove away, I plastered my fake smile on for Kali's birthday dinner, but she didn't buy it for a second. Like the good friend that she is, she ended dinner early, and us girls ended up having a sleepover in my room. While I cried myself to sleep, Kali stroked my hair, singing *No Scrubs*.

I thought he might call or text. I thought he might show up at home or work to talk. I imagined him telling me he'd acted like a dickhead and me apologising, and the two of us making out until Kali told us to knock it off, but those fantasies stayed as fantasies. I haven't contacted him, and he hasn't contacted me. I can't decide if that's a good or bad thing. I have no idea why he really had to leave Byron Bay, if he's still in love with his ex or how he feels about me. For all I know, he's wrapped things up with Lisa and is back in Sydney already. Lisa's been working from home for the week to oversee renovations at her house, so I haven't even been able to eavesdrop on any of her conversations.

Whatever's happening, I've had to resign myself to the fact that Patrick's got too much shit going on, in the present and his past, to be invested in anything else. He said as much on Saturday night. I said some hurtful things too. If I were him, I wouldn't want to contact me either.

Last Saturday afternoon, I'd been convinced I was developing something real for him, and him for me. Perhaps I was in a bubble of delusion, rather than clarity. I might never figure it out. I don't know whether we're playing a waiting game of who's going to crack first or if it's legitimately over before it began.

When the elevator doors open on the sixteenth floor, my brain can't compute what's playing out in front of me.

"Kali, I'll call you back." Before she can protest, I hang up and step out of the elevator.

People are everywhere.

Men and women in police uniforms are spaced around the foyer, talking to each other, or shuffling through papers. Lisa's office has about six people in it; a woman rifles through the folders at my desk and a man in a suit stands talking to Marketing Marcus, who looks absolutely dumbfounded at whatever he's being told.

My stomach churns, imagining the endless possibilities of what is going on; a data breach, a cold case being re-opened, Lisa being murdered, child extortion at one of our overseas properties. *God, I've got to stop with the true crime stuff.*

To my surprise, George Wilson spots me from across the waiting area and starts towards me. He's flown in from Sydney to witness whatever mess this is, which means it must be really bad.

"Hazel, I'm glad you're here," he says, pulling me to the side.

"What's going on?"

"The police have a warrant to search the place," he explains, and closes his eyes to take a breath before continuing. "They're throwing around words like *fraud* and *money laundering*." He whispers the last two words and then exhales, sounding tired.

I think my eyebrows almost fly off my forehead. "What?"

"I can't believe it either," he says, shaking his head. "The police said Lisa's been using her position to siphon money out of the company. She's been making private deals with overseas associates, costing things to be much higher than they are and taking a cut. For God's sake."

"Where is she?" I whisper, watching as people cart books and electronics out of Lisa's office. She hasn't been in all week and I realise 'overseeing renovations' was probably a complete lie. She never asked for my help with it, and that should've been a dead giveaway.

"Not sure," he sighs. "They think she was tipped off that she was under investigation because they can't find her. I can't believe I had a criminal right under my nose, and I didn't see it."

He's blaming himself? I'm her assistant and I never saw anything out of the ordinary. Yes, she's tough, sometimes cut-throat in her business dealings. She doesn't take shit from anyone. She could be considered mean on occasion. But fraud? Stealing money from the company she climbed to the top of in a matter of years? I would never have thought she'd be capable of that.

"Based on what that bloke said to me, it sounds like she was way ahead of them," George continues. "Her house has been cleared out and her car's nowhere to be found. She even dropped her dog off with a friend. The only thing they've found is a heap of cash in her office. Pretty sure he wasn't meant to tell me any of that, but I think he likes to chat."

Patrick.

The cash in the envelope. Did he know Lisa was involved in illegal activity? Are they in on this together?

Queasiness bubbles in the pit of my stomach. My mind is racing almost too fast for me to keep up with it.

No. It's not possible. *Calm down.*

I can't calm down. My anxiety and mind are getting away from me again and I don't think I'm being dramatic for once.

"Hazel, it'll be alright," George says sympathetically, tapping his hand on my arm. He's mistaken the look of panic on my face for concern about my boss, and that couldn't be further from the truth.

My mind is racing with so many scenarios when a police officer approaches us.

"Mr Wilson, we're nearly finished here," the man says to him. "We will need a list of all the people who worked with Ms Fox. We may have some questions."

I swallow. I'm her assistant. There's no way I'm getting out of that. I have nothing to hide, and yet the thought of speaking with police makes me sick.

"Of course, of course." George nods, concerned. "I'll ask Judith to get them for you. Anything else? Excuse me, Hazel."

George and the man step away from me and I sink down into

one of the lounge chairs, watching the curious faces of employees hovering in the foyer.

A few minutes later George returns and dismisses everybody on the sixteenth floor for the remainder of the day. He advises that some of us may be contacted by police if they need to ask questions and once again, I'm dizzy with nausea.

32

I DIAL Patrick's number before I even open my car door. Instead of ringing, it goes straight to voicemail. I curse loudly.

It's likely Patrick knew Lisa was up to something sneaky. He might even know where she is or where she's going. As much as it pains me to think it, there is also a possibility he's directly involved. The phone calls and conversations, his vague warnings about his work being complicated, the cash in the envelope and walking me out to the street, away from the eyes of witnesses or security cameras ... every interaction with him is now screaming at me.

Stop jumping to conclusions. Jumping to conclusions can end in disaster. I've watched enough crime documentaries to know that to be true enough. Get the facts first. Don't think about how people go to jail for fraud and money laundering for longer than most rapists and murderers. *Don't think about it.*

Okay, first, I need to get a hold of him. He's not answering his phone and he doesn't have social media. I never went to where he was staying ... I just know it's a something of a bachelor's pad with an ugly purple wall out the front. There's a passcode to the front gate. *What was it again? Blue balls? Ball sack! Am I crazy if I drive up and down the streets until I find the house?*

I dial Kali's number and she answers almost after half a ring. "Bitch, you hung up on me before."

"Shut up and get dressed," I order. "I'm coming to pick you up."

"Are you sure this is the house?"

"I'm not sure of anything."

Ten minutes of slowly driving up and down the streets of beach houses like mad women, Kali and I eventually find a house which matches Patrick's vague description. If this is the correct house, Patrick was right about the ugly purple wall. The towering house behind it looks modern, with a fresh coat of paint and white shutters covering the windows. The owners never got around to modernising the monstrosity out the front.

I park the car a little further up the street and Kali and I get out, closing the doors with quiet thuds. Every instinct tells me we shouldn't be here and should get straight back in the car and not get involved.

"Are you sure you want to do this, Hazy?" she asks. I know I have Kali's support, but she's worried about me. This isn't something straighty-one-eighty, rule-following Hazel would do.

"Come on. Let's do this before I change my mind."

My hand trembles as I punch the code into the keypad. Kali looks conspicuous as all hell as she whips her head back and forth, hopping up and down next to me. I hold my breath. The screen flashes green and the handle clicks, signalling it's unlocked.

"Oh, shit, it is *on*," Kali mutters as I push the gate open. We walk at a snail's pace to the front door, our unsteady breathing uncomfortably loud. I stand for about five seconds, unsure whether I should even be here, before reaching up and turning the handle.

The door opens.

The foyer is large and bright. It's all white walls and white-tiled floors, and staircases on either side of the entry meet on the second floor. Dubious pieces of art hang on the walls; splashes of colour, a warped bird hanging upside down. There's a golden vase perched on a pedestal on one side of a large hallway, which leads to the back of the house.

I hold my breath, listening for footfalls as the door creaks open. I don't hear anything, but as I step over the threshold, my stomach plummets, and Kali lets out a yelp.

I'm frozen stiff, my heartbeat hammering beneath my ribs. A tall, shirtless man built with lean muscle steps out in front of us. His sinewy frame is made more intimidating by the amount of inked flesh on display. Tattoos cover his entire top half, snaking up his neck and decorating his arms. His hands are absentmindedly playing with a fluoro pink string, reminding me of those elastics kids played with at school.

He gives us a cocky, lopsided grin filled with straight, white teeth. Dimples crease in both his cheeks, his crystal blue eyes twinkling with mischief. "By all means, come on in, ladies."

Kali straightens beside me, his casual demeanour lessening the sense of danger. I don't miss the half smile from my best friend or the way she takes in his ink.

"Is Patrick here?" I ask.

"Yeah, but I don't think now's a good time," he replies, stretching an arm to scratch the back of his shaved head. "We're kind of in the middle of something."

"Would it have anything to do with the police officers raiding my boss's office by any chance?" I quip.

The man straightens and steps closer. My breath hitches as the pleasant faint mixture of tobacco and aftershave hits my nostrils. "Not just a pretty face, hey Jonesy?"

I peer up at him. "Anthony?"

He grins even wider. "I did wonder if Patty ever mentioned his dropkick younger brother." Anthony's gaze settles on Kali, fleetingly scanning her from toe to head. "You must be Kali."

Kali's hands are on her hips. "Let's cut the bullshit, Anthony. Where is he?"

Anthony chuckles, twirling the string once again. "I've gotta say, you've both exceeded my expectations. Pretty ballsy, breaking and entering into someone's home."

"Oh, *please*. Your door was unlocked for starters," Kali scoffs, unimpressed and Anthony's wicked grin returns.

"Are you going to tell Patrick I'm here or not?" My voice nearly gives away the sound of fear, but I do my best to hold my ground. "Or do I need to call Mrs Healey to remind you of your manners?" The man's gaze wanders across my face and he grins again.

"I like you, Jonesy," he murmurs, stepping back. He surveys me, his smirk never disappearing. "If Patty asks, you forced your way in." He steps to the side and gestures for us to continue down the main hallway, where I can see the reflection of a pool flickering outside, a lush green lawn surrounding it. As I get closer, passing through an enormous kitchen, I spot Patrick outside.

He's not in a suit. He's in a loose, white button-up shirt that ripples slightly in the breeze, chinos cling to the muscles in his legs, and he's barefoot. He paces the grass, talking to someone on the phone as usual.

He must sense my presence because he whips his head up. He ends his call as he strides towards me, almost tearing the door open as he comes inside.

"Hazel, what are you doing here?" He demands, closing the distance between us.

Black circles encase his eyes and his five o'clock shadow has developed into something thicker. I'm distracted by the smell of his cologne and the widening of his eyes, almost as if he's relieved to see me. His hand hovers as if he's going to touch me, but he doesn't.

He glowers over my shoulder. "Kali? Anthony, I don't want them involved in this."

"Looks like you're not going to have much of a choice."

33

HAVE you ever had a moment that completely blindsides you?

I'm talking a knock the wind out of your chest, dump a torrent of dread over your head type of moment. A moment that is so profound and unnerving that you wonder if you're dreaming? Because that's how I feel right now.

I can't tear my eyes away from the sight in front of me.

Blood is rushing in my ears.

My palms are sweaty.

My breathing is becoming erratic; panic starts to settle in.

"Hazel ..." I hear his soft voice, but I don't respond.

"Hazel," he repeats.

"Is this part of your consultancy work?" I ask the question even though I'm not sure I want to hear the answer.

"Yes."

My heart sinks.

The sight lining the far wall is like something out of an occult drug-dealer movie. Piles upon piles of clear packages filled with colourful paper; packages from floor to ceiling, filled with money. Bags and bags of money.

"Holy shit," Kali whispers nearby.

Patrick edges closer and I reactively take a backward step, finally making eye contact with him again and registering the momentary flicker of pain on his face.

"I can explain all of this." It's almost as if he's terrified that I might explode, his large hands out in front of him as if trying to calm down a wild animal.

"Oh, I'm sure you can," I scoff, hearing the panic in my voice.

Where has this money come from? Has he stolen it? Is it drug money? Oh my god, all the jokes Kali and I made about him being in the mafia are true and I'm going to be murdered in this room.

"Do you ... are you ..." I struggle to find the words, looking back at the sight in front of me. "Do you work as a consultant for Lisa or not?"

"Technically, yes."

"Why doesn't that sound like an actual yes?"

He exhales deeply through his nose and casts another dark look over my shoulder. "Anthony, I am going to kill you."

Anthony swaggers up next to us, pulling a white t-shirt over his head. "They let themselves in!"

"Because you left the door unlocked," Patrick snaps.

"I didn't leave it unlocked."

"You were the last one in!"

Anthony smiles as he claps Patrick on the back, almost as if the tensest moment of my life isn't taking place right this second. "The boys are raiding her office. She already knows half of it."

There's a pause that feels like five hours long while Patrick and Anthony exchange silent words. When Patrick looks at me, his face softens. He pulls something out of his pocket and hands it over to me. It's an identification badge, with Patrick's photo and the name *Patrizio Bonetti* next to it.

"Wait ..." I stare at his photo, scanning the details on the card. My brain can't catch up to what's happening quick enough. "I don't understand."

Patrick's shoulders sag as he lets out a loud, drawn-out sigh. "I was a police officer for fourteen years, until three years ago. When I left, I went into accounting, specialising in property development."

From the armchair in the corner, Anthony elicits a snoring sound. "Could you imagine a more boring career move?"

Patrick rolls his eyes. "I'm good at it."

Kali lets out a whistle, gawking up at the bags of cash which almost reach the ceiling. "So, what, you've been robbing your clients and keeping the cash here?"

"My old captain contacted me nine months ago and asked if I'd be willing to help in a money laundering case they were having trouble nailing down," he explains, his gaze not leaving mine. "They needed someone to get close to their main suspect without arousing suspicion and offer services as someone who could get rid of dirty money. Given my expertise in police work and accounting, I was the best man for the job."

A few beats hang between us as I try to get my head around those words. I've watched enough crime documentaries in my time to know what he's getting at. Patrick's been playing the part of someone people call when they've gotten their hands on money by siphoning it, stealing it, or stumbling across it.

"Lisa's been stealing money from Green and Acre for years," Patrick continues. "Scoping out locations for stores, over-charging buyers and underpaying the organisation. She's in charge of an entire department and no one was any the wiser."

"Until she got greedy," Anthony pipes up.

Patrick gives me a grim smile. "Recently, she started taking cash bribes and payments from ... some unsavoury investors," he explains, nodding at the wall. "This money here is just some of the cash Lisa thinks I've been flushing for her."

The four of us turn to look at the wall of money again and

I'm unable to decide whether my boss is cleverer than I gave her credit for, or undeniably stupid.

My hands grip the identification badge in my hands, hot flushes dumping over my head in quick succession. Patrick's been working undercover in a huge operation to catch *my* boss, who's been stealing from the company I work for, and I had zero idea.

"We were days from making an arrest, but she got spooked." Anthony shakes his head, twirling the laces in his hand, creating a shape I recognise as a cat's cradle. "That's why Patty had to leave Byron last weekend. That wasn't a fun phone call to make. You were *pissed.*"

Patrick side-eyes me and I wonder if he's re-living our argument last weekend like I am right now.

I hold out his I.D card. "Is Bonetti your real surname?"

Patrick swallows loudly as he takes it from me. "Yes."

"But everyone knows you as Patrick Healey."

Patrick shrugs. "Most people don't even know who I am. They've heard of me through other people, or they've seen me around. People only really know me as Patrick. I was the silent founder and benefactor before all this.

"When I agreed to help my captain, he had some tech guys do some work in case people liked Lisa looked me up. They added Patrick Healey to my charity website and to a few images online. It didn't take much."

"Jesus," I mutter, bending over to put my hands on my knees.

Patrick moves hastily, his hand on my back as he bends down to my eye-height. "Can I get you something? Some water maybe?"

I shake my head, stepping back from him. "No. I don't want any *water.*"

Patrick nods in understanding, watching me carefully.

"What's your role in this?" Kali demands, glaring down at Anthony.

"Patty's right-hand man," Anthony replies.

"So, you're a cop?"

Anthony grins and winks. "That depends. Do you like cops?"

"He's not a cop. They'd never let him in with that shit all over his arms." Patrick nods at swirls of ink splayed on his brother's body and Anthony rolls his eyes. "Anthony's been assisting with some things on the case at my request."

"So, mainly an errand boy?" Kali asks, and Anthony's lips curl upwards, appreciating her jab.

My gaze falls back to Patrick, who's watching me. My body can't seem to decide which emotion to channel first, my mind can't seem to decide which question to ask next. Kali, on the other hand, can sense my paralysis, so she keeps the questions coming.

"How did you even get Lisa to trust you?" Kali asks Patrick. "You walked into her office and said 'Hey, I'm a crook too. Wanna hire me for my money laundering skills?'"

He peels his gaze away from me. "I've been friends with the CEO of Green and Acre for years, so I already had a way in."

George Wilson. Who he's known for *years*. He must know Healey isn't Patrick's surname then. Are Kali and I the only people who didn't know?

"Lisa attends my charity gala every year, so it didn't raise suspicion when I contacted her. We went to dinner. I told her I was schmoozing up a heap of the executives for extra donations and then steered the conversation towards her success. She's a smart lady, but she also likes to talk. It didn't take long for me to hint at what I could do to assist with her finances, and that was it."

The way he delivers his explanation so matter-of-factly is jarring. He's not boasting, nor is he ashamed. He's telling us how it is, what I've wanted from him the minute we met.

"So, you knew I worked for Lisa when you found me in the alleyway?" I ask.

Patrick hesitates, as if he's choosing his words carefully. "Not at first, but once you told me your name, it didn't take long to make the connection. You were flagged in our files."

It's a gross violation. He knew who I was the entire time. He knew I was the assistant of the woman he was investigating.

"Running into you was a complete coincidence," Patrick says sharply, as if he can read my mind. "Meeting you, taking you to the hospital ... you weren't part of any plan Hazel, I swear it."

"What about when I gave you the envelope that day? That wasn't part of some plan?"

His shoulders hunch. "That was at Lisa's insistence. I met you outside the office because it wouldn't have been safe for you to carry that much money on you, alone. I didn't want you to be caught on camera involved in it either, so I steered you across the street."

It's another blow to my ego. I'd been so busy falling over this man, and he was always working. Always on alert. Always *on*.

"So, you never used me to do a little extra digging? Not once?" I ask, bitterly.

Patrick clenches his jaw. "*Once*. After you fell asleep that first night, when you had your concussion? I looked through your laptop to try and get an idea of how much Lisa shared with you. But that was it."

I blink several times as I process what he's saying, mortification settling in. "You snooped through my things to see what my relationship with my boss was like?"

"I wanted to make sure she hadn't tangled you up in her mess," Patrick insists. "I was on auto-pilot. I didn't even know you then like ... like I know you now."

However true that may be, seeing our first meeting from his point of view makes me sick. He was annoyed with me and probably wanted to leave, but he stuck it out so he could hopefully get access to some more personal information about Lisa he couldn't get anywhere else. While I was busy fawning over the mysterious man in the suit, he was busy thinking about catching a criminal and making headway at work.

Tears blur my vision and I duck my head, embarrassed.

Patrick keeps talking. "I didn't think agreeing to meet Lisa at the office that day would matter, because I thought you'd take a day off for your concussion." I sense Patrick standing close to me, his voice low and gentle. "But knowing what I know now, of course you'd be as stubborn as a mule and show up to work. I swear I didn't think you'd be there. I was never meant to see you again."

I furiously wipe my eyes, glaring at Patrick. He doesn't waver or put up a wall or cower away. He stands before me, everything out on the table, waiting for my response. And I can't think of a single word to say.

"I think it's safe to say this is the first time in my life where I am also speechless," Kali chimes in, giving me a sympathetic head tilt.

Anthony smiles at her from his chair. "Lisa being investigated means the people around her will come under scrutiny. Jonesy, you'll be interviewed by police officers to find out what you know."

"I don't know *anything!*" I snap at him.

"Well, you know about Detective Dreamy Eyes here," Anthony replies, waving a hand towards his brother. "Not sure what the rules are on police sleeping with people close to investigations. Could be a slight conflict of interest."

"Anthony, enough."

Rubbing my forehead from the sudden headache pounding behind my eye, I exhale deliberately to try to focus.

My boss has been ripping people off and is on the run. The guy I *was* seeing was pretending to help her get rid of evidence, whilst being undercover and working for the police the whole time. He's a suave *detective*, playing the part of a sleuthing businessman. And then there's me. The idiot woman who, despite the warning signs, fell for his act too.

"Could you please give us a minute?" Patrick asks, turning to Anthony and Kali.

Anthony's mouth twists as if he's going to say something, but he pushes himself out of the armchair. Kali hovers, eyeing me with concern, before I give her a nod to signal it's okay. Anthony waves his arm to usher Kali ahead of him, and the two of them disappear down the hall.

"I'm sorry," Patrick croaks, catching me by surprise. His usually strong and fierce expression has been replaced by regret. "I'm sorry for putting you in this position."

"That's it?" I ask, after he doesn't add anything else. "That's all you have to say to me?"

"Don't listen to what Anthony said. Answer the detectives honestly, even about me. My captain knows we were spending time together and he can spot a liar a mile away. None of it will fall back on you, I promise."

"Is that what you think I'm worried about? About me getting caught up in something?"

Patrick frowns. "What are you worried about?" He looks genuinely puzzled and it takes me a few seconds to gather my thoughts.

Is this really one-sided? Am I really the only one who's upset about our relationship evaporating in front of our eyes? Did he even want to spend time with me, or was it a convenient pastime? Staring up at Patrick's face doesn't give me any of the answers to the questions I didn't want to have to ask.

"The whole way we met was a lie," I whisper. Patrick's face falters. "*Everything* was a lie, and the lying came so easily to you."

Patrick is silent, listening.

"Was any of it real?"

Patrick's mouth opens and closes several times before he stills it. The vein in his forehead pulsates, and any concern for me leaves his face in seconds. Patrick's eyes are cold and empty, and I brace myself for what's to come.

"I'm a very good liar, Hazel."

My body recoils as he says the words, and I take a couple of steps backward. "I don't believe you." I'm not sure if I even say the words loud enough for him to hear at first, because he doesn't look at me. He's staring long and hard at something outside, lost in thought.

But then, he speaks. "I never meant to hurt you. I'm sorry it's come out like this."

An audible gasp escapes my lips as the sensation of being kicked in the gut slams into me like a freight train. I've felt this before. When I caught Luke in the shower and when I saw the engagement ring on his fiancée's finger. It's a sucker punch to the entire body. Patrick is breaking my heart.

"You should go." Patrick's words are not a request. His gaze remains fixated over my shoulder to the view outside. He's checked out of this conversation, no longer interested in saying anything else.

"Right." My voice sounds hoarse and it's not until I taste salt on my lips, I realise I'm crying. Patrick's eyes flash with something as he looks at me, but he doesn't say anything.

And neither do I. Just like that, I'm rendered speechless again. Patrick is shutting me down without even having to say five words. He wants me out of here and out of his life.

Somehow, I find the ability to walk away. *One foot in front of the other*, all the way to the front door. As the door clicks open, movement to my right catches my attention and I look to see a blurry Anthony and Kali lingering near the staircase. I wonder, in my dazed state, if they heard our conversation.

As I open the heavy door, Kali curls her arm around my shoulders and steers me outside silently, right as the tears burst from my eyes like an overflowing dam.

34

"I CAN'T BELIEVE he was kind of like a mafia assassin this whole time."

"Christ. Me neither."

It's nearly nine o'clock and Kali and I are curled up on the couch facing each other. I've lost count of how many wines I've had. They did the job of making me feel numb, which I was going for.

Almost twelve hours ago, Kali drove us away from the purple house with me in a dazed stupor for the trip home. Kali barely said a word to me, but concern radiated from her body the entire journey.

"How did I not see it, Kali?"

"We're officially the worst true crime lovers ever." Kali smiles and squeezes my foot affectionately. "What are you going to do?"

I shrug. "What can I do? My relationship with Patrick was a lie, I'm pretty sure I don't have a job because my boss is a fraudulent criminal mastermind and I'm not getting any younger."

I've spent the past few hours reliving the conversation with

Patrick over and over. He dumped these revelations and then cut me off. Now his job is done. My heart literally feels heavy.

"I wish he said he cared about me or missed me or that what we had wasn't complete bullshit," I confess. "Does that make me pathetic?"

"Pathetic? You?" Kali asks. "Hazel Jones, you blew me away today. You took complete control of the situation. You scoped out the house, you led *me* up the path of danger. You are definitely *not* pathetic."

I snicker. "It felt good to take control."

Kali gives me a thoughtful smile. "Taking risks can be a *good* thing."

I eye her suspiciously. "What's your point?"

"You've got to start taking some chances, Hazy," Kali says. "Like the internship. What is the worst thing that could happen? So, what if it goes to shit and nothing comes of it? At least you would've *tried*. At least you'll know. You can try again. Go bigger. You never used to care, until ..."

"Until?"

"Until you did."

The intimacy of our conversation weighs on me unexpectedly, and I realise how much of a constant Kali is in my life. We live together, in every sense of the word. We argue and we laugh. Kali consistently lifts me up and all I do is drain her light with my problems.

"Thank you, for everything you've done for me," I whisper, and before I know it, I'm crying. *Again*.

Kali's eyebrows fly to her hairline with surprise, a half-smile on her face as she shuffles across the couch towards me. "I didn't mean to upset you, you big baby. Come here." Kali wraps her arm around my shoulders and kisses the top of my head before resting her cheek on it. "Why are you so upset?"

"Because I'm a fucking vampire who's done nothing but suck the life out of the people around me lately." Sobs break from me in embarrassing bursts. "I haven't even been a friend to you. I'm sorry I'm so shit."

"Shut up, you loser." I can hear the smile in Kali's voice as she gives me a squeeze. Proving she really is the best friend in the world, she holds me for however long it takes me to stop crying, which is an embarrassingly long time.

When my tears finally stop and my nose has a mortifying amount of snot rattling around in it, Kali releases me, a stern look on her face. "You have not sucked the life out of me, but I want you to promise you're going to start doing things for you again."

I wipe away the hair stuck to my face and nod.

"Also, as someone who enjoys many a fling, I can say with confidence Patrick didn't see you as a piece of ass to occupy his time with while he was working your boss. Guys purely interested in sex don't volunteer to go away with your friends for the weekend. Or drive you over an hour home at midnight and literally say goodnight to you without trying to get into your pants. Guys like that don't let their walls down and get upset when you get into arguments. He bought you a three-hundred-dollar notebook for God's sake."

"It's a handmade—"

"He fell for you, Hazy," Kali interjects. "I could see it in the way he looked at you. He lied to you because he had to. He didn't tell you any of it because he wanted to protect you. And now? He's cut you off because he thinks you're better off without him."

I hear what Kali's saying, but I'm afraid of allowing myself to hope what she's saying is true. "You really believe all that?"

A sharp rap on the front door stops her from answering. The two of us freeze, my entire body locking up as Kali's eyes widen at me, silently mouthing, "Who's that?"

"I don't know!" I mouth back. The knock sounds again and I bolt upright, putting my glass down on the table carefully. Is it

Patrick? Is it the police? Oh God, I'm not ready to face anybody tonight. I haven't figured out where my head is at.

Instantly sober with uncertainty, I tiptoe to the front door with Kali gripping my arm, the two of us holding our breath. Kali pulls me away from the door slightly as she reaches for an umbrella leaning against the wall in the corner.

"Hazel Jones, you left your dildo at my place *again!*" Even though that voice shouldn't bring us any sort of calm, we instantly relax.

When I swing the door open, Anthony's grinning face greets us both. He's playing with the string in his hands again. A dark shirt clings to the ridges of his torso, black pants accentuate his thighs. If I had to take a guess, I'd say he'd borrowed some of his brother's clothes.

"Do you think your neighbours bought that or nah?" he asks, stepping up to lean against the doorframe. He nods to Kali, biting his bottom lip suggestively. "It's a pleasure to see you again, Kali."

If his bad boy image hadn't already won her over, the dildo comment certainly did.

"What are you doing here?" I can't help but look at the road behind him, the image of a Mafia drug lord lingering near a car popping into my mind.

"I need a word; you got a sec?" he asks me. "Maybe after *we're* done talking, Kali, you and I could..."

"In your dreams." Kali smirks at him and backs away from us.

Anthony grins as he watches her saunter away and I shove him in the ribs, earning a groan. "Don't even."

He chuckles and juts his chin outside, signalling me to step outside with him.

"Did Patrick send you here?" I ask, closing the door behind me.

"Nah. Patty's back in Sydney. I'm on a flight out tomorrow.

Gotta tie up some loose ends here first." Disappointment expands from my chest through to my legs. The hope I didn't realise I was holding onto fizzles away right in front of me.

"Right," I finally say, sinking down onto the porch steps. "I guess neither of you have any reasons to stay any longer."

Anthony sits down next to me, titling his head back to look up at the night sky. "Oh, Jonesy. Please don't tell me you're as naïve as my brother."

"What is that supposed to mean?"

"Even if I wasn't Patrick's brother, I *am* a dude. He didn't break very strict work protocols for a quick shag. I bet my right nut he's into you."

"Well, he's excellent at playing a part. Maybe he's fooled you too."

Anthony shakes his head and closes his eyes with a smile, his head still angled towards the night sky. "Did Patty ever tell you I'm an addict?"

That's not what I expected to hear. "What?"

Anthony opens his eyes and gives me another one of his cheeky grins before straightening his left arm. The tattoos do a good job of covering up the scars, but I can make out the presence of a dozen or so marks in the crease of his elbow. "Just passed my three-year anniversary. Thanks to Patty."

"He never mentioned it," I say quietly, and Anthony retracts his arm.

"He didn't tell you about Chloe either, did he?"

I shake my head and Anthony nods, as if he suspected that already. He lets out a dramatic, long-winded exhale before starting his story.

"When I was at the peak of my addiction, I made some really stupid decisions. I worked as a courier and one day, my boss gave me a bonus stash. I didn't hesitate and took it straight home to stick in my arm."

The casual way he speaks is almost alarming, and yet I can

tell he's not proud of his actions. His shoulders lock up, his gaze drops to the in his hands as he fidgets. I suspect it's something he uses to keep his hands busy.

"Chloe lived with me and Patty at the time," he explains. "They'd been dating for a while and their relationship was ... heated. Chloe was an amazing woman, but she struggled with her own demons and somehow, we ended up getting high together in the living room."

I swallow down the fear thickening my throat. Anthony doesn't make me feel unsafe, quite the opposite, but the way in which he's explaining the horrific stories from his past scares me. It makes me wonder what else happened.

"I didn't know what had happened until I woke up in the hospital," Anthony mutters, tightening the string in his hands.

"She overdosed?" I ask softly.

Anthony scoffs and shakes his head. "You'd think so, wouldn't you? Turns out, the universe was in a spiteful mood that day. A car veered off the road and drove through the front window of our house. Somehow, it missed me and slammed into Chloe."

A sharp gasp escapes my lips, my eyes watering as I listen to Anthony's words. "Her injuries were critical. Her folks had to turn off her life support a few days later."

My hands tremble. "Anthony, I'm so sorry."

Anthony clears his throat, the emotion evident on his face. "If I hadn't been off my face, I could've done something. If I hadn't been such a prick and suggested we get high in the first place, she wouldn't have been sitting there or would've at least been sober enough to get out of the way."

Instinctively, I place a hand on Anthony's arm, and he stares at it, almost as if he hasn't been touched affectionately by anyone in some time. "That car coming through the window wasn't your fault. You can't blame yourself for what happened to Chloe."

Anthony nods, as if it's the millionth time someone has said that to him, but he doesn't believe it. "Her dad sure blamed me. Came after me one day with a kitchen knife. Patty saved my ass again. That's how he got the scar on his cheek."

So much of what Anthony is saying is clicking into place. It explains Patrick's initial reservations with me and lack of information-sharing. No wonder he shut down when I asked him about his scar.

"Patty was a mess after that," Anthony continues. "Different. Angry. Wracked with guilt. He quit his job as a detective and said every time he was at the precinct, he'd think about how he'd been there instead of at home with Chloe. He kept saying things like anyone who allowed their loved ones to get hurt shouldn't be allowed to be a cop. It didn't make any sense, but he couldn't cope with the grief."

Anthony's veiny hands gripped his string tightly, and his eyes flicker with his thoughts. "She was my friend and all I wanted to do was use after she died, but Patty wouldn't have a bar of that shit. He never once blamed me, but told me if I didn't get clean, he'd dob me in to the cops himself."

Anthony grins to himself and looks up at the night sky. "I went to rehab; I still have therapy and I battle my addiction every single day, but Patty is the reason I'm still alive and have a life worth living."

He nudges me playfully with his shoulder. "Patrick got permission for me to assist on this case as a civilian and if all goes well, his captain is writing me a character reference. It's not easy getting a job when you're an ex-convict, but a police captain's good word has surely got to help."

We sit in silence while I ponder this new information. Patrick shielded me from so many truths, but hearing the details from Anthony, I don't think any of them were purposefully deceitful. Telling me what he was doing could have jeopardised his investigation or ruined Anthony's career prospects. I constantly whined about Luke cheating on me and having a shitty boss, and he'd been to hell and back with the death of his ex-girlfriend, quitting his career and helping his brother stay sober. He's a goddamn superhero.

"I'm an asshole," I sigh. "No wonder he doesn't want anything to do with me."

Anthony tuts under his breath. "You're *not* an asshole. Patty kept everything from you because he's a bloody martyr and thinks it's easier for him to be alone and miserable forever. He pushed you away because he's scared of losing you, like he lost Chloe."

"But he said—"

"I know what he said." Anthony gives me a knowing glance. "He's a very good liar, remember?"

"Oh."

"The bloke has not stopped talking about you. I reckon you're too good for him. You're way too hot for him for starters."

My face heats and Anthony rises to his feet, stepping down onto the garden path. "Life isn't a fairy-tale Jonesy," he says, backing away from me. "Trust me. Sometimes good people do bad things, such as lie for the greater good."

"Speaking from experience?"

Anthony grins again. "Promise me you won't write my brother off just yet. Promise me you'll think on it. You owe me one."

"How in the hell do I owe you one?"

"Who do you think cleaned the vomit off the floor of the Merc?" Anthony gives me a wink and I stand up to walk back inside.

"Good night, Anthony."

I head back inside hearing Anthony's howl of laughter behind me.

Have you ever had a moment that completely blindsides you?

This time, I'm not talking about a knock the wind out of your chest, dump a torrent of dread over your head type of moment. I'm talking about the type that feels like a slap in the face. Like the universe has grabbed you by both shoulders, shaken you violently and screamed *wake the fuck up* right in your face, because that's my current situation.

I can't sleep from all the thinking and tossing and turning. Despite how conflicted I might feel about what's unfolded, it's made me realise the people in my life have been living their own lives without apology and my mind won't shut the hell up about it.

Patrick is selfless, driven and working to better himself and his future, despite his painful past.

Anthony, who has obviously been through a lot of shit in his life, takes things as they come.

Lisa. *Oh, Lisa.* I can't say I'd want to be in her shoes right now, but I can't deny I admire her balls either.

Kali's always done what she's wanted and fearlessly so. She doesn't hurt others in the process either. Well, her words sometimes cut people down, but she's got a heart of gold and is living her passion as a Pilates instructor.

Everyone does their own thing, and what have I been doing?

I've been stuck in a job I don't like.

I've been *wishing* I could use my skills doing something I love, instead of *doing* something about it.

I've been pining over men, putting my life on hold, and having it fall apart the minute they choose themselves over me.

I've been crying. I've been whinging and groaning.

I've been staying the same.

I whip my covers off and march across the room to my desk, plopping down in the high-backed chair. I open the leather-bound book in front of me and run my hands over the smooth surface of the blank page. Gripping a pencil, I let my hand flow across page after page, shapes and scribbles coming into formation in front of me. Patrick and Luke. Moments when I felt extraordinarily high and terribly low. I draw characters that have floated around in my head for years, and some of which are brand new. I envision what my life could look like if I were to move to Melbourne. I draw myself sitting at a graphic design table in the warm offices of Bookish Publishing House.

I draw until my hand cramps and my eyes droop.

I draw until I've got moments of good, bad, and ugly scribbled down on reams and reams of paper. It's then, I realise Patrick was right.

I'm not as much of a victim as I've told myself.

35

TWO MONTHS LATER

"SHOULDN'T you have left by now, boss?"

I look up from my computer to see Rachel's sea of vibrant red hair glistening under the office lights, a smile on her face.

"Stop calling me that," I order, furiously tapping at my keyboard.

"Why? Everyone else does."

"No, *Ella* does," I argue, referring to Green and Acre's newest employee. "And I can't exactly tell her not to when she's the actual boss's favourite niece. You should know better."

"But it's so much fun when you scowl and that frown line appears between your eyes," Rachel says mockingly, gliding into the room and sitting down in the chair across from me.

"You used to be nice to me."

Rachel laughs. "You know I'm teasing. After today, no one will call you, boss."

I exhale a shaky breath, halting my hands on the keyboard. "That's right."

"That's a good thing," Rachel reminds me.

I smile. "Thank you."

Rachel has become something of a confidante of mine while I transitioned into my new role. After the Lisa fiasco, things changed at the Gold Coast hub, starting when George Wilson offered me a temporary role in the marketing and PR team to assist with damage control. Given my role as executive assistant was no longer needed, I felt enormously grateful to him for making space for me elsewhere. The fact it was in the team I'd wanted to get into for years was almost too good to be true.

The shitstorm Lisa left in her wake meant life was chaotic at the office for several weeks. I was interviewed by police for several hours, but thankfully, there was no mention of Patrick or our relationship. At least not to me. They mostly wanted to know if I had seen anything unusual in Lisa's behaviour, what additional intel I had on our big accounts, and how her assistant of five years didn't know what she was up to. Whilst I'm pretty sure they were dumbfounded I didn't know anything, they seemed happy with everything I shared with them.

After my police ordeal was over, there was still the rest of the shitstorm to deal with. Media hovered outside the office building day and night for weeks on end, we worked ridiculously long hours and we had to quickly learn how to get along as a team in our new state of normal.

George hung around for a little while after it happened, overseeing the fallout with a hands-on method. Despite the seriousness of the situation, George did a good job of keeping everyone's spirits up with his grandad like sense of concern. He kept us fed and watered when we worked late and never shied away from dropping a cheeky comment or two about how messed up the situation was, commenting multiple times, 'I'm too old for this shit'. He also employed his niece Ella to run around as an extra admin person.

Rachel visited the floor regularly for updates, or to tell me what she'd heard thanks to her stalking/gossiping skills. She'd often bring coffee or a baked good from the café for George, so he never asked her to get back to her own job. Ever since he returned to Sydney, Rachel's continued to visit our floor, distracting most of the males and Ella, who has taken a particular shine to her.

"Seriously, shouldn't you be in a car on the way to the airport by now?" Rachel asks. A groan escapes my lips as I send off my final email.

"Yes, I should've left twenty minutes ago," I reply, standing to gather my things. "I've never left late for the airport in my life."

"Who have you become?" Rachel mocks, as Ella pokes her head around the door.

"Your car is still waiting downstairs, boss," she announces. It takes every ounce of strength to not roll my eyes at her use of the word.

"Thank you, Ella. I'm coming now." She nods and scurries away and I flip my middle finger at Rachel, who has begun to silently laugh.

"Don't you have a job to get back to?" I ask, collecting my handbag.

"Yes, I'm going." Rachel stands and surprises me by pulling me in for a hug. "Good luck in Melbourne. I am so excited for you."

"I'll be back at the end of April," I dismiss, to which Rachel squeezes me tighter.

"You're going to kill it boss," she whispers and steps back before I can take a swipe at her.

"The next time you get sent on a trip, all expenses paid, maybe ask if you can take a friend with you?"

"Kali, it's a trip to Melbourne," I reply. "Not a world cruise with business class tickets."

"I don't care! You're being chauffeured, put up in a fancy hotel for three nights and you're going through a huge life moment *by yourself.*"

"And come Monday, I'll be living in a tiny apartment, forced to catch public transport and officially be an intern, where I'll be forced to make coffees like a noob. Let's remember that, shall we?" I step forwards in the line at the airport, watching my screen as Kali sets up her phone in her empty Pilates room. She insisted on a FaceTime call *one last time,* as if we were never going to see each other in the flesh again.

"I know you're downplaying this because you're nervous, but you're going out there and living your dream," Kali says. "Huge life moment shit."

She's right about my nerves. Ever since Jess from Bookish Publishing offered me a position as an intern before Christmas, I've been a barrel of jittery energy. When I told George I had to quit because of this opportunity, he got so excited for me I thought he might have a stroke. To my complete surprise, he told me I could work right up until I had to leave and as a thank you for my work, booked my flight and a hotel for three nights while I waited for my apartment to be ready.

"I'm really going to miss you," I say.

Kali screws up her face in a dramatic fake cry. "I *already* miss you, but I'm so proud of you for doing this. I also can't wait to visit next month. Think of the shopping." She sits back to smile at me, and my eyes catch something bright pink in her hands.

"What's that?"

Kali leans in. "What's what?"

"What is *that,* in your hand?"

Kali stills and for a second I think our call has frozen, but then she blinks, her brain rapidly thinking of a response. "Oh, this? It's a fidget-thing. Helps keep your hands busy and calm your mind when you get worked up."

"Huh. Looks a lot like the one Anthony has."

Kali tilts her head. "Who?"

"Kali Cooper—"

"Next, please!" a woman calls, waving at me.

"You better go. Love you!" Kali ends the call before I can object. I can't help but grin as I trot up to the front counter.

"Hi, I tried to check in on the machines out there, but it said there was an error and to come to the kiosk?"

"No problems, name?"

"Hazel Jones."

"And where are you headed today, Hazel?"

"Melbourne." Butterflies of anticipation flutter in my belly about what I'm doing. I've quit my job, I'm leaving my friends and my heavenly comfort zone for an unpaid internship at twenty-seven (almost twenty-eight) years of age. Life has changed a lot in recent months. *I've* changed.

"Alright Miss Jones, you'll be in seat 2A and have the full range of the business lounge facilities before your flight. Please remember to be at your gate no later than thirty minutes before departure and you will have priority boarding."

"Sorry, business class?" I say, eyeing my ticket. "Someone else booked my ticket. Are you sure?"

"Most definitely. I guess it's your lucky day," the woman says with a wink and a smile.

It's just a two-hour domestic flight, so the difference between business and economy isn't enormous, but hey, I'm not about to complain about getting priority service and potentially free stuff in a lounge I've never been in before. I'll have to send an email to George to thank him for another pleasant surprise.

After getting through security, I locate the business class suite and am stunned they don't turn me away. The usher welcomes me into a large, brightly lit area filled with comfortable-looking armchairs and standing tables spread around the room. Passengers are scattered around the room, most of them enjoying after work drinks in small groups or sitting alone, typing on their laptops.

I've got just under an hour before my flight boards, but I intend on taking full advantage of what I can. I order myself a beer and score myself a comfy lounge chair in a private corner.

I can't help but think how much my luck has changed in the past few months. My job, my friendship circle, myself. I'm about to get on a flight to Melbourne for an opportunity people would kill for. I wish Patrick, a man who filled me with self-belief, was around for me to share it with.

Not speaking to Patrick, particularly in the days immediately after everything was revealed, was hard. Despite Anthony's visit, I was pissed off, and hurt, and felt like an idiot for denying my intuition when it said something wasn't right. It was easy to be angry.

My anger faded and the logical side of my brain lost out to the emotional side. My mind and heart couldn't stop drifting to the wonderful memories I had of Patrick, the way he held me, the pain on his face when we fought. I ached to be around him and ached for how I felt when I was with him. Happy. Wanted. I'd never felt my body and mind come to life like they did when I was with Patrick.

I couldn't get hold of him, and he never tried to contact me, so I decided to channel my emotions towards something more productive. I took what Patrick said to me in anger that night in Byron Bay, and turned it into something good. I *wasn't* as much of a victim as I thought I was. I just got comfortable staying there. Whatever happened that day, I was determined not to repeat what I endured with Luke, for my sake, and for Kali's.

Drawing became second nature again. I reactivated my business Instagram account and website and have already designed covers for a few independent authors. I created my own comic strip based on some of my recent experiences, and I found myself getting lost in it for hours. The work distracted me and gave me purpose outside of my busy day job, ensuring I had something of my own. It changed something deep within my soul.

I smile to myself as I take a sip of my beer and mentally salute myself for how far I've come.

36

WHEN I ARRIVE at the gate, I'm pleasantly buzzed from my two beers and one complimentary white wine spritzer the server gave me. Ordinarily, I'd feel a bit awkward about using the priority lane and cutting in front of everyone else, but the light buzz gives me a confidence boost. Damn it feels nice to feel important.

By the time I climb the stairs and get inside the plane, I'm out of breath. The craziness of work has meant training has taken a back seat lately. Once I settle in, I've got to get my ass back into gear.

The few seats at the front of the plane allocated to business are wider, and there are only two to a side, instead of three. We're also separated by a wall and a curtain that will give us the pompous privacy we so deserve up here. *Ha.*

"Excuse me sir, this lady has the seat next to yours," the stewardess sings. My eyes land on the man in the seat next to my empty one and my heart falls out of my ass.

His usual five o'clock shadow has been replaced by a heavier stubble, but it's as manicured as ever. A couple of locks of his mussed dark-brown hair flop onto his forehead. And of course, he's wearing a suit, with a white shirt underneath his dark blue jacket.

Whilst I'm busy completing my fast-paced assessment, Patrick's eyes lift and lock onto mine. Every minute of distracting myself the past couple of months with work and art and the internship and packing up my life to forget about him like he'd forgotten about me slips out of my hands in a millisecond. My contentment in the business lounge seems so far away.

The corner of Patrick's mouth lifts into a small smile and he stands.

"Of course." His voice is deep and smooth, and he steps aside to let me pass.

Butterflies explode in my stomach.

Heat catapults from my armpits to my fingertips.

I still want this man.

I ache to touch his warm skin again, to see his wicked smile and smell his cologne. I long to press my body into his and have him circle his strong arms around me. I miss his voice, his soft lips, the minty taste of his breath. I miss everything about him. Even the grumpy old-man attitude and the secrets.

Clumsily, I stumble over nothing as I edge forward, holding my breath the instant Patrick's familiar scent gets into my nostrils. I slide past him and sink into the seat, exhaling steadily as I lean back. *Seriously, universe?*

I feel, rather than see, Patrick sit down next to me and I pretend to be busy getting my giant handbag sorted to give myself time to process what the actual fuck is happening.

"So." The sound of his voice so close to me sends shivers up my spine and I turn to look at him properly. Like the first time I laid eyes on him, Patrick smoulders like a fucking superhero, with a jaw that goes for days and no dark circles or bags under the eyes to be seen. My gaze skims across on the scar on his cheek, and my body yearns to touch it.

"So." I shrug, clutching my handbag with sweaty hands.

"I hear congratulations are in order," he says.

"For what?"

"The internship," he replies with a smile. "George told me. You look like you're doing well for yourself. Business class for a two-hour flight."

I eye him suspiciously. "You didn't happen to have anything to do with this upgrade, did you?" Patrick's smirk gives me my answer. "Patrick—"

"Don't start. It was the least I could do."

"Thank you," I reply. "Still full of surprises, I see." Patrick tilts his head and smiles, his soft pink lips dragging my attention from his eyes for a split second. I hope he didn't notice.

"I didn't mean for her to put us together though," he says hurriedly. "I'm sorry if this is uncomfortable. I just asked if she could upgrade the ticket."

Embarrassed, I turn away on instinct, shoving my handbag under the seat in front of me. "Oh no, it's fine. Unless you're uncomfortable and want to switch with someone?"

"No, no, it's fine," he assures me, tapping his hands on his knees.

"Cool." The silence hangs between us while I battle internally between launching myself into his lap and suggesting he does switch with someone to avoid us getting into a heated argument about what the hell happened between us. Naturally, I decide to land somewhere in the middle, erring on the weaker side.

"How have you been?" I ask, daring to glance up at him again. Heat pools between my thighs from his dark-eyed gaze. I can hardly breathe.

"Good." He nods and his expression gives away nothing. "How about you?"

"Good," I say with more confidence than I feel. I notice the vein in his neck tensing, and I can't help but hope it's because he's as nervous as I am.

"How's Kali doing?"

"She's devastated I'm leaving, but I think she's secretly loving that she'll have the house to herself for three months." A part of me wonders what she'll get up to while I'm gone and if she's speaking to Anthony on the down low.

"You'll be back before you know it."

"How's Anthony?" I'm unsure whether he knows about his brother's visit to my house that night. Whilst Anthony doesn't seem like the type to fear much, I still don't want to get him into trouble.

Patrick looks pleasantly surprised at my question. "He's good, thanks for asking. He's starting an apprenticeship in carpentry."

"That's great."

A few beats of silence hang between us and I bite the bullet and blurt out what's on the tip of my tongue. "I hear Lisa's still unaccounted for."

I wait for him to flinch, to cloud over, to look guilty, to get angry, but he doesn't.

"Yes," he says, nodding. He glances at me and smiles again. "They'll find her."

Rachel heard from a friend of a friend that Lisa fled to Bali days before the police showed up. She's wanted on a bunch of serious charges, but a part of me hopes she's never found. She might have been a tough boss and done some terrible things, but I can't bring myself to wish prison time on her. Patrick doesn't seem too fazed that his investigation is up in the air.

The last of the passengers are filing into the plane, squeezing through the narrow aisles to get to their seats. I can't help the flicker of jealousy that comes over me when a stunning blonde woman flashes a smile at Patrick, who returns it politely.

My mind also can't help but think about how Patrick has been on the Gold Coast and didn't come to see me. How long has he been here for? Did he want to see me or am I thinking about him way more than he's thinking about me? *Amazing.* Two months of getting on top of my shit, only to have one encounter with the man and everything unravels.

I shake my head and attempt to stare out of the window casually, hoping I'm feigning enough casual disinterest that Patrick will think I'm completely unaffected by his sudden presence.

"Are you nervous?" his voice asks.

"What?"

He smiles and then nods his head towards my knee, which is jiggling up and down uncontrollably. "Are you a nervous flier?"

I force myself to still and smile sheepishly, fastening my seatbelt. "Must be."

Once we make it into the air and the fasten seatbelt sign is off, Patrick presses the button for an attendant.

"Four of your finest beers, please," he purrs.

"Four? Jesus, Patrick. Tough day?"

He winks at me as he folds down his tray table. "Three are for you. Figured it'd help settle your nerves."

"My nerves?"

"For the flying," he says.

"Oh, right. Thanks."

A stewardess delivers our beers and Patrick opens two of them, pouring mine for me without saying anything.

"So, are you excited for Melbourne?" Patrick asks, breaking the obvious tension.

"Yeah, I am. Now that I've gotten organised, I'm excited," I reply. Patrick smiles widely, giving me a look of what I would guess is pride. "It's just an internship. They might find I'm not suited after one week."

"Stop selling yourself short, I've seen what you can do."

Patrick raises his drinks in celebration, and we tap our cups together. "Congratulations."

"Thank you. So ... how long were you on the Coast for?" I ask, not meeting his gaze. Did that sound as casual as I hoped? I don't think it did.

"A couple of days." Patrick tops up his plastic cup. For someone who usually avoids alcohol, he's drinking quickly. "Managed to get some new sponsors onboard for Henchman and I'm meeting up with John about a property investment this weekend."

I nod in understanding, curious to know if he's still working with the police or has hung his law enforcement boots up for the second time.

"I wanted to see you."

My eyes snap to his and I melt at the expression on his face. Tension sits in his jaw and my thoughts about him being nervous earlier could have been true. He's on edge and his eyes are so focused on mine they feel like they're piercing straight through me.

"I know I don't have the right to see you after what I said that day. I'm selfish for even saying it ..." He drops his gaze and clears his throat, adjusting the collar under his jacket.

My heart beat drums in my ears. "I wish you had. You know ... seen me."

Patrick's eyes widen with relief and it weakens me even further. There's a thumping in my chest and I can already feel every rational thought about how I didn't miss him becoming fuzzy. Those thoughts are slipping away and I'm not putting up much of a fight to keep them.

"Your brother came to see me," I blurt out. Patrick's eyebrows bunch together, like he's trying to figure out how, when, and why. "He told me about his addiction and how you helped him. How ... dark things got for the both of you." Patrick swallows loudly. I can't tell if he's angry or not, so I keep talking.

"He told me about Chloe," I say, watching the tiny streams of bubbles rise in my cup. "About how you blame yourself and how he blames *himself*. How you look out for him because that's what you've always done. Protected him."

Patrick lowers his cup. "When was this?"

"Right after ... right after everything came out," I reply. "I thought about calling you, but—"

"I was a total asshole to you."

I can only nod in agreement, finishing the rest of the amber liquid in my cup and topping it back up.

"I'll kick Anthony's ass for going to see you," he growls, giving me a small wink to show he's joking. "I really am sorry for everything. I lied a lot and whilst I know it's not an excuse, I had reasons for keeping you in the dark about everything. I tried to protect you."

"I know."

And I really do know that. After what Anthony said and seeing the visible battle Patrick seems to be going through with his past, I believe he struggles to allow happiness in. A trait I'm all too familiar with.

"I didn't lie about how I felt about you though," he says, and I have to consciously try and slow my breathing. I start questioning whether I'm really here, having this conversation. "You really drive me crazy. Good crazy." He grins and I chuckle.

"I wish I'd been more honest and told you about Chloe. About Anthony. More about Lisa." He stares into his cup. "Would you have wanted to keep seeing me if you knew the truth?"

"I honestly don't know," I reply. "For what it's worth, I'm glad I know everything now. Even if some of it's still a little hard to swallow."

"I'm so sorry," Patrick whispers, and I meet his earnest gaze, forcing myself not to close the gap between us by lifting the armrest up and jumping into his arms.

I offer him what I hope is a kind smile. "I forgive you."

"I know you're busting to pee."

I smile up at Patrick as we walk out of the catwalk side by side. I guess my attempts at acting like I wasn't busting up to my eyeballs failed.

"I'm about to wet myself," I admit with a giggle.

After the initial awkwardness on the plane, and after several more beers, we relaxed into more casual conversation. It felt so nice. Patrick was different, more at ease than I'd ever seen him. I couldn't help but wonder if it was because it was the first time we'd spent time together where there was nothing to hide.

I was enjoying the unexpected time with Patrick so much that instead of ducking to use the toilet I held onto it for dear life, which was an absolute rookie error. Even business class passengers can't get off the plane quick enough when they're dying to go.

"I won't keep you; the bathrooms are just over there."

I glance at the bathrooms and feel intense despair. For half a second, I imagine wetting myself in the middle of the airport for all to see, just so I don't have to part ways with Patrick.

But logic wins out this time.

"Take care of yourself," I say.

"And you. It was really lovely seeing you again."

"You too."

Without thinking twice, I reach out to hug him and feel such relief when he pulls me into him. His grip around my ribcage is almost crushing, and for a second, I swear he inhales the scent of my hair.

A million thoughts race through my mind. Does he still miss

me? Like, *miss* me where it hurts, like I miss him? Would we have worked out under different circumstances? Are we just going to go our separate ways now and never talk about this again?

I might not like the answers. I don't know if I'm ready to hear the truth in some of his responses. I don't want to shake things up right when we've found a good common ground. So, I don't ask anything.

We stand for several, perfect moments and I close my eyes to imprint the smells, the sensations, and every other minute detail to replay later.

My bladder screams at me again and I reluctantly let him go. Silently, Patrick and I back away from each other, neither one of us wanting to be the first to turn away. Just when I think my bladder can't take it, I remember something. Something worth wetting myself for.

"Wait a second!" I cry, still walking backwards. "You never told me what you said to that guy at the gala that night! Remember? What did you used to say to Anthony when you beat him in fights?"

Patrick throws me a devilish smile, still backing away. "Run home to mum, you little bitch!"

I throw my head back and cackle loudly, Patrick's booming laugh ringing like a favourite song in my ears. I replay his laugh on my entire run to the bathroom, making it just in time.

37

"Ella, I told you it's fine. I'll catch a taxi or an Uber and reimburse the company."

When I finished having a mini freak out about my time with Patrick and looked at my phone, I found I had several missed calls and messages from Ella, explaining she'd made an error when booking my transfers from the airport.

"I know, I just feel like such an idiot," she cries at the other end.

Bless her. She's George Wilson's niece, fresh out of high school and hates messing up. I remember how I used to get worked up about the same things and do my best to comfort her.

"It's not a big deal, I promise," I assure her as I grab my bag from the carousel. "Ubers are how I get around at home. I'll message you when I get to the hotel." I hang up before she can apologise again and head outside into the warm city air.

I make my way to the Uber rank. When I open the app, I grunt with the estimated price of a fare into the city. Yep. Green and Acre will definitely be reimbursing this one.

As I'm about to book in my driver, the prickly sensation of

being watched washes across me and I look up. A sleek, black Mercedes is parked several paces to my left, and a dashing man in a suit emerges from the driver's side.

For the fiftieth time this evening, my heart flutters.

With anticipation? Fear? Excitement? I'm not entirely sure as I remain frozen for a few beats, weighing up my next move. But my body knows what I'm going to do before my brain does. I can't help myself.

I walk slowly towards the car, watching the smirk on Patrick's face get bigger.

"Some things never change," I say. "Do you have a Mercedes in every state?"

Patrick cocks his head to the side. "Maybe."

My palms are sweaty as I tighten my grip around the handle of my suitcase.

"Do you need a lift to your hotel?" he asks politely, moving so he is standing on the path in front of me. He glances down at his flashy watch. "I don't need to start saving damsels in distress for a few hours yet."

I grin at his reference to how we first met and take the moment to survey him, and his features, and the memories I have of him. Patrick sleeping soundly next to me, the sound of his laugh ringing in my ears, the way his lips felt on mine.

Patrick must sense my mind whirring, and he steps closer to me. "When you asked me back in November if any of what we had was real ..."

Wait.

"All of it was real."

What?

A choking sound comes out of my mouth.

"The way I felt ... the way I *still* feel about you, is very much real, Hazel."

Holy. Fucking. Shit.

Surprised tears spring to my eyes, but I make no effort to wipe them away. I can't believe what I'm hearing.

Patrick sees them but continues. "I hated every time I had to lie to you. I hate that the lies came so easily and that it was part of the job. I hate that my past stopped me from loving you as wholly and completely as you deserve."

Now Patrick's eyes are brimming with tears, but he shows no sign of relenting. "My relationship with Chloe wasn't without its problems and we weren't without our issues, but she was perfect to me. After she died, I was convinced I could never love anyone else again, the way I loved her. I was in a world of pain and my life was an absolute fucking mess. Until I met you."

I'm sure my watery eyes bulge out of my head with what I'm hearing, because he chuckles. He tucks a lock of hair behind my ear, his hand lingering on my neck. "I love you, Hazel."

I want to capture how I'm feeling right now and bottle it up to use anytime I want. My skin is warm, my heart is no longer heavy. It's like all the crooked puzzle pieces are finally slotting into place.

"When we first met, you changed something in me," Patrick says. "Your obsession with true crime made me *laugh*. You helped me forget about all my baggage for a few hours. To be fair, it probably helped that your sass was second to none that night."

An ugly snort escapes me, and he laughs, bringing his other hand up to cup my cheek.

"Excuse me! You can't stand here; you need to keep moving!" A traffic warden standing further up the ramp shouts. She's waving a bright red stick in her hands and looking at the two of us crossly.

"Yes, ma'am!" Patrick replies.

He turns back to me. "I felt I didn't deserve you and maybe I don't, but I would rather beg for forgiveness, ask for the slate to be wiped clean and take the *risk* of you rejecting me, than walk away. You, Hazel Jones, are absolutely, one hundred percent worth that risk."

My body floats off the ground as my insides turn to mush, happy tears rolling down my cheeks and onto his hands, still cupping my face and neck.

"Sir! Ma'am! You need to get in your vehicle, *now!*"

Patrick lowers his hands, glancing at the woman briefly. "What do you think?" he whispers hoarsely. Nervously. "Can you forgive me? Do you *want* to forgive me? Could we... maybe start over?"

Patrick presses his lips together as he waits for my response; waits for me to say something. Anything.

I vaguely hear the traffic warden coming closer, speaking loudly and firmly into her radio. She's probably calling for assistance to move us along. Or have us arrested. We *are* at an airport. They don't fuck around with security here. But none of that matters because Patrick is standing in front of me, asking if we can give us a real go and my heart can't take it.

He's waiting patiently, albeit slightly on edge, for my answer.

I step forward and grab the lapels of his jacket with both hands, yanking his face to mine. I kiss him harder, deeper than I've ever kissed anyone in my entire life. I don't even need to coax his mouth open, because he welcomes me hungrily, wrapping his arms around my body and squeezing me tightly.

"I love you," I breathe. Patrick pulls back and looks down at me, his eyes wide as a strangled gasp releases from his throat. He grabs my face again and kisses my cheeks and my nose, before gazing into my eyes, his expression filled with absolute *joy*.

"You can't stay here!"

Patrick peels away from me. "We should go."

"Yep!" I spin the handle of my suitcase towards him and race around to the passenger side. I spot an extra two traffic wardens heading along the pathway towards us and squeal with excited panic.

Like déjà vu, I slide into the passenger seat of the black Mercedes and close the door behind me. Patrick joins me seconds later, firing up the car and laughing at the officers heading our way.

"Go, go, go!" I shout, as Patrick pulls away from the curb. I giggle and squeal like a big, stupid, happy idiot. What tops the moment? When Patrick reaches over and interlaces his hand with mine, like it's the most natural thing in the world.

"Alrighty, let's get out of here, Jonesy," he purrs, just as the car's central locking kicks in.

I shoot Patrick a cheeky side glance, and he smiles knowingly as I unlock my door.

"Don't even think about it."

EPILOGUE

"I DIDN'T THINK three months in Melbourne would turn you into a Melbournite, but I was wrong."

I'm sprawled on Hazel's bed, watching as she unpacks one of three enormous suitcases. Beautiful, expensive-looking items of clothing keep coming out, most of which I recognise from her Instagram feed. Some of them I picked out for her on one of my visits. Others she clearly purchased before she flew home, tags dangling from the hems.

"I couldn't help myself. Once I bought one thing, I couldn't stop. Don't act like you're not eyeing every one of these items." She hangs a knee-length, caramel-coloured coat on a hanger, slinging it into her wardrobe. I can't wait to wear it in winter.

"You've left me little choice," I sigh. "I love you being a self-employed boss bitch, but the lack of free clothes from Green and Acre has been a real bummer. Before you know it, you and Patrick will live together, and I'll be naked and alone."

Hazel grins as she shakes her head. "We're not moving in together anytime soon. I don't want to rush things with him. We're still figuring each other out."

"He's re-locating here permanently. It's only a matter of time before he asks you to move into his new place. And I'm all for it, but if you're going to abandon me, make sure you give me enough notice to replace you."

Hazel tuts under her breath. "Moving in together is way off. Relax, you lunatic."

Whilst the idea of my best friend moving out of our home is a bit of a downer, I couldn't be happier for her. She's beaming from her internship, where she excelled, surprising no one except herself. She nabbed a part-time gig with the publishing house to assist with designing book covers for some Australian authors, and since re-launching her own graphic design business, is booked out with clients for the rest of the year. Working things out with her brooding, sexy man is the cherry on the icing on the cake.

"Speaking of lunatics, how's Anthony doing?" Hazel's gaze drops to the fluorescent pink string I'm twirling between my fingers.

A snort escapes my nostrils. "I have no idea. We still haven't spoken. I've received nothing since the Rubik's cube."

Anthony and I don't talk. We don't even have each other's phone numbers. After he visited our house a few months ago, random packages started showing up. The first one was a large piece of string connected at the ends, the same as the one he twirled in his hands when I met him. A fidget spinner and a Rubik's cube followed in two separate parcels. A note has never accompanied them, but I know they're from him.

As I stare at the bright pink knots I've formed with my fingers, I wonder why I'm not more concerned. A guy I met on two occasions under the most bizarre circumstances sends me random gifts with no explanation. Any other time, I'd be throwing these red flags in the bin, setting it on fire and telling Patrick to warn his brother to back the hell off.

"Kalina Cooper." Hazel's hands are on her hips, a knowing smirk on her face. "You've got a thing for Anthony Bonetti."

I grin as I roll off her bed. "Calm down, heart eyes. I love receiving gifts and the whole mysterious game he's trying to play, but we legitimately don't speak. You've spoken to him more than I have."

"You think he's sexy," Hazel sings.

"I'd love to lick his face off," I confirm, images of me doing exactly that flashing before my eyes. "But that's about it. We're not all looking for love just because *you're* madly in love."

I'm stoked for Hazel and her newfound happiness, but it's not something on my radar. I enjoy spending time with my friends and having the freedom that comes with not being in anything permanent. I love meeting new people, having good sex and then being able to get on with my own thing. In my experience, monogamy has always been a goddamned drag.

"Be careful with Anthony," Hazel says sternly, her light expression replaced by concern.

"Oh, please. He's harmless. I'm not afraid of him."

Hazel folds her arms and frowns. "I know he's harmless. I meant you. *You* be careful with *him.*"

A laugh escapes my lips as I wait for Hazel to tell me she's kidding, or to elaborate on her advice, but she says nothing else. "Are you being serious?"

Without missing a beat, Hazel says, "Just be gentle with him. He might have a tough-guy exterior, but I think he's a big softie underneath it all."

"What makes you say that?"

Hazel's expression tells me she knows a lot more than she's letting on, but all she's ever mentioned to me is that he's a good guy with a troubled past.

Several knocks on the door stop Hazel from responding, her face almost cracking from the smitten grin now plastered on it. "That'll be Patrick! I'm gonna pee. Can you let him in?"

Hazel ducks into her bathroom as I make my way to the front door, twirling the string in my hands and pondering

Hazel's words about Patrick's brother. During the past few months, I've thought a bit about Anthony, mainly his cheeky smile and ripped body and what it'd be like if he slammed me up against a wall. I generally follow those thoughts with ordering myself to calm down. Imagining things about a person you don't even know leads to disappointment or crazy town. Or both.

I've got to hand it to him, though. He's kept my interest longer than any other man in a long time. Sending me unsigned gifts could be considered stalkerish, but I'd be more concerned if his brother wasn't a former detective who keeps a close eye on him. And the gifts have been kind of cool. I've been on YouTube looking at how to master a hammock string figure, and I think I've finally done it.

With my hands interlocked with my latest design, I awkwardly fling back the front door. Standing on our front porch is our tall, dark, and unfairly handsome mafia assassin.

"Patrizio! I think I've nailed the hammock!" I cry triumphantly, wiggling my string covered fingers in his face.

Patrick glances at my creation and offers me a small smile. I'm not sure what his feelings are about his brother sending me gifts, but somehow, I don't think he's as enthused as Hazel. "Looks like you're getting the hang of it. She's a quick study, Anthony."

I drop my hands, my attention solely focussed on the tall figure hovering behind Patrick's right shoulder. My memory didn't do him justice. I'd forgotten how sex oozes out of him. I slowly take all of him in, from his close-shaved head, to the tiniest dimple in his stubble-covered chin, to his lean arms covered in black ink. His hands are in the pockets of his low-hanging pants and his dark t-shirt stretches across his chest, accentuating the muscles beneath it.

When my gaze falls on Anthony's face, I note a grin threatening to break out. Probably from me unabashedly checking him out and getting into the spirit of hand string games so openly.

"Nice work." Anthony nods towards my hands, mischief in his ocean-blue eyes.

I offer him a polite smile as I unravel my creation. "Two Bonetti brothers in one day. This can't be a good sign."

"I promise those days are long behind us both," Patrick says.

"They'd better be." I step aside to allow Patrick across the threshold. "Hazel's in the bathroom." He takes off toward her bedroom, clearly unable to be apart from Hazel for another twenty seconds. Or to avoid whatever awkward conversation his brother and I are about to have.

When I turn to Anthony, he's leaning against the door frame with his arms folded, inches away from me. I can smell his minty fresh breath and woodsy cologne and it's doing crazy things to my concentration.

"What are you doing here?" I ask, holding my ground.

Anthony peers down, his piercing gaze staring straight through me. "I landed myself a job in Burleigh Heads, working for a builder."

Excitement flutters in my belly. "You live here? Since when?"

Anthony's smile takes over his face. "Since about two hours ago."

Hell. Yes.

If Patrick and Hazel's voices weren't travelling up the hallway behind me, who knows what I might do or say. Being in Anthony's presence is enough to get my heart racing and my panties damp.

"Anthony!" Hazel cries, running towards him and throwing her arms around his neck. Anthony visibly stiffens, like he's surprised by her reaction, but he gives her a quick squeeze before releasing her. "What are you doing here?"

"We were just discussing that," I mutter.

"Anthony's decided to start afresh on the Gold Coast too,"

Patrick says, curling an arm around Hazel as she presses into his side. "I figured we could all go out for a drink to celebrate."

"I don't know that Anthony moving here is something to celebrate," I counter.

"I'll place a healthy bet that you'll change your mind soon enough," Anthony replies, giving me a wink. I'd think that wink was tacky and over-the-top if he wasn't so hot.

"Well, let's celebrate Hazel's success," Patrick suggests, ignoring his brother. "Or Kali mastering a hammock. I don't care what it's for, I feel like celebrating." He stares down at Hazel and gently kisses her on the mouth.

"Are you guys always going to be this nauseating?" I ask. Patrick and Hazel grin into each other's mouths, but neither of them respond. "I think I preferred mafia assassin Patrizio. Sure, let's go for a drink to celebrate my hammock string."

I grab my bag from my room, silently thanking myself for the low-cut top I put on today and add a layer of gloss to my lips before I head back to the hallway, shaking my shoulders out with nervous energy.

I love this part. The beginning of new things. The teasing, the games, the electricity. My body hasn't responded physically to someone in several months. I've found people attractive and have gotten giddy and excited. I've gotten aroused and feisty, but something about Anthony has another level of crackling energy to it. I'm a sucker for a bad boy.

When I return to the front door, Hazel and Patrick are already strolling down the front path together. Anthony is standing on the porch with his back to me, watching them.

"How long do you think it'll be before he kicks me out because he wants Jonesy to move in?" he asks, still watching them. I laugh as I close the door behind us, locking it with a resounding click.

"Three months max."

"I thought two."

"The way they're carrying on, it could be tonight."

Anthony turns and captures my gaze, an unmistakable heat blazing behind the blue. "Who knows what tonight could bring."

Oh, he's good.

"I like the string." He nods to the limp string clutched in my hand. "Looks good on you."

"Thanks. It's been kind of therapeutic."

"That's the idea."

I grin. "Are you saying I'm someone who needs therapy?"

"We all need therapy," he replies, without a hint of irony. "I'm saying you strike me as someone who would appreciate the patience it takes to master some of those tricks."

He takes a step towards me, swallowing the space between us, and gently reaches for my hand with both of his. His fingers dance across my palm; a current of electricity shoots up my arm. My body tenses.

"Taking your time ..." He curls the string around his fingers.

"Practising patience ..." He threads the string between both our hands, creating a criss-cross pattern. I'm struggling to breathe evenly.

"Being consistent ..." He gently manoeuvres my hand until it's encased by a net-like shape, held up by his own. "Those are excellent skills to master."

He grins at his creation before looking up at me. "Look at that. I've got you all tied up, and I didn't even have to buy you dinner first."

If I was a betting woman, I'd say the look on Anthony's face reflects how I feel. Like we should blow this celebratory drink off and head back inside.

"All this talk makes me think you must be good with your hands," I whisper.

"You have no idea." Anthony's raspy voice sends a blazing bolt through my limbs, straight to my panties.

"Guys, hurry up!" Hazel shouts from the footpath.

My best friend's yell breaks my trance and I wave a hand at her to signal we're coming, unable to speak properly because I'm pretty sure Anthony's boldness is hurtling me towards a climax.

Anthony untangles my hand before stretching his arm out in front of him, smirking as if he can read my mind. "After you."

He's got trouble written all over him.

And I'm one-hundred percent ready.

Did you enjoy *Hazy Love*? I hope so!

If you liked this book, please consider leaving a review on any retailer site. Reviews are pure gold to indie authors and help get our books get noticed. Even a few words make all the difference.

Thank you.

ACKNOWLEDGEMENTS

I'm writing acknowledgements in my own published novel. It's like having an out of body experience.

First of all, thank you to every single person who picked up, ordered, downloaded or borrowed this book. A lot of blood, sweat and tears (and I mean, a *lot*) went into getting this out into the world, and I'm so grateful to each and everyone one of you for reading it.

To my editor, Rachel Collins. You taught me so much and I am forever grateful for your patience, wisdom and kind words. I swear I'll keep working on my passive voice.

Thank you to my designer Emily Wittig, for producing a cover I fell in love with, and for putting up with my pedantic requests. You have the patience of a saint.

To my beta readers: Erin O'Connor, Jen Quilty, Katie Garrett, and Tara Byrne. You're all very busy women whose opinions I greatly admire. Thank you all for your time, feedback and support.

To the writing community. I never knew such an amazing group of people existed and I am SO GRATEFUL that I found you all. A special mention to Jen Morris for letting me send messages at all hours about the most tedious of things. You are a wonderful friend (even by way of a virtual friendship) and a brilliant author.

I've got to say a fangirl thank you to K.A. Tucker, whose book *The Simple Wild* was the catalyst in me deciding to write my own romance novel. It was the book I didn't know I needed and I'm so glad you, Calla, and Jonah, exist.

To my wonderful ARC readers. Thank you for volunteering your time to read my debut and provide reviews from the heart. It means more than words can express.

To my parents, for always encouraging us kids to do whatever we dreamed of doing. I didn't make it as a storm chaser, but I sense you'd prefer me writing in the safety of my home anyway. Thank you for your endless support and for always feeding me when I visit.

Jen, Sian and Fraser—love love, blah blah, ew emo. Let's get matching siblings tattoos if we haven't already by the time this comes out (sorry Ma).

JM, thank you for your constant encouragement and support and for letting me rant, rave and sob about this for the past couple of years. I couldn't have done this without you.

And Maxi, I know you can't read or understand, but thanks for cuddling me for hours on end while I typed away. You're the actual best.

Finally, thank you to all my friends, family members and every person who sent messages of encouragement over the past two years. It means so much when people take a vested interest in your passion and I am so grateful.

No one could've truly prepared me for the journey that was self-publishing my first novel. It was hands down one of the hardest and most rewarding experiences of my life. There have been long days and even longer nights of wondering if I could ever get this done, and I still have moments of not believing it's real. The fact that I made it to this point is honestly, mind-blowing.

Time to do it all again.

ABOUT THE AUTHOR

Hannah Smith realised her love for writing at a young age. Her stories follow strong women on journeys of self-discovery and love, because women are bad bitches and she loves romance.

Hannah lives with her partner Josh, and their rescue dog, Maxi, on the southeast coast of Australia. When not writing, you can find Hannah watching true crime documentaries or reading a book with a cup of tea in hand.

Sign-up to Hannah's newsletter for the latest updates, sneak peeks and giveaways: www.hannahsmithauthor.com

BOOKS BY HANNAH SMITH

The Wipeout Series

The King Contract

Hazy Love Series

Hazy Love

Crazy Love